Shades of Blue

Dana Tanaro Britt

To That Husband o' Mine—my Hero, my Anchor and
always my Number One Fan.
This simply would not have happened without you.

Chapter One

"OH, JACK."

In that moment, Gabe Montgomery would cheerfully have given his right arm to be whoever this Jack guy was. The husky voice had him stopping mid-stride, holding his breath and listening intently.

There it was again—barely audible.

"Oh, Jack."

What had first sounded sensuous now seemed broken and sad.

Standing absolutely still amid the ferns and bamboo shrubs between The Painted Parrot beach cottages, Gabe winced, the sobs twisting his heart.

Man, this Jack guy sure had his hands full dealing with that range of emotions.

He debated investigating further, hating to hear someone in such pain, but clearly it was a private matter.

After a moment, when no further sounds joined the ever-present island music of the waves, Gabe shrugged and resumed his path through the foliage, the distant, brightly colored banners of his beach-side restaurant and bar beckoning him in the breeze.

* * *

Grief is a thief. A thief that saps the very energy needed to breathe, much less move. Who could know such things until grief became your own?

Oh, how she wished she didn't know these things.

Waking on a pillow soaked with tears while feeling achingly aroused at the same time was not a good way to end a nap in paradise—or anywhere, for that matter.

Naps are supposed to be refreshing, not heartbreaking.

Pillows that smell of island breezes should be soothing, not tear-soaked.

Eyes closed, Charlie desperately hoped, yet again, that she was awakening from a bad dream instead of into one. As the tropical breeze dried the tears on her face, the sensuous feeling faded and all she could do was sob his name.

Chapter Two

"HEY GABE!" Jill—a bona fide Jill of many trades—called out from behind the bar.

Gabe flashed her an impudent grin as he bent to pet his ever-present shadow, a black lab named Jake, who then flopped down in his spot just outside the bar.

Gabe made his way across the open-air bar set barely out of the water's reach, pausing to talk to both repeat customers and newcomers alike.

Reaching the long bar, he caught the glass of lemonade Jill slid to him and drank deeply.

"Met the new tenant yet?" One of Jill's many hats was management of the rental cottages.

"No, tell me about 'em." Gabe stepped out to intercept a runaway toddler intent on escaping the adjoining restaurant.

His path blocked, the little boy attempted to dart around Gabe's legs but was scooped up into strong arms just as the flustered mother rushed up, apologizing.

"No worries, we love kids running amok." His easy manner reassured the lady as she took the blur of movement from him.

Jill smiled as she watched the boy, resting her hand on her slightly rounded belly.

"Nothing to tell. Just one person, haven't met her myself. We made all the arrangements via email and I got everything ready, key on the counter as usual."

Gabe considered the sobs he'd heard earlier and decided to keep it to himself for the moment; nobody likes strangers to know about private moments.

"Just her, huh? I might have to stop by there after a bit, y'know, in the name of hospitality 'n all." His grin was devilish.

Jill rolled her eyes and swatted at him with the bar towel.

"She'll have to surface sometime, there's only so much stocked in there and she did specify a few things repeatedly when I offered to stock particulars." Jill tossed the words over her shoulder as she turned to greet a customer with a sunny smile.

As was his habit, Gabe carried the lemonade glass with him as he walked through the pub, again stopping to talk with various customers.

Listening to the honeymooners gush about their stay and the older couple thank him for personally delivering their order from the restaurant the night before, he was in his element.

A born and bred New Englander, Gabe had sea salt running in his veins but had fled the harsh winters in favor of the tropics. He loved everything about the sea and shore living; he was made from it and for it.

After the horrors of 9/11, he'd left the city and the fire department in search of peace and sunshine and had found it in spades out here in the outlying islands.

Nothing like a paradise getaway, he thought for the millionth time since buying the properties a few years ago, his gaze taking in the ocean as he left the pub, snapping his fingers for Jake to fall in at his side.

Now he had an excuse to check on the origin of the sobs—Gabe always made a point to introduce himself and welcome his tenants, why should this one be any different?

The scene he'd overheard earlier was made even sadder by the fact that she was alone.

Waving to beach volleyball players, Gabe made his way across the sand to the wood shop that did triple duty as his home and office.

He planned to finish the project he'd started in the sleepless hours before dawn.

* * *

After the harrowing events of the past few months, Charlie desperately wanted a place to simply exist. A place with zero demands outside of herself, as selfish as that sounded.

A hideaway, because she planned to do just that—hide.

Aside from checking in with Troy and Cassidy at their insistence, she didn't intend to see or speak to a single soul for a while.

She took a deep, shuddery breath, then another one and swung her legs over the side of the hammock. Her head ached, her skin tight with the dried tear streaks. Apparently even paradise doesn't guarantee a better wake up. Breathing was no easier here, either.

She sighed heavily, feeling trapped under the overwhelming, pressing sadness that was a part of her every moment—waking or sleeping. Shaking it off just wasn't an option.

While she wouldn't call it refreshing, the nap had restored her body a bit and she was ready to check out her temporary home.

Upon arriving at the cottage that morning, Charlie had stepped out of her shoes and sank deep into the hammock, dropping her bags right there on the porch.

Now, she stood slowly, gratefully noticing how truly secluded the porch was. Vines covered the far end, spreading in a tangle across half the front to the steps. The other half of the porch sported a gauzy fabric curtain that fluttered slightly in the breeze. The view beyond the fabric was astonishing, the turquoise sea and clear blue sky almost magical.

Inside, the cottage was simple yet colorful and with the ever-present breeze blowing gently, the space was both airy and comforting.

More deep breaths and a few steps later, Charlie had unpacked her two bags, putting her few clothes and two pairs of shoes in the walk-in closet and setting out her toiletries in the spacious bathroom. Setting up house, so to speak, gave her a measure of control yet also set her free to just be.

Stepping out of the bathroom, her steps slowed at the sight of a small indigo blue glass bird on the nightstand next to the bed. Walking slowly to the table, she picked it up with trembling fingers, the cool glass burning a fresh hole in her already ravaged heart.

Jack had often called her his bluebird in their early years together, her perky disposition making her his own bluebird of happiness.

She sank to the bed and curled into its softness, lost in a memory of Jack's laughter as he teased her yet again.

"Blue, no matter how long you stare at her, that kitten is not going to tell you where it came from."

Hot tears flooded her eyes and harsh keening sounds tore from her throat as Charlie embraced the memory, the missing him a physical pain that made breathing feel like shards of glass were buried in her chest.

Sometime later, she became aware of the bluebird's edges pressing painfully into her hand. She set it back on table, rubbing the red creases in her hand absently.

"Okay, Charlie, let's think about food before you fall over, shall we?" she admonished herself, returning to the kitchen to see what she could find.

The woman she'd emailed when making her reservations—Jill? Was that her name?—had cheerfully agreed to Charlie's request to stock the fridge and pantry with a few things before her arrival.

Jill had told her that in addition to The Painted Parrot restaurant and bar, the island boasted a well-stocked grocery store, several good restaurants, and dependable mail service for online orders.

Charlie hoped not to think about such things and had asked if the other woman could stock a small list of items for her—offering to pay extra for the service. Jill had been happy to help, brushing off her offer of extra pay.

Taking a bottle of her favorite chocolate milk from the fridge, she went back out to the deep porch, intending to walk onto the beach.

Gazing at the sea, she instead sat on the step—absently setting the chocolate milk between her bare feet.

Since she'd stepped onto the cottage porch, her travels done, no responsibilities waiting, her mind seemed to know it was free from suppression and memories had begun to come in waves.

This particular one was full of laughter—hers, Jack's and the kids'—inevitably, though, it would end in horrifying screams or wracking sobs.

She embraced every memory, every dream, for this is why she had come to this haven at the edge of the world.

Chapter Three

DURING THE BRIGHT DAYS, he could almost believe he'd lived this idyllic life forever. It was the long nights that kept it from being a flawless paradise.

With a stretch, Gabe headed back to the bar, thinking about food as he walked–he was always hungry. A cheeseburger would be perfect—one for Jake, too. On that thought, he tugged a half-smushed granola bar from a pocket of his cargo shorts and absentmindedly ate as he walked, tossing bits to the dog gamboling about at his side.

The bright tropical foliage along the rustic path was pleasing to the eye and also served to keep a high level of privacy between the eight cottages on Gabe's property. Each cottage was well-hidden from the others, providing seclusion for guests from all windows and porches. From couples of all ages to families with children, Gabe's cottages were almost always booked year-round.

As he righted a crooked statue of playful frogs, he was stopped by a sound that twisted his stomach into knots.

Not a cry or a shout, but a soft sound of soul-deep anguish.

Twice in one day?

Hidden from sight yet still able to hear such a soft sound, Gabe figured it must be coming from Sea Glass, the smallest of his cottages, through the vines several feet to his right.

The new tenant. Standing still with his hand on the statue, Gabe figured it had to be the same person he'd heard earlier—and he fervently hoped so, because two people feeling like that in one place made for a sad situation to say the least.

The sound came again.

A sigh—more like a whimper at the end of a crying jag—and the name he'd heard earlier, "Jack," exhaled on a deep shuddering breath.

Gabe desperately wanted to find this Jack person and punch him senseless for whatever he'd done to cause such pain. Lord knows, he himself hadn't been an angel over the years, but he damned well did his best not to hurt anybody. While he stood soundlessly, the sighs escalated to less-quiet gasping sobs. Even Jake whined at the sound.

His every instinct wouldn't allow him to ignore a person in such pain; keeping his voice calm and low, he spoke. "Don't cry."

The sobs hitched in surprise.

He quickly added, "I won't intrude, I was just walking by. But I gotta say, whoever this Jack person is, I'd love to punch him for making you cry like that." Gabe continued his path slowly, listening for any response.

There was none.

He'd wait for a better time to introduce himself.

* * *

Charlie gasped at the low, soothing voice that came from just beyond the porch. She reflexively swiped her hands over her face and turned in the direction his voice had come from, dreading coming face to face with anyone right now. She'd shed her mask upon her arrival to the island and had no desire to tug it back into place.

No steps came closer, only a slight rustle as she heard him walk away. She felt an overwhelming sense of relief.

Despite her efforts, she was used to people witnessing her grief and she was, quite frankly, sick of that. She didn't mind the crying; it was Jack's absence and witnesses to her grief she couldn't stand.

Hence the running away to this island, to get away from well-meaning looks, pats, and advice. Oh, the advice. It made her head hurt even now, many miles away from anyone she knew.

Breathing was all she could ask of herself, making a face as she remembered the recent and horrifyingly public breakdown that led to her finding this getaway.

She just wanted to be left to mourn in peace. If there was such a thing.

Her stomach rumbled, reminding her of the chocolate milk she'd let fall to the step. It wouldn't do to get sick, so she opened the bottle and drank deeply of the still-cool milk.

Watching the waves of the sea sweep in and out, unconsciously matching her breaths to their cadence, she felt her muscles begin to relax a fraction.

She was here to just breathe.

*   *   *

"Charlie, is there possibly a surface in this room I could sit on?" She heard Jack's teasing voice as if he were in the room with her. He'd come in to her writing study in their first home to tell her something and stood looking about.

Chaos was her habit when working. In fact, Jack used to say chaos followed Charlie wherever she went.

She'd stuck her tongue out at him, grabbed him by his shirtfront and proceeded to very deliberately show him just how well he could sit on the small space of unoccupied floor.

With no idea of how long she'd stood there, Charlie came back to the moment, leaning heavily on the table where she'd put her laptop and the bag filled with notebooks, pens, sticky notes, pencils and books. The rest of her books and things would arrive on the mail boat within the week.

Grief was funny that way, for she barely remembered to eat, often left water running and rarely noticed the time of day, yet when planning this trip, she'd been coherent and precise in her plans. Some, like her friend Trudy, would be eager to say that meant she was moving on, but Charlie knew better.

It simply meant she was eager to escape, to create a new world to call home for now. Jack was gone, Charlie was here, and all she had left of their life together were grown children and her memories.

Facts were facts.

Charlie decided to set up her laptop on the square wooden dining table instead of the little computer nook she'd seen in the bedroom. The mid-sized table wouldn't be needed for anything else and it would afford her plenty of room to spread out books and papers as was her writerly habit.

Little comforts and quirks often acted like Band-Aids, holding edges of a gaping wound together in hopes that it could begin to heal.

Although, from where Charlie stood, healing wasn't something she was hoping for right now. She had no intention of healing, for the pain of her loss was all that remained of Jack.

The setting sun found her back in the hammock, worn out from the trip across the globe and the small efforts she'd made at settling in.

Her eyes drifted closed as the hammock swayed slightly in the breeze, and the only sounds were the waves of the sea and the chirps of the tropical birds.

Curling into the hammock, she allowed an exhausted sleep to claim her, whispering brokenly, "If only..."

****Chapter Four****

THE FISHING, THE EARLY MORNING when the world was quiet, was his anchor—it had been nearly as long as he could remember. No matter what went on in the world, being out on the sea was a balm to his soul.

On this particular morning as they motored back to shore with the morning's catch, Gabe thought again of his mystery tenant, as he had several times over the last few days. He couldn't help but wonder what her story was. He'd only heard her voice, but that alone left him both eager to help and hopelessly intrigued.

The sun glinting off his shades, he turned to scan the sea once more, filling his soul with the peace of the morning before the day's pace picked up a bit.

He tossed the boat's lines to Nash, who had jumped ashore, Jake at his side.

"Nice catch o' the day, Arch." His long-time friend and business partner called him by an old nickname, tying off the JohnB.

He clapped Nash on the shoulder in agreement as they unloaded the day's catch of mahi mahi and snapper, the local buyers for shops and restaurants already waiting nearby. Business was completed easily out of long-standing habits and easy relationships, and in a short time the buyers were loaded up and headed inland, leaving Gabe and Nash to go on with their day.

"How's our Jilly this morning?" Gabe asked as the two cleaned the boat, readying it for a later charter.

"So far, so good." Nash made a praying motion with his hands, eyes rolling heavenward. His newly pregnant wife's battle with morning—well any-time-of-day—sickness was a thorn in all their sides, most especially Jill's.

"Fair weather and smooth sailing," Gabe wished fervently; it'd been a wild few weeks thus far.

The two men talked over the day's plans as they walked, until Nash veered off in the direction of his house with a shove to Gabe's shoulder, planning to check on Jill before he headed to the bar for the morning. "Get outta here." Gabe shoved back, turning into the trees along the path to his own place.

As he walked, Gabe tugged his phone from his cargo shorts pocket and answered a few texts, most importantly the one from his sister in New England.

Tally and her husband, along with Gabe and Tally's parents, Sheila and Robert, ran the family's B&B back home. Sheila hadn't been feeling well lately and Tally was asking her brother to chime in and help her talk their mother into a rare doctor visit. Gabe made a mental note to call his sister and give her his ear to talk about it at length.

Lost in thoughts about his family and the day's business, he realized he was about to walk past Sea Glass cottage.

Admittedly, he was intensely curious about his tenant, and not only because she was one of the rare ones to ask for an indefinite stay.

This time, though, he heard no sounds from the cottage.

Shrugging, he continued on, his mind already on what he might find to eat.

It was then that he heard a laugh that stopped him in his tracks, sending him a brief, vivid vision of bright swirling skirts and dancing eyes.

Well, that was different—enchanting, even.

He waited, absently rubbing the dog's ears, hoping to hear it again. After a few moments, when no further sounds came from the direction of his mystery tenant, he resumed walking.

He shook his head; a woman he'd never even seen had him all curious and confused with her heart-rending sobs and magical laughter.

He was pretty sure he'd lost his mind—and suspected he was okay with that.

*   *   *

When the dreams were good, they were very, very good.

In the hammock, Charlie slowly came fully awake, her body soft with remembered touches, her smile fading as she desperately tried to hold on to the feeling just a bit longer.

No matter how hard she tried, the warmth that particular recurring dream brought her could not be kept beyond the first few waking moments, nor could it be called forth when she was awake.

With a sigh, she stood and did a few yoga stretches, her sky blue sundress falling damply away from her legs. Hours upon hours in a hammock felt great until you tried to move. *You're not twenty-five anymore, Charlie*, she thought ruefully as she finished stretching and faced the sea.

A walk would be great for body and soul; it was early yet and few people would be out. After all, weren't morning beach walks part of why she'd come here? Pulling her unruly curls into a messy knot, she secured the mass with an ever-present elastic hair band and stepped off the porch onto the sand.

The sea breeze caressed her face and lifted the dress from her body as she walked along the edge of the surf, looking right through the stunning sunrise and the boats that dotted the water.

After so many weeks of trying to pull together amid friends and family, she felt unbearably fragile and cracked—as if she might just shatter and blow away on the breeze under the onslaught of newly freed feelings.

Yet somehow, she also felt solidly real, truly present for the first time since she'd lost Jack. Grief sucked hairy donkey balls, but it was here and demanding its due.

"FINE!" Charlie startled herself by screaming out to the sea. "Fine, here I am, you bastard! Bring it on!" After several days spent totally alone, her voice sounded oddly rough to her ears.

She automatically glanced about to see if anyone had noticed before reminding herself that it no longer mattered if anyone did.

She stood motionless, her head bowed, wayward strands of hair blowing around, watching the sea swirl about her feet.

For the foreseeable future, she had no plan—not one single plan beyond keeping herself breathing.

Incredibly sad and incredibly freeing, she thought, sinking to sit in the sand at the water's edge.

Incredibly alone.

*   *   *

Showered and fed, with lemonade in reach, Gabe moved about behind the bar taking stock of the day's inventory while Jimmy Buffet cheerfully gave cheeseburgers in paradise their due from the radio mounted above the supply shelves.

Jill came in, dark circles under her eyes despite her sunny smile.

Raising an eyebrow, he wordlessly put together an ice cold ginger ale on the rocks and rounded the bar to rub her shoulders.

Seated on the barstool, she sipped gratefully before speaking. "How does a city girl like me get lucky enough to live on island time with two studs waiting on her hand n foot?"

Gabe grinned. "I think the luck is all mine—I slept well, bet Nash can't say the same."

Jill burst out laughing and punched his shoulder as he went around the bar to resume opening tasks.

"Have you seen our new tenant yet?" she asked, sucking on a cube of ice and looking a bit more steady.

He paused, leaning on the bar, and took a long drink from his glass. "Well, not face to face, I haven't."

Jill looked at him quizzically.

"I heard her on the porch in passing a couple times but haven't gone to be neighborly just yet," Gabe clarified, avoiding Jill's curious gaze. "What do we know about her?"

Jill finished her ice cube and replied, "Nothing beyond the usual tenant stuff—she's from St. Louis I think. Paid three months in advance but asked for an open-ended lease, asked repeatedly about privacy. All via email, so I've not talked to her or met her yet myself."

Gabe gazed out to the beach, where a few people walked and one lone person sat at the water's edge. He considered whether he wanted to share with his friend what he'd heard coming from Sea Glass.

"What is it?" Jill nudged his arm with her empty glass, their years of friendship giving her a clue to his mood.

Deciding to keep the details to himself just yet, he refilled her ginger ale and handed it back to her with a shrug. "I just figured with the extra inquiries about privacy that maybe I'd not knock on the door but wait until she comes around."

Jill raised her glass and slowly stood. "That might be awhile; with the supplies I laid in for her, girl could exist without leaving the place for quite a while if she wished."

She waved and walked away from the bar, calling over her shoulder, "You have me curious, ya know."

"Yeah, well, join the club."

*   *   *

The heat of the late morning sun made Charlie's skin prickle as she realized she'd been, yet again, sitting at the water's edge for a long time.

Hot and more than a little thirsty, she made her way back to the cottage, noticing how truly quiet her little stretch of beach was, with just a few people walking or running past.

The tile floor was cool on her sandy feet, the wide-blade fans gently stirring the air in a perpetual breeze.

Filling a tall glass of water from the front of the fridge, Charlie drank it down and refilled it, drinking deeply as she leaned against the kitchen island, welcoming the coolness of the dark blue and yellow tiles against her body.

Some moments she noticed such small things, other times she noticed nothing, blinded by her grief and memories.

A shower would be a good thing, she thought vaguely, feeling the tightness of her sun warmed skin.

Open to the sky but with high walls, the outdoor shower was peaceful and private. Charlie leaned back on the broad bench, letting the water rain over her body as she mused. *Jack would revel in making love to me out here*—the resulting grin faded instantly as if she'd been slapped.

Reality bit sharply as she acknowledged she would never again be loved by Jack. Her sobs came hard and fast, tearing through her battered throat, her voice hoarse with repressed screams she'd yet to set free.

The next lucid moment found her back on the porch in the hammock, clad in t-shirt and capris, her damp hair beginning to dry in curly sprigs. She shook her head, momentarily amazed at how a person could function on such oblivious autopilot so much of the time.

Exhaustion took over and she drifted into her dreams.

Would she wake smiling or sobbing this time?

****Chapter Five****

THE DAYS PASSED in the timeless island groove that was the very definition of paradise. The sun shone, the sea moved to and fro, children turned brown as they played in the waves, parents relaxed amid few distractions, couples delighted in the many hidden spots to be found around the island.

After the morning fishing and opening the bar, Gabe decided a trip to the other side of the island was in order. He waved to Jill, mouthing the name "Amos" and headed up the dunes to his truck, Jake at his side.

Gabe remembered with a pang that it was only last summer the old man they all considered an adopted grandfather would make his way to his favorite barstool at The Painted Parrot promptly at 3p.m. every day for food and conversation.

This year Amos wasn't physically up for driving himself anymore and refused to let Gabe fetch him and keep up the routine more than twice, maybe three times, a week.

He was missing the old fella, thus heading out early in hopes of spending some one-on-one time with him before they came back to the bar for the afternoon. He might even tell Amos about his mystery tenant—*well, it is a curiosity*, he thought defensively, a little perturbed by how much she was on his mind.

Gabe spent a relaxed few hours with Amos, helping him fix a broken board on the porch and talking about the week's catch before they washed up.

Amos ran a comb over his sparse hair before replacing his ever present Red Sox cap and climbing into Gabe's old blue Ford for the trip across the island. Jake jumped into the truck bed, sticking his head inside the open back window for Amos to pet from time to time.

"What's for lunch today, Gabriel?" Amos settled into the truck gingerly.

"No idea, menus are Jill's realm. I just show up to eat," Gabe laughed.

"That Jilly's a good egg." Amos nodded with a grin.

Living alone all these years, he did love being fussed over from time to time.

"That she is." Gabe turned up the radio, knowing the old man would doze as he drove.

After depositing Amos on his customary barstool with Jake sprawled on the sandy floor at the old man's feet, Gabe took his sandwich in hand and headed out for his afternoon charter. Jill and Amos waved in his direction, busy catching up while Jill set the old man up with a plate and fussed over him.

This time, Gabe purposely walked the secluded path next to the Sea Glass cottage, treading carefully and listening closely.

You're an idiot, man. Just go introduce yourself or move on. He rolled his eyes in annoyance at himself and continued walking—almost missing the sound he'd been waiting for.

The first had been a heartrending sob, the second a fetching laugh and now a slightly hoarse, composed voice came through the trees, "Well, that's definitely good news, honey, I'm so thrilled for you."

So that's what her voice sounded like normally, huh?

Gabe shamelessly stood still and listened in as his mystery guest talked to what was revealed in the conversation to be her daughter. He wasn't eavesdropping, really—he just liked the sound of her voice.

Man, did he like the alluring, almost smoke-edged voice fading behind him as he walked on.

*   *   *

Charlie paced in and out of the cottage as she talked on the phone with Cassidy, who was excitedly reporting news of a new job and new apartment in St. Louis.

After assuring her daughter that all was well and that yes, she'd visit the new place before long, Charlie ended the call and sighed deeply. Had she never noticed how exhausting a phone call could be?

Keeping up pretenses takes a lot of work—even from afar.

Charlie fervently hoped her daughter would be too busy with her new job and setting up the apartment to concern herself with trying to visit her mother off on a tropical island getaway, but her mother's heart would never let on to Cassidy how much she wanted to be alone.

Seated cross-legged at the table, Charlie checked her email, having promised Trudy that she would stay in touch.

Sure enough, there were three messages from Trudy, each one increasing in intensity—Charlie's friend tended to worry. Trying to remain stubbornly shameless at how she'd ignored her friend's texts since arriving on the island, Charlie took a moment to reply to the emails, assuring Trudy that she'd arrived safe and sound and would be in touch now and again. And, yes, she was certain she didn't need company.

Shaking her head, she wondered yet again how on earth she'd managed to hold things together as well as she had over the past few months when clearly mere texts and emails from her best friend irked her.

Whatever, no more of that fake stuff.

In spite of having slept most of the day away, Charlie felt heavy limbed and tired; the perpetual exhaustion grief seemed to have deposited on her body left her with a feeling of walking through molasses, every move and thought a struggle. Feeling slightly light-headed and woozy, she realized she hadn't eaten any real food since before her travel to the island.

Despite her complete lack of desire to prepare a meal, she didn't want to get weak or sick.

That being that, she examined the pantry and decided to make an Alfredo that she and Jack had always loved.

They'd often enjoyed a variety of pasta dishes such as fettuccine Alfredo or pasta primavera made at home and eaten out on the patio or in the cozy kitchen nook—sometimes even standing at the kitchen island.

And there it was.

Finally, after months of yearning and wishing for something of Jack to reach out beyond her dreams, she actually felt him.

Mid-reach to the stove burner knob, she could feel Jack's hand at her waist and hear his voice rumble in her ear laughingly, "I get to kiss the cook."

She whirled around, certain she'd find her husband's brown eyes twinkling in merriment, as they so often had at her expense.

Finding only emptiness, her hands covered her face as she sank to the floor with a low, keening wail.

Her initial reaction to realizing she was on the floor was to gasp and breathe deeply, to control the wail and the tears before she remembered she was alone—she was finally totally alone.

So she sat.

And she wailed.

*   *   *

As the day waned into evening, Gabe drove Amos home with at least two days' worth of food packed in individual containers and placed into an insulated carry-all. Jill considered it her mission to take care of everybody who crossed her path.

After helping the old fella to the porch where he settled into his rocker with the newspaper, Gabe put the food in the fridge and promised to be back, day after tomorrow. He strode back to the old blue Ford, waving and laughing at Amos' protests that he was fine, whatever.

Gabe stopped in town at the bakery, feeling the need for something sweet and wondering if Jill's sweet tooth had returned yet.

"Hey, Gabe! Where you been hiding these days, man?" the cheerful ponytailed baker called out as she placed a tray of dough on the cart to rise and crossed to the counter.

"Hey, Katie, you know how it goes—tough gig, this paradise life." Gabe bent to blow a raspberry on the cheek of the wriggly toddler being held up by the young girl standing next to him.

"Miri, darling, you have got to stop getting prettier all the time!" Gabe ruffled her hair, taking her baby sister into his arms.

"I'm a princess, they're always pretty," the eight-year-old laughed.

Gabe shrugged. "No hope for the rest of us, then!"

Pointing to the fresh batch of blueberry lemon scones Katie had just placed in the case, Gabe said, "I'll take the dozen, Katie . Jilly can put 'em away when she's feeling up to par. "

"Speaking of Jill, how is she?'.

Gabe gave her a shrug and a grimace, "As well as expected, I guess? She either eats nothing or a ton at once."

Katie laughed at that. "Tell her I'll be by in a couple days to chat."

"Will do." With a wink and another giggle-inducing raspberry, Gabe handed the baby over to Katie and waved his fingers at the little girl.

Back at the cove, he stopped by the wood shop to change shirts before heading to the bar to take the evening shift.

A fresh white t-shirt sporting an ad for his fishing charters and a cold glass of lemonade in hand, he chose the path that wound next to Sea Glass Cottage, having made it a habit of sorts to listen for her every time.

In any other situation, the first responder in him wouldn't have hesitated to check out the keening sound coming though the bushes, but in this case he recognized that intruding wasn't the answer.

She was clearly in pain, and Gabe had a growing hatred of the man named Jack, certain the guy had something to do with the whole thing. That was all he knew and that would have to be enough for now.

The keening was gone, replaced by sobs that sounded closer this time—she must've moved out onto the porch.

"There now, it can't be all that bad, can it?" His desire to fix things overrode his intention to give her privacy this time.

The sobs hiccupped and stopped.

Moments of silence passed before a hoarse, shaky voice said haltingly, "Oh, yes it can ... and then some."

Gabe debated stepping out of the trees into the dusky light in front of the cottage, but instead he stayed put and said, "I'm sorry for eavesdropping, but it wasn't intentional ... at first."

A deep sigh came followed by a rustling sound. "It's okay; I just didn't think to control myself out here. I'm sorry for causing you concern."

He shook his head, even though she couldn't see him. "I don't mind. If I weren't a stranger, I'd offer my company and my shoulder. In fact, I'm offering anyway. If you've need of either, or anything else I can help with, you've only to ask at the bar. My name is Gabe."

With that, he walked on and left her in peace.

* * *

Just on the other side of the trees, Charlie peered into the dimming light, expecting him to come out into her line of sight.

Instead, he had offered her comfort, told her his name and continued on his way.

Huh, she thought, *that's interesting*.

Gabe. Wasn't that the owner of The Painted Parrot's name?

Charlie remembered from Jill's emails that he was friendly and would likely pay her a visit early on during her stay to introduce himself.

She was glad he hadn't done so yet.

From the steps of the cottage porch, she drank her chocolate milk and considered a twilight walk along the water's edge.

Tomorrow would be soon enough, she decided, leaning against the porch post wearily.

"Jack, I've made a decision," she said aloud, holding her bottle up in a toast.

"That decision is that I'm making no decisions anymore." She laughed without humor, realizing how ridiculous she sounded, yet she was completely serious.

"I'd love to just walk into the sea, to float away, to find you wherever you are. I can't do that to our children, but oh, I wish with all my heart that I could."

****Chapter Six****

BEHIND THE BAR, Gabe laughed with his customers, offered sightseeing tips and poured drinks handily, all the while hearing her voice in his head.

Even given the fact that she was clearly upset, her smoky voice had stuck with him. Not to mention he had a soft spot for damsels in distress.

Nash joined him behind the bar, playfully shoving as he popped the top on his own bottle and slid a freshly iced ginger ale across the bar to his wife, who ate robustly, having had no appetite all day.

"Damn, Jilly, don't forget to breathe," Gabe teased.

"You see how they treat me?" she lamented with a wink to the customer sitting next to her.

The evening wore on, the bar and adjoining restaurant aglow in the darkening evening, the sea a glittering jewel dotted with boat lights as a few pleasure cruises and locals enjoyed the night.

At one in the morning, Gabe gave a last call holler and tossed his bar towel to Nash, Jill having long abandoned them for her couch and television shows.

"Close up? Will Jilly mind?"

Nash resisted doing a double take, catching the towel easily.

"No worries—you okay?"

Gabe did most of the closing, allowing Nash and Jill to settle in together at night.

"All good, just want to head out a bit early tonight—need to check on Mom." Gabe waved his phone in the air and made his way through the bar out onto the sand.

He stood a moment beside the sea, wondering if he should just go back in and let Nash head home instead of doing what he was thinking about doing.

It just wasn't in his nature, or his training, to let someone hurt like she was hurting and not try to help; it just wasn't going to happen.

Resolute, Gabe strode down the beach until he reached the stretch of sand in front of Sea Glass Cottage.

He stopped at a spot he knew made the cottage visible to him.

There were no lights on in the darkness besides the tiny fairy lights around the porch.

Well, it is late, you idiot, Gabe scolded himself as he neared the cottage, intending to walk on around towards his own place.

In the trees, Gabe was almost past the porch when she spoke.

"I should thank you."

She spoke from the porch, her profile barely visible in silhouette.

"I was hoping you'd be out here," he said.

"Oh I'm here. I'm not going anywhere for the foreseeable future." Her laugh was humorless and sad. "I just wanted to say thanks for talking to me earlier."

He then heard footsteps that went into the house, the screen door closing behind her.

Gabe shook his head and continued on to the shop. Once there, he fed Jake and fell into a rocker on the porch, pulling his phone from his pocket to call his sister—it was only late afternoon there, with the time difference.

The call lasted awhile, as Tally told her brother details about their mother's health, the B&B, and shared news about her own family— his three nephews and tiny niece kept her hopping. He promised to call and nag his mother about her doctor visits. Laughing at the antics of his nephews and niece, he bid his sister good night and went inside the shop, leaving the door open for Jake to come and go as he pleased.

Forgoing sleep in favor of crafting wooden toys, the night slipped by him in a haze of top shelf scotch and loud music, the only release he could find when his neck tightened up and wouldn't let go.

*   *   *

Things were changing.

Though she found herself sitting motionless in tears time and again, as the days passed, there were changes. Changes she felt were both good and not.

Good changes in that it seemed she was getting stronger, remembering to eat more often—even if it was usually just her standby toast—noticing the sunrise and enjoying her walks.

Not good in that she felt traitorous to Jack in enjoying the world without him.

Getting stronger was a good thing, as long as she didn't lose Jack's presence in her dreams. Logically she knew life was for the living and she couldn't live in the dreams forever, yet her heart couldn't help but try.

She'd had the bad dreams from the moment she lost him, but had only recently begun to truly feel his presence in the good ones. Those she wished would stay.

The hammock had become her solace, swaying gently through the nights and days. After her morning walks, she settled there until the need to eat drove her inside.

The rest of the day was always a blur, with her waking up from dreams several times only to fall back into them again. Her grief, combined with exhaustion, made sleep always within reach.

Over and over, the same three dreams haunted her sleep, yet over and over Charlie did not want to give up a single one.

Change the sad reality of the bad ones, yes, but give them up when they were almost all she had left at this point? Hell, no.

She had no idea if person could live in dreams but she fully intended to find out.

****Chapter Seven****

SEEING A LONE FIGURE down the shore, Gabe thought that even from afar she looked sad, her slumped shoulders and bowed head showing more than words could say. He suspected it was his mystery guest, but hadn't the heart to intrude and find out.

"Hey!" He jumped as Nash bumped him.

"Wake up, Arch, let's go eat."

They ambled off towards the restaurant side of the bar, in search of a hearty breakfast.

Jill waited for them at a table there, steaming pot of coffee at the ready. Her empty plate was pushed aside, no way was she letting a good appetite sit waiting on the men to return.

"Good fishing?" she asked, smiling as Nash leaned in to kiss her cheek, taking a moment to nuzzle her neck in the process. "You smell good," he murmured against her ear.

"Get a damn room, will ya?" Gabe rolled his eyes, pouring coffee in both his and Nash's waiting mugs.

"We could abandon him, Nash. Just leave him here to eat all this breakfast by himself, hell, he can run the place without us for the day. What do you say, dear?" Jill teased.

A petite woman with short, tousled red hair brought plates to the table just as they sat down.

"You're the best, Jane. I ever tell you that?" Gabe groaned appreciatively at the plate filled with his customary eggs, bacon and toast. He and Nash were creatures of habit when it came to breakfast— simple fare, lots of it.

"Not since at least yesterday." Jane laughed, setting an identical plate in front of Nash.

"Joining us, Jane?" Jill asked her friend, who was also the general manager of both the bar and restaurant. A long-time resident, Jane was practically an island native—red hair and all—making her a huge asset to the expats when they'd arrived to rebuild the hurricane-wrecked property a few years ago. It hadn't taken the women long to become fast friends then close as sisters over the years.

"Not today, just feeding the bosses—all good?" When both Gabe and Nash nodded, mouths full, Jane waved a hand and headed back over to the restaurant side of the place.

After breakfast had been eaten and the coffeepot replenished, Jill left the men to their refills; today was office day for her—setting up reservations, helming her crew that cleaned and prepped the cabins.

* * *

At the end of the night, Gabe closed down the bar and dropped the shades to discourage bats and birds from taking up roost in there overnight. His steps were heavy as he walked through the darkness.

If he'd let it, the damned nightmare would have him fighting the same fire over and over, hoping for a different outcome. The anniversary of said fire always ramped up the nightmare. So he simply didn't sleep during that time—not much, anyway.

Instead, he spent most of the nighttime hours in the wood shop, music loud, drink cold.

Operating in the fog of exhaustion and melancholy, he almost missed the voice that came from Sea Glass tonight. "Did you know that chicks have a temporary egg tooth that helps them poke their way out of the egg?"

"I—Well, I'm not sure I did know that." He laughed, the inanity catching him off guard.

"Did you know that pineapples don't grow on trees?"

"I did know that one thanks to a curious nephew. Did you know it takes forty to fifty gallons of sap to make one gallon of maple syrup?" he countered, leaning against a coconut palm tree.

"I did know that and should warn you that I'm full of such enlightening tidbits." She laughed lightly.

The pause that followed was companionable, both simply resting in the dark.

She spoke first. "You know, earlier today I realized it's been almost two weeks since I've spoken to another human being. While that was by deliberate design, it does make me wonder at my sanity a little. So when I heard your footsteps this time, I thought I'd say hello and see if you're a figment of my imagination or not."

Gabe was so attentive to her voice that he could almost hear her slight smile as she spoke.

"Your sanity is fine, I'm as real as it gets."

"As real as what gets? Things in one's head are still there, whether others see them or not." Her voice was teasing in response.

"As real as Davy Jones' locker?"

She laughed then, a hesitant musical sound that made him want to give her the world on a string just to hear it again.

"Good night, Gabe."

He heard the screen door close behind her, momentarily startled that she'd remembered his name.

He wondered what her name was for a moment before he realized he could easily look it up in his files.

Damn idiot, you've lost your marbles over a disembodied voice with a fetching laugh?

Shaking his head, he sought his bed, refusing to allow himself to plot when he might talk to her again.

Chapter Eight

ENOUGH. CHARLIE DECIDED this had gone on long enough. Pushing herself up from the hammock, heart racing, she struggled to wake fully.

Waking up screaming in terror with her heart pounding just flat out pissed her off.

That was a new dream, not one of the three she was used to having. In fact, it wasn't a dream at all but the reliving of the moment she knew her husband was dead, the moment she first saw his strong, vibrant body motionless and colorless.

Just that moment was all she'd been able to recall from the night of the accident. Her doctor said the memory might return or it might be gone forever, nobody could know for sure. She knew she'd been there, knew she'd witnessed her world fly apart but just that moment was all she remembered. Now for it to invade her dreams? Absolutely not.

Since Jack's death, sleep had been an inviting escape where the dreams brought comfort amid the sorrow. This dream did nothing of the kind. She was not going to relive that every night, oh no, she wasn't.

It seemed sleep was no longer the refuge of memories that, while they hurt more than she could describe, brought Jack close to her.

Hair firmly in a ponytail, lips pressed together, Charlie brewed a pot of coffee and fired up her laptop. The thing had been largely untouched in the past weeks, save for one email reply to Trudy, in which Charlie had faked flaky internet access to avoid further contact.

With the desire to stay awake, Charlie suddenly felt charged and too alert, like her nerve endings were firing willy nilly on all cylinders, with no rhyme or reason to them whatsoever.

She fixed a plate of cheese and crackers, noticing how low her stash of both was getting. Ugh. She wasn't ready for the world, by far.

Forcing herself to breathe evenly as she'd learned to do when coping with her grief in front of others, Charlie was angry that she had to control her feelings once again, but she preferred that to reliving the night her life as she knew it had ended.

With a sigh, she sat in front of the computer and decided it might be time to learn a new hobby. The hours ticked away as she clicked page after page.

As dawn began to streak the sky, she stretched and carried her coffee cup out onto the porch—dream or no dream, she wasn't going to miss dawn breaking upon the sea. It was a magical sight every time.

Putting her cup down on the tiny table, Charlie sat back in the hammock and just as the sunrise broke over the horizon, fell hard and fast into sleep.

* * *

He really shouldn't be surprised by now, Gabe thought as the sounds from Sea Glass Cottage reached his ears.

He was going to have to do something different, either stop walking this way—which wasn't really an option—or go to her in hopes of being helpful in some way. Where does a guy draw the line between helping and minding his own business?

Needing to shower and get back to the beach for charter day, Gabe had decided to let it go once more when her voice came again.

"Mmmmm, you can do that all day." Throaty and sensuous, the sound was far different from what he'd been hearing.

If he didn't know better—did he, really??—Gabe would've thought he was over-hearing two people enjoying themselves amid the privacy the place afforded.

Sea Glass girl could have company or be on the phone with someone obviously special to her, he acknowledged when the satisfied murmur came again, causing him to shrug and move restlessly towards his cottage.

He didn't need to listen in or interrupt, he told himself sternly as he showered and pulled on a gray t-shirt, this one advertising The Painted Parrot in bold colors.

Charter day was always a good day, filled with a variety of interesting people and the wide open sea. He looked forward to it.

Walking to the shore, he texted his nephews:

Knock Knock!
Boys: Who's there?
Gabe: Cowsgo.
Boys: Cowsgo who?
Gabe: No, they don't, cowsgo moo.
Boys: GROAN!

He laughed loudly, imagining the groans across the supper table in New England.

Jill set up the bar, greeting him on his way. "Morning, Gabe!"

He waved and called out, "It's a beautiful day to be out on the sea!"

He was rewarded by Nash's voice replying, "It's always a beautiful day to be out on the sea!"

They were truly happy to be here, building this life together.

Aboard the JohnB, Gabe spent the next couple of hours answering questions and pointing out whales and shipwreck sites, the Sea Glass girl's sensuous voice lingering in the back of his mind right next to the heartbreaking version he'd heard more often.

She really had a hold on him, it seemed.

He shook his head slightly as if to clear it and focused on the elderly couple in front of him who were determined to learn every detail he might possibly know about the island and the surrounding sea.

Next to them bounced a boy full of pirate questions who reminded him of his nephews. Gabe grinned at them all and continued to answer and point, fully in his element.

*   *   *

This time the dream was sweet and sexy, leaving her with an intense longing so deep she felt like she might never breathe again, ever.

It was these dreams that were her complete undoing; these were the essence of the entity that was—that had been— Charlie-and-Jack.

Just her and Jack. No children. No neighbors, no students, no missions. No dog or cats. Just Charlie-and-Jack, making love as if nothing else existed.

It seemed no matter what was going on in the world around them, Charlie and Jack came together at the end of the day seeking one another. Often wordless until after they'd made love, sometimes talking over the day—always deeply connecting.

Sometimes sweet, sometimes desperate. Sometimes tender, sometimes laughing. Always seeking.

In the aftermath of this sweet dream, Charlie's tears would not be slowed or checked, her hands curled under her chin, holding the pillow close, wishing for the dream to return yet hating the point-less arousal it brought. Wishing to wake up to what life had been.

Reluctant to give up time spent dreaming of Jack, Charlie let the anger at the horrifying dream from earlier lead her to sleeping less. Drinking more coffee, she spent more time online researching both her desired hobby as well as her budding writing project.

She carried her toast out to the porch steps and sat watching a boat come closer and closer to shore before it veered off out of her sight line, the trees obscuring the view. Sighing, she knew she needed to venture out and face people at the seaside bar soon, for that's where Jill told her the mail run would be.

Maybe later. For now, toast, coffee and the view were enough to clear away the dregs of the dream still clinging to her.

****Chapter Nine****

CHARTERS DONE, boat cleaned and ready for the next morning's fishing, Gabe jumped off the boat and headed for the bar that was filled with customers as the supper hour, followed by after dinner drinks and just plain fun for the evening.

He greeted customers as he made his way to the bar where Jill slid him a cold bottle with a smile.

"You're looking good tonight, Jilly-girl." He raised the bottle in salute and drank deeply.

"Sshh! Don't tell this imp I'm carrying or he might wreak havoc." Jill laughed, putting a finger over her lips with a wink.

Gabe blew her round belly a kiss, turning to the man who'd walked up to his side. They talked of charters and Gabe gave him a card with the details, a parting handshake, and turned back to Jill just as she came down the bar, laughing at Bill's joke. A fixture about the place, Bill and his late wife had owned the bar before Gabe. They'd sold it with the intention of moving closer to grandchildren, but Margie had died before they could do so. Gabe had encouraged Bill's desire to stay on the island, assuring him he'd still be a part of things. He helped out from time to time and was often in charge of the bar's evening game time.

"You're bad, Bill, so bad. Hey, Gabe, a couple of boxes came on the mail boat for our mystery gal in Sea Glass. Looks like we'll get to see her soon."

Gabe cocked an eyebrow in response. Hmm, he could linger about the bar tomorrow in hopes of seeing her. Or, maybe he could be of help after all by taking the boxes to her. That was a thought.

Then again, didn't she need to get out for her own sake?

Gabe shrugged, figuring it wasn't up to him to decide such things.

"I'll take the boxes to the cottage, Jilly," he said, rising from the barstool, headed for the shelf where they stashed the mail deliveries.

The two boxes stood on the floor, one a bit larger than the other. The return labels gave away nothing, for just about anything could be ordered from that online giant warehouse.

Gabe pushed away a moment of guilt at not sharing what had happened so far with his friends, winked at Jill and carried the boxes across the sand, humming along the way.

As he drew closer to the cottage, he had second thoughts about his gallant gesture.

What if she didn't want to be seen—especially knowing he'd heard her private pain several times?

Five minutes ago he was convinced taking the boxes to her was a good idea, but now he wasn't so sure. His steps slowed as he approached Sea Glass, the fairy lights twinkling in the darkening twilight.

"Do you know if the island grocery has chocolate milk in bottles?" Her voice came from the darkness, just as soft, yet much stronger than before.

Gabe was a bit taken aback by the question and it took him a moment to answer. "You want chocolate milk?"

Her light laugh came across the porch railing. "In bottles. I live on the stuff."

"Well, I do have a couple of boxes here for you, not that I think you ordered chocolate milk through the mail." He waited for her reply before walking any further.

"Thanks, you saved me from having to face people. After these last few weeks alone, I'm afraid I'm not quite suited for conversation." She spoke slowly, as if choosing her words carefully.

"Alone? You've not left that cottage since you got here?"

"You got it—besides walks down to the water," she said. "Jill did a great job of supplying me with the things I needed but chocolate milk doesn't last forever—especially my chocolate milk." She cleared her throat, after so little talking in almost a month, it felt like sandpaper.

"Have you talked to anyone but me?" Gabe couldn't help asking.

"My adult children on the phone every so often. But, you see, Gabe, that's what I came here for. Solitude. Silence."

He wasn't sure what to say next.

"Remember last time? When you said you wanted to punch J-Jack?" her voice hitched on the name, squeezing his heart more than just a little.

Gabe lowered the boxes and leaned against a tree next to them before answering, "I remember and I still want to punch anyone that'd cause you such hurt."

Moments passed with only the sounds of the waves and the sea birds settling in. He heard her take a deep shuddery breath and realized she was crying.

"Aww, don't cry. He can't be worth this much pain." Gabe's hands fisted.

"Oh, he is ... worth it and so much more," she whispered, barely loud enough for him to hear.

"But you're hurting so much. Nobody should cause someone they love so much pain." Gabe forced his voice into calm when he really wanted to shout some sense into her.

She cleared her throat again. "Jack..." A sigh. "Jack would never hurt me in any way." Her voice rose in emphasis before falling silent.

Just as Gabe opened his mouth, she said softly, "But he has. He has shattered my heart ... beyond any hope of repair."

Gabe swore, "Damn it." Pushing off from the tree, he stepped toward the porch.

Her voice stopped him—that was becoming a habit.

"Jack ... Jack is d-dead. He's dead and I'm all alone." Her voice was emphatic, fading to a whisper.

"Oh, honey, I'm so sorry." Gabe was shocked, realizing he'd been blind, or deaf rather, to the signals.

He'd assumed it was a breakup, never considering such a tragic, final loss.

The sobs slowed a little and she hiccupped. "Can you leave the boxes?"

"I can."

He heard the screen door close, the conversation ended.

It seemed that for now they were going to remain only voices, and that had to be okay with him.

*　*　*

If she could possibly care about another person's feelings, Charlie would feel terrible about the way she treated him, simply dismissing him after he'd saved her an outing by bringing the boxes practically to her doorstep.

If.

She had to admit the sound of Gabe's voice had been a kind of comfort. It had been nice not to be alone, even if just for a few moments.

That surprised her, for she'd truly relished the last few weeks. Letting go and just being had been so hard yet so freeing. She wondered again if, just maybe, she was actually getting stronger. Not that she had any desire to change her status quo, but that maybe she'd do more than cry and dream ... although she still fervently wished she could inhabit those three dreams.

Wasn't there a movie or three about that somewhere-people preferring to live inside their dreams instead of reality? Inside their fantasies, like Avatar or something—isn't that pretty much the same thing as in your dreams?

Charlie shook her head. *Too much thinking going on here, girl*, she told herself as she stood to fetch the boxes.

Her chocolate milk dilemma remained, with only two bottles left in the fridge.

As she unpacked the boxes of snack crackers, candy and a few paper goods, she decided she was going to have to brave the public and make a trip to the island store the next day. She knew the store was within walking distance but figured carrying a load of chocolate milk bottles back wasn't an option, so her plan was to walk into town, shop and then hire a cab to come back out.

That decided, Charlie sat atop the kitchen table with her computer, refusing to dread the outing. She didn't have to go; chocolate milk was her choice.

She blew out a breath, resuming her research, adding things to her online order list. Absorbed, she worked online through the night into the morning—marking articles, making lists and reading.

She moved from the table to the floor, to the couch and back to the table. She even started writing a new article series about reading for all ages, even though she'd taken an indefinite leave of absence from her steady magazine writing jobs.

As the morning sun splashed through the window, Charlie looked up in surprise.

She surveyed the table before her, littered with the last of the chocolate milk bottles, some candy wrappers and scribbled papers.

"Well, that felt good," she remarked to the walls, stretching as she rose to start a fresh pot of coffee—pouring out what little had gone untouched last night.

She spied the boat just before it veered out of her line of sight and walked off the porch onto the beach to see it reach the shore.

The sun was already warm and steady at just after sunrise. That's the tropics for you, she thought as she watched the same two men jump off the boat, calling back and forth to the vendors as they worked. A young boy ran up to them, carrying cups of coffee; they ruffled his hair and laughed as he ducked and ran away.

Would she ever feel as carefree again, Charlie wondered.

She wandered to the water's edge, walked down the beach a ways and sank to the sand as had become her morning habit. She pulled her hair back with a blue hairband and raised her face to the sun while the water lapped at her feet.

The sea and the sun were long reputed to be healing, and while she couldn't imagine life without Jack, she was a mother. So here goes whatever healing might be found.

Chapter Ten

"GREAT MORNING FOR FISHING!" Nash grinned as he cleaned and stowed the gear.

As he expected, Gabe's answering grin was wide. "It's always a great morning for fishing!"

"Come on over to the house. Unless something changed, Jilly was feeling good when I left and said she'd have breakfast ready."

"Don't have to ask me twice," Gabe replied, noticing the lone woman down the shore a ways. He'd seen her every morning for a while now, never with anyone, always seeming so solitary.

Nash followed his gaze and commented, "She one of ours? She's been around most mornings for a while now."

Gabe shrugged. "I wonder. I've noticed her, too."

It didn't really occur to him that the lone figure might be his Sea Glass mystery girl, because this lady he was watching had walked quite a bit further down the beach past Sea Glass. With the Sea Glass girl's adamant avoidance of people, he didn't expect she'd venture out that far from the shelter of the cottage.

The two men talked about their progress on the wooden toy donations for the FDNY toy drive as they joined Jill for breakfast, both relieved she seemed be feeling well thus far into the morning.

As the trio finished eating, Jill said, "I'm going into town this morning for a doctor appointment. You two want anything while I'm out?"

She picked up her tea mug and pushed aside her plate, smiling at Nash as he stacked plates and took them to the sink.

"I'll take you if you want, I've a craving for Katie's praline scones and I want to pay Amos' grocery bill before he can do it himself." Gabe stood and finished clearing the table while Nash loaded the dishes into the dishwasher the two of them had installed last year.

"I'll meet you at the truck in fifteen?" he called as Jill disappeared into the bedroom.

"Sure thing," she called back.

"Hey, Arch, if she goes all pale 'n stops talking, pay attention, man," Nash said low-voiced, glancing warily in the direction his wife had gone.

"Reading you loud n clear, pal. No worries." Gabe grinned, lightly punching his friend and heading to his cottage to shower quickly and change.

Fishing was stinky work no matter how beautiful the location.

*   *   *

Later, Jill told Nash about how, while in town, their dear Gabe had purchased a flat of thirty-six bottles of chocolate milk and ordered more to be delivered to the bar the next week.

"We stock chocolate milk here at the bar?" Nash asked. "I know the restaurant side might, but we don't—do we?"

Jill gave him a look and said, "He didn't explain, just muttered about needing it on hand and got all close-lipped on me!"

Wasn't that interesting? The two of them considered this as Nash carried their groceries home while Jill prepared to open the bar for the day.

The more Jill thought about it, the more she thought there was something more going on than Gabe's sudden, inexplicable need for chocolate milk. It occurred to her that she had stocked their mystery tenant's fridge with the stuff, but Gabe hadn't mentioned meeting her. Interesting.

Maybe she just hadn't noticed amid dealing with her near-constant morning sickness followed by eating everything in sight.

"See what you're doing, already causing havoc?" She patted her belly and laughed as Bill approached the bar.

"Hey, Bill, how goes it?" She bantered with the 70-year-old as he found his place and settled in for the afternoon.

Jill eyed the dozen or so bottles of chocolate milk in the bar's glass front cooler and wondered anew what Gabe was up to and why didn't he tell her about it?

*   *   *

Gabe carried two dozen bottles of chocolate milk in a milk crate through the trees near Sea Glass Cottage, stopping to see if he heard any sounds and trying to decide how to approach his mystery tenant this time.

He could hear the outdoor shower running on the other side of the cottage. He could either wait and actually meet her or he could leave the chocolate milk on the porch and hope she found it soon, or he could walk around and call to her.

The shower was well-protected from any outside view whatsoever with a high, thick wall but she'd be able to easily hear him if he called out. That seemed creepy, though.

He probably should've given in to Jill's pointed curious looks and asked her opinion on what to do, but Gabe was protective of the Sea Glass girl and not ready to tell his friends about their talks in the dark.

Then it hit him and Gabe groaned aloud. Why didn't he just put the damned bottles in a cooler of ice and leave them for her? With a sigh of disgust at himself, he stalked back to the bar and placed the bottles in the glass door cooler, pointedly ignoring Jill's puzzlement and shooting her a grin as he strode out to join the charter customers gathering at the shore—the chocolate milk run would have to wait.

The sea was sparkling blue as usual, bidding sea lovers everywhere to lose themselves amid the waves and shining sun. Gabe adjusted his shades, fired up The JohnB, and turned to welcome his guests.

Chapter Eleven

FROM THE EARLY DAYS of their marriage, Jack had usually joined her in the kitchen when he was home—either helping to cook or charmingly reading her snippets from the newspaper while she cooked. Once the babies came, he'd play with them while talking to her. This had been their routine from the beginning, through raising the babies up until his last night on Earth.

In the last year since Cassidy had left home, they'd cooked the evening meal together every night he was home—it became a sensuous dance, foreplay of sorts.

These memories, so much a part of the person she was, so many that she couldn't recall cooking without him, made it hard for Charlie to set foot in a kitchen. She hadn't cooked once in their home kitchen in the months since Jack's death, and she intended never to do so again.

Thinking of their bright and inviting kitchen, done in her favorite colors of blue and yellow, Charlie buried the recurring budding idea that she was considering selling the house without ever returning to think about another time.

She paused, looking about the bright kitchen, and decided courting ghosts was not on tonight's agenda. With that, she took the peanut butter jar and spoon with her to the porch.

Since the first time she'd fallen apart in the kitchen, sure she'd felt Jack behind her, she'd yet to cook a meal for herself, existing on toast and the staples Jill had stocked for her. It wasn't the worst or the best way to be, but she was doing okay.

That had to be enough for now.

As she curled up in the hammock, she reached out for Jack, thinking of each and every one of his features. One of her greatest remaining fears was that she'd forget what he looked like beyond the pictures.

Every time she felt that she was forgetting, she'd envision him fully in her mind's eye, running her fingertips all over his face, cupping his broad shoulders in her hands, filling her arms with him, memorizing the feel of his short-bearded jaw against her cheek, trying to see the details of him over and over.

The jar falling to the porch, Charlie brought her hands to her own face and whispered, "Please, please, please let this be a nightmare you'll wake me from this time, please…"

* * *

Music and lights spilled from the bar out on to the sand where people of various ages played volleyball and further down others tossed horseshoes, kids ran amok and lovers sneaked kisses in the shadows of the trees.

Paradise never looked so good as Gabe served drinks and joked with his friends and customers, trash talking Nash as Bill and company challenged him to a rousing round of darts. Gabe never turned down a challenge. Even though pool was more his game, he was no slouch at darts.

The restaurant next to the bar kept both its patrons and the bar patrons supplied with delicious food, the bar offered fresh snacks every evening and drinks of all kinds from aged rum to freely-flowing draft beer.

This plus the fantastic staff made The Painted Parrot a hot spot of the island's beach hangouts. There was something for everyone, and Gabe was very proud of that fact.

As the hours passed and the crowd waned, Jill and Nash cleaned up and left the bar together, Gabe, Bill and a handful of regulars hooting in jest and waving as, arms around each other, they slow-danced off into the shadows.

Gabe watched his friends go with a smile as he returned to the bar and finished up the process of closing down for the night. Sometimes witnessing the deep connection between them made him think about his failed marriage. Was Tabitha right in her accusations that he hadn't even wanted to try to make things work? He saw it as a mutual problem—neither would compromise. But sometimes, he wondered.

The last of the customers gone, he wiped down the tables and readied things for the next day, his motions accompanied by the sounds of the radio and the ocean waves.

After everything was finished up, Gabe filled a portable cooler with ice and loaded the chocolate milk bottles from the bar cooler.

He thought for a moment then scribbled a note and taped it to the top of the ice chest with a slight smile. Sea Glass girl was going to get her chocolate milk tonight.

Society always said that was a bad thing, hiding, but he understood how hiding—even to the extent she took it—was often a survival tactic that needed to happen before healing could go on. As if after a traumatic event the tiny soul flickering to survive inside needed shelter from the storm in which to mend.

Gabe refused to analyze why he was so determined to help her hide from the world, but he was going to help her however he could.

He wheeled the portable cooler cross the sand and into the trees. He figured he'd leave it on the porch steps and go on his way, planning to check in with Tally and his mother before it got too late over there.

As he reached the edge of the trees next to Sea Glass, Gabe sighed, hearing her heartbroken voice begging that she be awakened from her living nightmare.

He was finished tiptoeing around.

Taking a deep breath, he cleared his throat and spoke quietly, "Did you know that when the alpha female of a wolf pack has a litter of pups, all the females in the pack will have a pseudo pregnancy so that they can take over if the mom gets hurt or killed?"

Her breath hitched and the sobs slowed.

He could swear he heard a slight laugh.

Not waiting for a response, he said, "I've got something for you, another box. I'm going to leave it at the top of the steps, okay? It's a little heavy to leave at the bottom."

She made a sound of confusion. "I'm not expecting anything."

Gabe grinned in the dark as he walked to the bottom of the steps and hefted the cooler up to the porch, then walked away.

"Trust me, you want this."

*   *   *

Curiosity got the best of her and, after hearing him leave, Charlie went to the box. She pulled off the taped note and held it close to the fairy lights.

"Magic elixir," she read, opening the cooler lid and immediately clapping a hand over her mouth.

"Chocolate milk!" She laughed out loud—nearly scaring herself with the sound.

Not only was she relieved beyond words that she didn't have to venture out, she was completely charmed by Gabe's thoughtfulness.

Could you consider someone you'd never laid eyes on to be a friend? she wondered as she opened the first bottle and drank deeply.

Ah, chocolate milk. She really did live on the stuff. Jack had often called it her happy juice. She sobered at the thought, yet it brought a smile, however small and tremulous, to her face as she remembered.

Jack was never, ever off her mind, but she could at least think of him for longer periods without dissolving into a basket case on the floor.

While on one hand, Charlie thought that kind of progress took Jack further away from her, the other hand knew it was part of the process of living with her loss. Was she moving on? Oh hell, no, but she was surviving, and that was important, with Cassidy and Troy in the world.

Sitting on the porch steps, looking across the moonlit sand, she felt antsy and stiff, in need of a walk. It was at least two a.m., and she was not walking the beach in the dark, she thought crossly.

Stretching into a sun salutation yoga pose, she decided that would have to do until morning. As she moved her body through the poses, she was soothed by the stretching and warming of her muscles. The yoga had made a difference during all of these trying months, keeping her feeling strong and healthy.

It wasn't long before she felt the blood moving and her mind quieting a little. Her body soothed, she pulled the cooler on wheels into the house and put the bottles into the fridge, a bemused smile on her face.

After the effort of putting the bottles away, she felt the need to curl up in the bed, cocooning inside a cave made from the lightweight quilt instead of reclining in the hammock where the air was fresh and the space wide open. She didn't analyze the feeling and did just that.

As soon as her eyes closed, she saw a field of daisies and a sun-warmed patchwork quilt; Jack was laughing, reaching his hand out to her, the laugh lines beside his eyes crinkling sweetly as he tilted his head and entreated her to join him. Charlie laughed with him, took his hand and followed him, leaning against his broad, strong back, his soft navy t-shirt warm with the sun's rays.

He pulled her down to the quilt, his arms coming around her as she lay against his chest, watching their small children sleep curled together like kittens in the sunshine. Jack kissed her, his lips tasting slightly salty from the pimento cheese picnic lunch they'd shared with the kids and slightly sweet from the wine they'd shared with each other.

She kissed him back fervently, her arms around him, holding him to her tightly. He pulled back a bit and looked at her with a question in his eyes, and her hold on him tightened. Then his image faded and her arms were left empty.

As his body faded from her arms, suddenly her senses were filled with a whipping cold wind, helicopter blades and her own screams.

She awoke in her borrowed bed, clutching the pillows and gasping for air, the shattered shards of her heart piercing her chest, her throat on fire from the screams.

The details of that horrible day were trying mightily to return to her memory and she fought them just as mightily, fearing that once she remembered all of the details, the good dreams would stop and leave only the nightmares.

Pushing the smothering covers and pillows away with vengeance, she made her way out to the porch, taking great gulps of the salty air.

Dawn was slowly breaking and the silhouettes of fishing boats were visible against the sky. She watched them but her mind's eye was burning with the image of Jack lying on the ground, lifeless and unseeing.

"Oh, dear God. Jack! Why?!?"

Enough was enough, how much pain could one person take? She wanted to run, to scream, to pray, to curse.

And she wanted him back right this minute.

Chapter Twelve

IN HER FIGHT to both grow stronger and grieve at will, Charlie subconsciously developed a routine of sorts—one that frequently included crying jags or the realization that hours had passed unawares, but a routine nonetheless.

Mornings she spent watching the sun rise and the boats come in, followed by a long walk down the beach.

She'd walk back to the stretch of beach just below her cottage and sit at the water's edge, the sea lapping at her legs. When she grew sun-weary and hot, she returned to the cottage to shower and eat something from her stash of boxes and bags.

She still avoided cooking or spending much time in the kitchen. Allowing grief to come freely was one thing, purposeful punishment of one's self was quite another.

The rest of the day was spent researching and writing with the hammock naps that always brought dreams growing fewer and farther between. Later she'd take an evening walk, being sure she was back on the porch before night fell.

Every night around one a.m., Gabe's voice would come through the darkness.

She found herself actually listening for his footsteps among the trees, sometimes even speaking to him first.

They talked of general things, passing the time lightly.

Gabe told her about the antics of his impish nephews and their tiny sister, details about tourists at the bar or stories of those he took out on the charter, anything to keep her talking to him. After the first few conversations, he almost always made her laugh.

He seemed to know he'd become a touchstone to reality for her.

It amazed Charlie that he never tried to come any closer into the light, not that any light more than the fairy lights was ever on.

After he left, she would be wide awake and grounded, spending a few more hours on her computer, writing and reconnecting in bits and pieces with her world before dreams would overtake her again.

It was a life, of sorts, and she was loath to think beyond it.

* * *

As it became habit to talk to her every night, to himself Gabe likened their friendship to online social media in that it was a very real thing to build a friendship without meeting in person for a long time, if ever. He figured the day would come soon enough and was bound and determined to leave that decision in Charlie's court.

One night after he'd sheepishly told her he thought of her as Sea Glass girl, she'd laughed a little and introduced herself.

She told him how she was a writer, about her young adult children and her nutty friend Trudy.

She didn't mention the husband she'd lost except briefly when Gabe caught her in the moments following a dream.

Gabe's heart ached for her when he overheard the dreams, which appeared to be random memories that brought her to her knees every time.

He wondered what it was like to love and be loved like that, where the world seemed to make no sense when you'd lost your other half. He was certain he and Tabitha hadn't loved like that.

****Chapter Thirteen****

CHARLIE FOUND HERSELF humming along with the radio—when had she turned that on—while considering how she'd get to town.

Well, actually, she considered how she'd return with her groceries, for the store was easily within walking distance, she knew.

It was as good a time as any to look around the island, and she could stop in at the restaurant to ask for the number to the cab company—wait, restaurant!

She had no need to brave the kitchen, only to brave The Painted Parrot. Surely she could get take-out and be in and out within minutes.

Charlie did a little dance and stopped short. She was excited about facing the world? No, she was excited about real food that she didn't have to cook.

After her shower, clad in a sundress of various blue-green shades of the sea that flowed to mid-calf, Charlie pocketed her back-up hairband and found her long-neglected flip flops.

Then she sat in the hammock.

Suddenly overwhelmed and anxious, she remembered the last time she was around people—before her trip. After weeks of putting on a mask, a brave face, she'd fallen apart, sinking to the floor in the local Panera sobbing Jack's name over and over into her hands while Trudy shielded her as best she could, frantically calling the kids.

Up until then, Charlie had allowed no one to see her fall apart.

Like a volcano long dormant yet simmering, her grief had burst forth in hot, destructive lava, searing everything in its path. All she had wanted to do was escape.

She'd managed to pull together and convince Trudy and the kids that all she needed was some time away from daily life.And here she was, weeks later, still randomly sinking to the floor—but at least in wasn't in public surrounded by people who knew her.

Shaking back her hair, Charlie resolutely stood and walked in the direction she first came from weeks ago.

She smiled at the sight of toddlers tripping in the sand, children running in and out of the surf, parents close at hand.

She'd always been so afraid for the children at the water's edge. At her insistence, Jack had stood out in the water a few feet, keeping between them and the sea—playing with them, yet keeping them safe from harm.

Blinking back tears from behind her aviator shades, she took another deep breath and kept walking, The Painted Parrot coming into clear view. Her stomach rumbled at the smells wafting her way on the tropical breeze, reminding her just how long it'd been since she'd eaten a real, freshly made meal.

Her steps faltered a bit as she approached, but she straightened her shoulders and walked through the open doorway, the hostess stepping up to speak to her. Charlie's voice sounded odd and creaky to her ears as she spoke to the woman, but she answered her query and was seated in moments. She'd chosen a spot in the far corner of the restaurant, against the half-wall that was open to the sea.

Having intended to ask about take-out, Charlie was surprised to find that, once seated in the corner, she felt like staying.

Music played in the background as kitchen sounds clattered and diners talked and ate. The mood was exactly what you'd expect in paradise—carefree and happy.

Bypassing the fresh catch-of-the-day, she chose her favorite pasta dish and sat with the cold tea glass in her hands. She closed her eyes for a moment, her shades still firmly in place. So many sounds, so many voices, it was a little overwhelming—okay, a lot overwhelming.

This is all on your terms, she reminded herself. *You can go right back to the cottage and stay there, or you can sit here and eat something worth eating for a change, Charlie. Take your pick.*

Keeping her eyes closed a bit longer, she tuned in to the sounds around her, acclimating to what seemed like chaos after her self-imposed exile.

It was then she heard him—after numerous conversations in the dark, she'd know that voice anywhere.

Gabe.

Upon her first venture out, it was poetic that her only friend in the world right now was within reach—and just out of sight.

Charlie kept her eyes closed, unsure of what to do next, feeling exposed and vulnerable before she remembered that he had no idea what she looked like—as far as she knew.

Breathing deeply, she opened her eyes and looked around, not moving or lifting her shades. She loved the privacy the shades afforded her; who didn't like looking around without being noticed?

She heard him shout out a laugh, apparently joking around with someone named Nash, but she still didn't see him.

It was then that she realized the bar was just across the bamboo wall a few feet in front of her, and that was where his voice was coming from.

"Here you go, ma'am, all fresh and delightful." The waitress smiled brightly.

Charlie lifted her shades to the top of her head—there was something to be said for manners, no matter the situation—and smiled.

"Thank you so much," she said softly, purposely keeping her voice low.

The steaming pasta drizzled with fresh Alfredo and tossed with grilled chicken sent waves of pleasure through Charlie with the first bite. She momentarily forgot Gabe's presence as she took another bite and moaned softly. "MMMmmm."

The waitress, refilling her tea glass, laughed. "Believe it or not, that's a common reaction to Matteo's cooking."

Charlie continued to eat, listening to Gabe's voice rising and falling from time to time amid the other noise. Her curiosity was beginning to override her desire to hide. She thought maybe she could peek without letting him know she was doing so, then chastised herself for being silly.

For a moment she heard Jack's voice. "Don't over-think things, Charlie, just do it."

Swallowing carefully, she took a drink and managed to make it past the moment without tears falling.

Baby steps, she told herself calmly as she nodded in answer to the waitress asking her if she wanted her to box up the remainder of the meal while she enjoyed her tea.

It occurred to her that she could easily take the tea and move to the tables outside the bar without anyone thinking twice. The view to the sea was even better out there and the area was fairly empty at the moment. Then, perhaps, she could catch a glimpse of Gabe, to put a face with the voice that soothed her and kept her anchored to reality night after night.

She chided herself for feeling shy after all their talks, but at the same time, it made sense that she'd feel vulnerable after her shattering loss followed by seclusion for so long.

Baby steps, Charlie thought again, smiling in thanks at Sandy and taking up her glass and the bag containing her food.

Go or stay? Charlie bandied about the thought as she walked across the restaurant and out the open doorway. Turn left to the tables or go straight, heading to the cottage? Left or cottage, left or cottage. The words became a chant in her head as she paused mid-step.

Charlie took a deep breath and turned to the tables.

She settled herself facing the sea, where she could turn her head to see inside the bar whenever she chose.

Shades down, feet up on a chair, she watched the water and listened to Gabe's voice as he bantered with customers.

The man sure did laugh a lot; she couldn't help but smile just listening.

Finally, after several slow-ticking minutes, she turned her head and looked into the bar.

Being midday, the place was filled with tourists eating lunch and enjoying a drink or two. She looked past the tables and the bar stools to the two men behind the bar.

At that moment, neither man happened to be speaking, so she had a minute to observe and try to guess which one was Gabe.

One had dark hair covered with a red ball cap, a ready laugh and a tattoo on his forearm, shades hanging from a cord around his neck.

The other was taller and broad-shouldered with short, wavy hair the color of dark gold that looked like it'd curl more if it grew longer. He, too, had a tattoo on his forearm and laughed easily.

A pair of aviator shades perched atop his head, the golden-haired one laughed again and threw the bar towel in his hands at the other one. "Some skill you have, Nash-Man."

And there he was, her voice of reason in the dark.

He looked so familiar. She wanted to hug him and wanted to run away at the same time, her feelings unsettled and strange.

Secure in the knowledge that she could retreat to the cottage at any moment, Charlie lifted her face to the sun. There was no need to decide if she'd make herself known to Gabe, or at least not right now. *Go with the flow, girl, go with the flow.*

She watched the activity on the beach, listening to Gabe's voice in the background—realizing that because of that reassuring, familiar voice, she was mostly relaxed and enjoying herself instead of feeling tense and needing to escape.

The psychology junkie in her was interested at that, but she pushed it away and concentrated on the moment. On the feeling of the warm sunshine, on the cold tea glass in her hand and the children calling along the shore.

She was absorbed, watching the sea as the sunshine scattered like golden glitter across the gentle turquoise waves, letting the sun warm her endlessly cold bones, and she didn't see Gabe ending his shift at the bar with a wave, only hearing his voice from afar and not comprehending the words of farewell he spoke to Nash and the customers as he headed out for the afternoon charter.

She didn't notice when he stepped from behind the bar and walked in her direction.

*   *   *

Before it could occur to him that Charlie might not want to be noticed, Gabe had walked up to the table and wordlessly set a bottle of chocolate milk in front of her.

She didn't look at him, but her hand moved, fingers touching the bottle, a slight smile on her face as she continued to gaze out at the sea.

How he'd known it was her, Gabe couldn't say for sure, but he was certain.

Her curly hair—What were those colors? Cinnamon? Chestnut?— fell across her face, a blue scarf having fallen askew in the breeze.

Gabe waited, suddenly afraid he'd freaked her out—but, after all, it was she who'd ventured out in public, wasn't it?

Charlie gestured to the other chair, still not looking at him.

He pulled the chair out and sat, reaching out with one finger to toy with the whimsical sea glass in the shapes of shells on the bracelet adorning her wrist.

"Hello, Gabe," the familiar husky voice spoke softly, her gaze yet on the sea as if she were still gathering her courage to look at him.

"Hello, Charlie," he replied just as softly, looking at her, waiting. He let go of her bracelet, his hand resting on the table between them.

Tentatively, she put her hand in his and used the other one to lift her shades, pushing back her hair and finally looking at him, her eyes a dark sapphire blue.

Her fingers gripped his tightly, surprisingly strong.

He smiled, watching her worry the edge of her bottom lip with her teeth—a mannerism that somehow seemed to suit her.

She took a slow, deep breath and started to speak, but stopped, her lip quivering slightly before she caught it in her teeth again.

Gabe looked down at their linked fingers rather than stare at her as she battled for composure.

"It's gonna be okay." He repeated what he'd said to her many times in the dark, looking back at her face to see her tremulous smile, her eyes back out to the sea.

He muttered in frustration as he saw the charter group begin to gather.

"I've got a charter in fifteen and Nash has the bar—Jill isn't around to take over for either of us or I'd take some time right now to properly say hello. You're welcome to ride along..." Gabe's voice trailed off, it didn't feel right to walk away from her at this moment without offering further company, but he knew she wouldn't join him on the boat with all those people just yet.

"Maybe next time." Charlie gave a small shrug of apology, meeting his eyes, yet not feeling ashamed for turning down the invitation.

"Same place, same time." Gabe winked and squeezed her fingers as he answered the hail of a repeat charter customer walking by the table.

"We sailing, Skipper?"

"We're sailing, Professor." Gabe laughed, turning back to find that Charlie had already started back toward Sea Glass Cottage.

He wasn't sure what the feeling was in his chest when she turned and gave him a little wave, but he liked it.

*   *   *

Charlie reached the cottage in short order, admittedly making a pretty hasty retreat from the overwhelming emotions threatening to take her down.

She dropped her shoes on the porch step and went to put the food in the fridge—she'd thank herself later—before seeking solace in the hammock, the fabric shades swinging free, casting the porch into slight shadow.

Collapsing into the hammock, she curled up tightly, reaching under the pillow for the shirt of Jack's she kept there.

Her breathing slowed as she gave in to sleep—the outing had been good yet exhausting. Her nerves were on high alert, feeling as if she'd been through an ordeal. Seeing Gabe at the end had been completely overwhelming—good but overwhelming.

What on earth had she expected? He did own the place and it wasn't like it was a big place; he was sure to be within reach just about anywhere on the property, Charlie thought as she drifted off, reaching for Jack as always.

*   *   *

Gabe jumped aboard the boat, automatically starting things up, but his thoughts were still with Charlie and the thrill of seeing her face-to-face after all these weeks—tanned from the island sun, her jewel blue eyes so serious and sad, all cute and whimsical with her sea glass bracelet (he was a sea glass sucker, without a doubt), that multi-colored hair that seemed to have a life of its own despite the blue scarf tied in it, the way she worried the edge of her lip repeatedly.

Noting all of that in five minutes meant she had made an impact on him, Gabe knew. While he was always attentive to details, admittedly he was human and thus sometimes selective in his memory.

Not so with his first look at Charlie. If he'd thought he was smitten before, he was down for the count now.

His chest tightened, thinking about how she'd tightly gripped his hand, like a drowning person grabbing on for fear of being swept away.

While the charters were always a fun time for Gabe, when this one was over, he barely remembered interacting with his guests, but everyone seemed happy and went on their way.

His thoughts consumed with one particular sad blue-eyed tenant, he barely waved to Nash as he walked by the bar on his way to enjoy a few minutes of downtime before he came back to relieve the man and rock out the evening shift.

*   *   *

Nash watched Gabe walk by the bar without a word.

Turning to his wife, he asked, "Our boy seem oddly distracted to you lately?"

Jill hooted with laughter as she wiped glasses and put them under the counter. "I seem to remember asking you the same question last week 'n you dismissed me as—and I quote—'hormonal and nosy.'"

Nash grinned, popping his wife's jean-clad rear with the bar towel and ducking out of the way before she could retaliate.

"But, yeah, I agree, something's on his mind and it's odd that he's not telling us. He's told us most of his every thought for the past 18 years it seems—with the exception of 9/11, and that took a bit longer for all of us." Jill shrugged. "I don't think it's worrisome, he seems in good spirits, so I doubt it's anything significant. Maybe something to do with Tally or his mother?"

Nash pitched his voice low and said, "Maybe so, but I saw him stop and talk to a woman over at the tables earlier."

Jill rolled her eyes. "Gabe talks to everyone."

"No," Nash continued. "He stood there for a few minutes, sat down and toyed with her hand. The body language was familiar, and he reached out to hold her hand.

Jill raised her eyebrows. "Hmmm, Super Sleuth, we'll have to see won't we?" She caught him off guard and popped him back with the towel as he turned to leave the bar, headed to check in with the maintenance crew. Nash stuck his tongue out and waved.

"You're nosy," she called out.

Thankfully the daily sickness that had plagued her had begun to settle down more often than not. She was glad, not only to be feeling better, but to have her husband and Gabe relax a bit and stop hovering over her every step.

She loved tending bar in the afternoons and hated it when one of them felt the need to hover over the entire shift, effectively rendering her nearly useless.

Boys! Jill shook her head with a smile; she'd not trade either of them.

Chapter Fourteen**

THAT NIGHT, instead of stopping in the dark between the cottages, Gabe walked up to the porch steps.

"Gabe?" He was surprised when her voice came from inside the cottage instead of from the hammock. "Come on in," she called. With a shrug, he climbed the steps and walked through the open door.

The cottage was lit with lamplight, the bright colors muted in the glow.

Gabe's eyebrow arched as he saw that Charlie sat atop the table in front of her laptop, books and papers spread all over, as well as bowls of candy and empty chocolate milk bottles. Her hair was twisted into some kind of complicated knot, secured with what looked like a pencil.

Wearing a navy t-shirt that was clearly not her own and cutoff denim shorts, she looked impossibly young and vulnerable as she looked at him through black-framed glasses.

"This," she explained, waving a red pen in the air, "is genius at work."

Gabe laughed despite his tiredness; the day had been a long one. Besides the worries of his mother's health weighing on his mind, his own demons had predictably kept him from sleeping.

"Is this awkward? Should we go out in the dark?" Charlie stood, retrieving two bottles from the fridge—one water, one chocolate milk, handing the water to him.

Her eyes sparkled in jest, yet her voice was hesitant.

"I don't find it awkward at all." He leaned against the counter. "I'd have come to you after the charter but wanted you to have some space after such a big event as being out in public."

Charlie grimaced. "Yeah, about that…" Her voice trailed off as she looked away.

Gabe took the hint and changed the subject, gesturing to the table. "Got a project going?"

Charlie waved her chocolate milk bottle in the direction of the couch and led him to sit down. "Writer; always a project going on," she said as they both settled into couch corners facing each other.

"I don't know what I expected to see when we met face-to-face, but you're exactly it," Charlie told him, absently twisting a strand of her hair around a finger. She'd never given much thought to how eyes could smile, but his dove gray ones were doing just that.

"Yeah? Well, you're smiling, that's enough for me."

Charlie cleared her throat. "Gabe, before I saw you today I'd planned to tell you this tonight … I admit it's harder face-to-face, but it seems silly to talk in the dark now."

She closed her eyes a moment and opened them, meeting his questioning gaze.

"I know we've talked about everything but J-J." She stopped, hand to her throat, and began again. "Everything but Jack and I wanted to say thank you. Your voice in the dark has been exactly that, a voice in my darkness." She paused, seemingly searching for the right words.

"I came here to hide and I'm still hiding. But your voice at those times kept me from feeling like I'm losing touch with reality. I just wanted you to know how much it meant to me. It was a gift; I could keep hiding yet not freak out." Her voice had become a whisper.

Gabe sat quietly and companionably for a few minutes, suspecting that was the best thing he could do, just be there.

He spoke gently, "You don't owe a single soul an explanation, Charlie. Ever. That being said, I'm glad you told me Jack is dead."

Charlie flinched at his bald words, making him wish he'd chosen different ones, but he pressed on— "Otherwise I'd have had to hunt him down and beat the shit out of him for hurting you."

She gave him a ghost of a smile for that.

"It occurred to me that while I want to hide and keep myself away from everyone, a guy who simply offers me comfort with his presence time after time at least deserved to know that important detail. After 'keeping up appearances'," she actually used air quotes with an eye roll, making him smile, "I came here with the intention of not seeing a single soul for as long as possible. A dramatic public meltdown of epic proportions and I realized I couldn't truly grieve in what was—had been—our normal world."

Gabe took her hand in his, both resting on the couch between them.

Charlie looked at him and shook her head. He merely raised an eyebrow.

"I can't believe you're sitting here. Seeing you face-to-face was so hard yet so natural."

His smile was warm, his presence easy. Charlie felt connected to someone for the first time since Jack had left the planet. Shaking off the thought, she gently pulled her hand from Gabe's and pushed back her hair with both hands.

"So tell me about your life before this island; you've not talked much about that except to say you're from New England."

Charlie settled back into the couch cushions, cross-legged, pulling a soft throw from the back and covering her legs with it.

Gabe looked at her expectant face and sat back, propping his feet on the coffee table. "Okay, what do you want to know?"

"What was your childhood like?"

"Wildly idyllic. Mom, Dad, sister. We ran amok along the shore, Tally and I, along with our friends. Friends who still live there or we're still connected with—like Nash and Jillian."

"You've been friends with Jill since you were kids?" Charlie's expression was incredulous.

"Her husband, Nash, grew up down the shore from me. Jilly didn't come along until we were about 19 or so. You don't have any friends from childhood?"

"No. I'm a Navy brat, I hail from all over the world. Before email and Facebook were a thing, it didn't seem as easy to stay in touch, I guess." She shrugged. "Your parents still live on the shore?"

"They do. Tally and her husband Sebastian help them run the B&B these days. Dad retired from full time fishing for the local businesses a few years ago, spends his time woodworking and fishing as he pleases. Mom takes care of everybody. What about your parents? Siblings?" Gabe turned the questioning around.

Before Charlie could reply, a muffled ringtone made Gabe frown slightly.

"Jillian at this hour?" He fumbled in his pocket for the phone, pushing to his feet and answering it in one motion.

"What's wrong?"

Charlie stayed where she was, watching him pace as he listened to Jill's voice.

"Wait, who? I'll be right there." Gabe ended the call and pocketed the phone.

Turning to Charlie, he said, "That's odd. Jill said an attorney—not ours—has left four voicemail messages trying to reach me. She returned the call only to be told he'd only speak with me and that it's urgent. With the time zone differences, I've only a few minutes to catch him. I'm going to go to them so we can speakerphone when I call him back."

"Go, it's also late. We'll talk later." Charlie walked him to the door.

"See you soon." He squeezed her hand as he stepped off the porch and broke into a light jog, the phone call taking over his mind.

Chapter Fifteen

"MY WHAT?" Gabe bit the words into the phone, causing Jill to sit down in her chair and Nash to rise and stand beside him.

"Can you give me a second?" Gabe muted the phone and looked at the concerned faces of his friends, his face pale, gray eyes stunned.

"He's telling me..." He swallowed hard and fumbled for words.

"What is it, Brother?" Nash brought his hand to Gabe's shoulder.

"He's telling me I have—I have a nine-year-old daughter. A little girl who's just lost her mother." Gabe's voice was thick and halting, as if he couldn't force the words out.

Jill gasped, her hands flying to her mouth.

Nash's grip on Gabe's shoulder tightened. "Finish the call, Arch."

Gabe nodded, licking his dry lips and returning the phone to his ear.

"Of course I'll come. I'll be there as fast as I can get a flight. Email the paperwork plus directions to me and copy my attorney, Damien Sharp. I'll meet you at his office as soon as I land."

Gabe called his own attorney and tersely relayed what information he had, making arrangements to be in his office as soon as he landed.

Ending the call, he set the phone down on the counter and just stood there. Nash poured him a shot of whiskey, which he drank down in a gulp before rubbing his face briskly.

Nash exchanged a look with his wife, his hand steady on Gabe's shoulder as Jill pushed the coffee cup closer.

Gabe scrubbed his hands over his face again and sipped the coffee as he struggled for words, looking as if he'd seen a ghost.

"So apparently I have a nine-year-old daughter. If that's not surprise enough, her mother died in a car crash four days ago. And to top it all off, there's a will outright begging me to take her if anything ever happened. The attorney is emailing me the will and the letter right now."

Gabe looked from Jill to Nash. "How in God's name do I have a child, a nine-year-old child I never knew about? And she's sitting there all alone."

"I've got to get to her." His eyes were wild as he tried to gather his ricocheting thoughts and figure out what to do next.

Jill put a hand on his arm. "Let's read the paperwork, Gabe, okay? Take a few minutes to figure out what's going on." She went to the computer as the email alert chimed.

She came back to the table with several pages from the printer. "Looks like the will, a letter addressed to you and then the attorney's note about meeting him when you get there."

She handed the pages to Gabe and went over to the kitchen, slicing up coffee cake. What was it about bad news that meant food needed to be on hand?

Nash settled in the chair next to Gabe's as his friend read the pages, dragging a hand through his hair time and again.

"Oh, dear God. Lilith," he whispered, setting the pages aside.

"Is that her name?" Jill asked gently, setting plates in front of them and refilling coffee cups. She rejoined them at the table, skimming the pages Gabe handed to her.

Gabe pushed away the plate, his appetite gone for the first time in recent memory.

"Remember that night after 9/11 and the Melbourne Road fire— the one where we just couldn't take it anymore, and we all ended up at Ray's place?"

Nash nodded, remembering all too well how the raggedy band of exhausted, grief-stricken firefighters had gathered at Ray's bar, unable to hardly sleep, eat or speak.

Ray, a former firefighter himself, had watched the hugs, the vacant stares, the need to just be together, and quietly locked the door to the bar, making his place a sanctuary from the world for a few hours.

"Well, later, when Ray put me into that cab, it was occupied. All I remember are scents and touches."

Gabe measured his words, remembering. "Long story short, I woke up a few hours later in the Gold Leaf, naked in bed with said cab occupant. I got up, made eye contact, kissed her and walked away. We might've said five words to each other and that was that. Until now."

Gabe forced himself to drink more coffee, both to give his hands something to do in order to calm himself and also knowing he wouldn't be sleeping anytime soon.

Nash would man the boat and take him to the mainland airport at daylight so he wouldn't have to wait for the morning ferry, which didn't run until 9a.m.

He'd be there for the first flight out.

"I can't believe you never told us about it." Jill was floored at his secrecy, yet mostly concerned for him.

"In the haze of exhaustion, grief and Johnny Walker Blue Label, I barely remember it myself." Gabe shrugged. "What memories I have are shadowy. I wanted mindless escape, apparently she did, too. It's not something I'm proud of—I've never used a woman like that before or since. I put it away with the rest of that time, like we all did."

Nash nodded his understanding.

Gabe vibrated with energy, pacing the floor. "Her name is Aurora Dawn, she's nine years old. Right now she's with her mother's parents, who she hardly knows and apparently against her mother's wishes, according to this paper."

Jill frowned at that. "So she's pretty much with strangers?"

"Yeah. He'll tell me more in person." Gabe returned Jill's hug.

"I'm going to pack a bag. Meet you at the boat at daylight?" He glanced at Nash's nod then strode to the door, turning back to pick up his phone from the counter.

"Gabe, wait a minute." Jill worried her lip in her teeth, arms wrapped around her robed body.

"What is it?" he asked absently, entering the attorney's information into his phone.

"I'm coming with you. I'll be at the boat come daylight." She held up a hand as Gabe's mouth opened to protest.

"There's no way you need to be alone dealing with this. You're going to be overwhelmed with trying to figure out what's going on. Plus a grieving, confused nine-year-old girl needs a friendly aunt like me."

"No, Jilly, the baby—plus I need you here," he protested, looking to Nash for backup.

"I can cover things here, let her go with you. So help me, you'd better take care of them." Nash pulled his friend into a hug, holding him tight a fraction longer than most guy hugs go.

Gabe nodded as he went to get his things.

"He's going to be okay." Jillian moved to wrap her arms around her husband's waist.

"You take care of him—and of my girl and our baby," Nash whispered, his arms tightening around her. His entire world was getting on that plane.

Chapter Sixteen

IT'D BEEN A LONG TIME since he needed to wake from a dead sleep to fully alert. It was good to know he still had it. On his feet, he realized the sound that had stirred him was coming from Charlie, curled up on the couch.

He'd been drawn to come back and tell her his earth-shattering news and, upon doing so, had found her asleep. He'd sat down on the couch beside her and, despite all that was on his mind, fallen asleep himself.

The wail came again, ending in a series of heartbreaking whimpers. He couldn't stand it anymore.

She was curled up smaller than he could imagine, the blanket clutched tightly in her hands, covering her mouth as she rocked back and forth.

He kept his voice soft. "Charlie."

Her eyes flew open, confused and unfocused as she sucked in a breath and held it.

"Charlie, breathe!" Gabe shook her gently, more than a little worried at her glazed expression, and the fact that she was clearly not aware of him. He'd seen such night terrors before, but that didn't make him worry less for her.

She gasped for air, then burst into tears, covering her face with the blanket as she rocked back and forth. "Oh, my God, Jack, Jack, Jack. No, no, no, no."

There was no consoling her as she keened, completely oblivious to his presence. Gabe knew that forcing somebody to wake mid-nightmare didn't usually help anything, so he simply sat there, keeping her from falling off the couch, his hands on her upper arms gently yet firmly—hoping she might find his touch grounding and comforting as she came out of the dream bit by bit.

She cried out Jack's name again and sat up straight, coming awake abruptly and training unfocused eyes on him.

"Gabe..." she straightened and pulled back from his grasp. "I'm sorry—"

"Don't apologize."

She sighed, her breath still coming in hitches.

"Want to tell me about it?" He stroked her arm gently.

She pulled her legs up, resting her head on her knees as she breathed through the panic attack, her breath finally coming easier.

"My-my memories of the accident have been pretty much non-existent. While I've dreamed of Jack every time I fall asleep since the moment I-I lost him, the dreams were sweet memories except the one where I just keep hearing myself screaming for him. About the time I got here to the island, I started dreaming bits and pieces of the night he died, as if I'm trying to remember it. It's horrifying, even more horrifying than waking up to realize he's gone because I see him clearly but I can't reach him."

She paused and took a deep breath. "I'm in this silent bubble; I can see him falling but hear nothing. I see his body going slack and falling in slow motion to the ground, and I know. I scream and scream but nobody hears me and I can't g-get to him." She covered her face again.

Gabe stroked her arms, cleared his throat and said what was on his mind, "Charlie, are you sure being so adrift and alone all the time is helping you?"

She glared at him through the chestnut curls that had fallen over her face. "You think anyone needs to witness this?!?" She shook off his hands and the blanket, standing in a fury. "Gabe, who on Earth needs to witness this time after time after time? My children?"

While he was taken aback by her anger, he welcomed the fire in her eyes and the color coming back to her skin. He could take it; bring it on.

"In keeping them from witnessing this, I pulled up a mask that took me weeks to get free from. I don't want to move on right now. I need to grieve in my own way, in my own time without worrying about other people."

"And you being alone for days upon days, weeks upon weeks is a good thing, Charlie? Your heart being shattered again and again, over and over while you try to sleep? Nobody should wake up from reliving the greatest horror ever visited on them and have to be all alone." Gabe knew he was risking their new, fragile bond, but time was against him. He couldn't imagine leaving her alone after all he'd seen her go through.

Gabe dismissed the thought that this was exactly what happened to him in his nightmares time and again. He was floored that she'd torture herself to keep from making somebody else uncomfortable.

"If that's what my life is now, then so be it. I'd die before I'd give up one single moment of these dreams, Gabe. They keep Jack near, they keep me from forgetting him." She pulled her wild hair back with an elastic and stomped to the fridge, tearing open a bottle of water and draining it in three long gulps.

Rising from the couch, he crossed to the kitchen counter, leaning on it, watching her pace the floor and tear open another bottle. She stopped pacing and looked at him, her dark blue eyes glaring.

She enchanted him.

Even amid her broken love and grief for a dead man, amid his confusion and worry about a child he hadn't known existed, Lord help him, he was enchanted.

*　*　*

Charlie felt alive for the first time in months—her blood was pounding, her feet stung from stomping the floor, and Gabe, devil take him, was just smiling at her.

"Stop it," she ordered, sitting on the counter and crossing her legs and arms, glaring at him.

"Okay." He nodded.

As she calmed down, welcoming the distraction as there were hours before daybreak, Gabe took her hand and said, "Tell me what happened; tell me what made you run far away months after his death."

She took a moment to marvel that she was fighting mad in the middle of the night on a tropical island with a man who, until tonight, had been only a voice in the dark, keeping her from shattering into a million pieces.

"My memories begin the morning of the funeral, six days after the accident. I remember waking up alone and screaming in my bed as if I'd just realized that my husband was gone." She drank the rest of the water.

"My children both rushed in, terrified beyond words. One look at their faces and I knew what I had to do. I pulled it together, and that was the last tear I've let them see. I became the goddess of the grieving widow mask. I was screaming inside but, damn it, I was pulled together every waking moment."

Gabe squeezed her hand. "I'm so sorry."

She nodded and continued. "While I did take some time off my tutoring and writing deadlines, I resumed them within a month. The kids returned to their lives in the city, my friends slowly stopped calling except now and again, and there I was, alone in this life I didn't recognize. Jack was my everything; my best friend, my lover, my children's father, my neighbor's friend, you name it and Jack was it. Oh, he wasn't perfect, but he was MINE." Her eyes glittered as she battled tears again but let her anger lead.

"So what happened to bring you here?"

"Well, a few weeks ago, my friend Trudy and I were in Panera Bread for lunch—our usual Thursday thing. I still don't know what triggered it, but suddenly I was on the floor screaming his name over and over and over. Right there in the middle of the restaurant."

Gabe winced. "Oh, man."

Charlie sniffed, a tear trailing down her cheek. "I lost it. Management called 911, Trudy called my kids. I apparently refused to get up. Rescue came, checked me out, by then I managed to refuse medical treatment. When they argued with me, I looked them dead in the eye and said 'Are you going to give me back my husband? Because if not, let the hell go of me and leave me alone."

He grinned. "I knew you had fire; you're a survivor."

Sticking her tongue out at him, she continued, "I went home, let my kids hover over me until they went to bed. I got online, did a little research and when morning came I told them I was getting away. Within an hour, I was on my way here."

She shrugged. "You know the rest."

"I'm curious to know what you expected to happen when you ran far away, when you decided to live through this alone."

She sighed, 'Well, it's not like it was a logical decision. It was and still is my attempt to live on my own terms, to live with no mask, to let Jack come to me any time in any way. I don't want to have to push back a memory because I'm tutoring a kid, to miss a dream because I'm afraid of scaring someone else with my cries. I just … I want whatever I can get of him."

He nodded, resting his chin on his hands.

"No more pulling up a mask. For these past weeks I've been sinking to the floor in the shower, I've been crying in the hammock all night, I've been crumpling to the sand at the water's edge until my scalp prickles from the sun. And, Gabe, I'm finding me."

She straightened. "You know how I know? Those times are getting less and less. As much as I want the dreams to stay with me, they aren't. As much as I don't want to do this, I'm learning who Charlie is without Jack."

*   *   *

He grimaced, imagining her doubled over with grief in the shower, at the water's edge. All alone with her shattered heart.

He spoke the thought that, before now, hadn't been fully formed but had been growing in the back of his mind every time he heard her heartbreak at night. *Come stay with me.*

"I have to go away for a few days, I don't know how long I'll be gone. Come with me."

Her brows raised. "Gabe, I don't need rescuing and I don't need an avenging angel. Jack is dead and I just want to keep him close for a while longer." To ease the sting of her words, she touched his shoulder. "Do I need a friend? Sure. But I don't need to be babysat, that'd only set me back—don't you see?"

"Damn it, Charlie. I need to know you're safe."

Charlie's color rose dangerously. "It's not about what you—or anybody else—needs," she said coldly as she shoved him back and hopped down from the counter. She stalked into to the bedroom, slamming the door behind her.

"Charlie!" Gabe called out, running his fingers through his hair, knocking his shades to the floor. Picking them up, he walked to the bedroom door and leaned heavily against it.

"Charlie, I'm sorry for pressuring you, but standing by, doing nothing? That's not me," he said.

"So, again, it's about YOU? Forgive me for not sparing a moment out of missing my HUSBAND to think about how it affects YOU!" she shouted, and something thunked against the door.

Having had enough of this day, Gabe slid to the floor against the wall, elbows on his knees, leaning his head heavily in his hands.

He'd take a five alarm fire call any day over this. People he cared about needed him and, for the first time in a long time, he had no idea what to do about any of it.

* * *

When she opened the door after an hour or so of silence, there he sat, on the floor, his head in his hands.

He didn't move. "Forgive me, Charlie. I'm lashing out where I shouldn't be."

Charlie realized she'd forgotten his earlier dash off. "Your phone call?"

He nodded, still not looking up. His voice was quiet. "Apparently I have a nine-year-old daughter I've never known about—and she's just lost her mother."

Charlie instantly forgot how angry she was at him, sitting down at his side.

"I feel like I'm failing you miserably right now," he said sadly. "Every fiber of my being says I can't leave you to deal with this alone, yet every fiber of my being is already on the way to New England to stand with my child. Fuck this." He fisted his hands.

Somewhere deep inside, Charlie found a mask, dusty from disuse, and pulled hard. He needed her.

She touched his knee. "Tell me about her."

Gabe told her what little he knew, pushing to his feet to pace the room while she leaned in the bedroom doorway.

When he finished, she stepped into his path to hug him, offering him comfort, his solid warmth also a comfort to her.

"You'll do right by her, Gabe. Now, you need to eat something before you go? There's bread for toast."

Gabe snarled, gritting his teeth, "Stop it, Charlie. Stop putting on a show for my benefit. Don't insult me."

She simply looked at him, her gaze steely as she moved to sit cross-legged atop the counter. "I've listened for you to walk by every night since the first week or so. I admit your voice has been my one hold on reality—one I didn't even realize I needed, much less wanted. I admit that holding your hand last night made me feel less unmoored. However, I'm afraid after all that, I still welcome unmoored right now. My battle is mine to fight. You've got your own. I'll be here when you get back."

He nodded, accepting that he was out of line—and out of time as dawn broke in the sky.

"Nash will have your chocolate milk brought to the door. If you need or want anything, you've only to call him, here's his number and Jill's—as well as mine." Gabe pulled a card from his shirt pocket, scribbled three numbers on it and laid it next to her on the counter.

"Okay." Charlie fervently hoped he hadn't asked either Nash or Jill to check on her.

Reading her mind, he said, "I haven't said a word to them about what you're going through, Charlie. Not one."

He touched her hand and left the cottage, turning once at the door to meet her gaze. He smiled slightly at the view of her resolutely sitting straight, that hair keeping her from the semblance of seriousness he knew she was striving for. She made a shooing motion as she uncapped her chocolate milk and drank deeply.

"Bye, Charlie. See you soon."

He wanted so badly to ask her to let him call, but even in his frustration he knew that could cause her to shut down on him, for it was clear she really intended to keep herself immersed in her grief and dreams. She wrapped any iota of Jack around her tightly and held on.

Who was he to tell her to do any different?

* * *

Bag at his feet, coffee in hand, Gabe stood on his porch to gaze at the sea. It always helped, but somehow he didn't expect answers to come forth on this one.

His mind spun with thoughts—what could he possibly do to help a grieving little girl he'd never met? *His* grieving little girl who'd just lost her mother?

How could he have expected Charlie to listen to the demands of a man she barely knew? How could he explain the feeling of protectiveness that had tethered his heart to her since the first time he'd heard her in the dark?

As he stood and hefted his bag to his shoulder, he fervently hoped Charlie would hang on and he prayed that he'd think of some way to let to his sad little girl know she'd never be alone again, as long as he had anything to say about it.

Helplessness was not something Gabe was used to feeling—and he didn't like it one bit.

Chapter Seventeen

ONCE THEY WERE SETTLED on the plane and in the air, Jill squeezed his arm and snuggled into her seat to sleep, her head resting on his shoulder. Being almost five months pregnant, she could drop off to sleep just about anywhere at any time.

Moving carefully as to not disturb her, Gabe pulled the letter from his pocket, needing to see the words yet again, trying to work through his shock and disbelief.

He couldn't even recall what Lilith Baxter's voice had sounded like as he read the note she'd written with hopes that he'd never see it.

Dear Gabe,

I hope you're able to forgive me for keeping such a secret from you. Actually, your forgiveness doesn't matter, your acceptance does.

Four months after our night, I found out I was pregnant. After much thought, I decided to raise the baby on my own. You and I were literally strangers passing in the night; I didn't see any need to try to find you.

On May 1st, Aurora Dawn was born and my life was changed.

As a single mother, I had to make provisions for my daughter in the event something happened to me, because you're her next of kin.

My parents and I are estranged. I don't want them to have any say in my—our—daughter's life. Don't let them spend one minute with her. Trust me, they will make her life hell. I've named you as her father on her birth certificate and taken care of paperwork with my attorney, Kevin Blade. You shouldn't have any problem taking custody.

Please take your daughter and give her a happy life. She's a treasure, the greatest gift.

I can't say I'm sorry for keeping such a secret from you, I wouldn't have chosen differently if I had it to do over.

I kept a journal and every year, I've noted things about her— personality traits, something cute she did, her favorite foods, favorite color. Things so that she'll know I treasured her and that you'll know a few things about her to start with. I know it sounds morbid, but as her only family, I had to be prepared.

Love her, treasure her.
Lilith

Gabe couldn't believe the almost terse tone of the letter bequeathing him his own child.

Forgive her? If this child was his, he'd lost nine years of her life. Forgiveness was going to take some doing.

* * *

"What do you mean she's not here?" Gabe was seeing red as he paced in his attorney's office, Jill seated nearby.

Damien Sharp held up his hands and spoke calmly, "For God's sake, sit down and take a breath. You'll do nobody any good if you spontaneously combust on the floor. You have my word that I'll tell you everything and I'll take you to her. You know my word is gold, man."

As a long-time friend, Damien's stare bade Gabe to trust him. Gabe ran a hand through his hair yet again, the waves already standing on end, but sat down and tried to calm himself for at least the thousandth time since he'd gotten the call.

"First things first, I assume you'll want a DNA test before you take custody of her." At Gabe's nod, Damien called his assistant to the door and put that task in motion.

"Damien, I don't want her in that house while we wait for answers. If her mother was adamant that she not be with them—why is she there?" Gabe stood again to pace.

The attorney leaned his hip on the desk with a sigh. "That's likely my fault. I was out of reach when Lilith died. I found out on the day of the funeral, which was yesterday. I opened the file from her attorney and contacted you as soon as I knew, then I went to the funeral. I didn't talk with Aurora about you, but I did tell her I would be back to talk to her today. Unless I involved Child Services, I couldn't just take her from them until you got here. If you hadn't responded so quickly, I would've had to call on Child Services or let the grandparents keep her—there's no one else."

Jillian went to Gabe's side and took his arm. "Then what are we waiting for? We'll go get her and stay at the hotel until the DNA results are in."

"We'll do the test as a formality, but I'm not waiting on the results. You have my proof of identity plus the will; I'm taking custody right now. There was no need for Lilith to lie; she didn't ask me for a damn thing. I believe the girl is mine. Let's go get her." Gabe was nearly breathless with fury.

Jill nodded, eyes filled with emotion for both the motherless little girl and the confused father who was determined to stand for her.

"I'm to meet with them in half an hour. You can follow me there and wait in your vehicle for a few minutes, give me time to talk to the girl and to the Baxters, hopefully stem some of the fallout. They have no idea this is coming, due to their nature, I thought it best that way." Damien knew Gabe wouldn't be left waiting.

He picked up the file he needed and headed for the door.

Gabe stopped him, holding out his hand. "I appreciate your efforts. I know I'm being difficult, it's been an earthshaking few hours."

Damien shook his hand with a smile. "Let's get you your girl."

* * *

"I'm done waiting."

In the circle driveway of the two-story Colonial house, Gabe waited exactly ten minutes before he opened the door of the rental car, leaving Jill to wait there as they'd agreed.

Not bothering to knock, he shoved open the front door.

Gabe didn't know what he expected to see but it wasn't a small dark haired girl sitting alone on the enormous staircase.

Angry voices from the sitting room off the entryway stopped as Damien and the Baxters heard the door slam back against the wall, all three hurrying to the foyer.

Gabe glanced at Damien with silent inquiry and upon the attorney's nod, walked to the girl. He squatted down to her eye level, oblivious to Damien's need to physically block the furious grandmother from rushing over.

In the girl's face, his own darkly lashed slate gray eyes looked back at him unflinchingly, even though they shone with unshed tears and the tip of her nose was pink. Her bottom lip quivered slightly before she caught it in her teeth.

"Hello," Gabe said softly. "Are you Aurora?"

The girl nodded, shifting slightly, scratching her leg where the stiff pink dress touched her skin.

"I'm so sorry about your mom, kiddo." Gabe put his hand on her other hand where it clutched the banister, keeping his eyes on hers.

"I've got a question for you—and you only." He glared at the Baxters in warning before meeting those mirroring eyes again.

The fear and tears in them was about to undo him.

"Damien says you know I'm your father. Do you want to stay here or do you want to come with me?"

"With you." The girl didn't hesitate or look away from his gaze.

"Then you'll go with me." Gabe smiled in reassurance as he stood and held out a hand. She took it and stepped down to stand beside him as they turned to face her grandparents.

Stuart Baxter's face was red as he blustered, "That's our grandchild, you can't just walk in here and take her."

Gabe held up a hand and said with barely suppressed fury, "Be right back."

The girl at his side, he walked out to the car where Jill waited.

"Aurora, this is my good friend Jillian. Will you stay out here with her while I go let your grandparents shout at me?"

The girl returned his grin with a slight smile and said, "Better you than me, they shout a lot" in a way that would've been cheeky if she hadn't seemed so heavy-hearted.

Gabe left her there and strode back inside the house, not bothering to push the door closed behind him.

The Baxters stopped shouting at Damien and turned on Gabe, who simply waited for them to realize he wasn't going to say a word until they shut up.

Damien stepped outside, deciding to let this play out for itself. Gabe had every legal leg needed to stand on and he clearly could handle the Baxters on his own.

Once the Baxters stopped talking and just looked at him, Gabe looked from one to the other, determined to say his piece and get out of there once and for all.

"While I don't know much about this whole thing, I do know that Aurora's mother didn't want her here for one second. Unless that little girl asks to see you, this is the last you'll see of her." Gabe turned and strode out the door, leaving the older couple standing in the foyer in stunned silence.

Damien and Jill turned as he came down the steps, the wide-eyed girl standing between them.

He crouched down to her level. "Okay, kiddo, do you need to go in and get your stuff?"

The girl shook her head sadly. "They d-didn't let me go back to m-my house."

Gabe swore, the child's stricken face the only thing keeping him from storming back in the house to let the Baxters know just what he thought of them, in case they weren't sure yet.

Jill gently nudged the girl into the car and got back in herself, leaving Gabe some privacy to talk with Damien.

Damien smiled and winked at the child through the window as he spoke to Gabe, "Everything is in order. If they file custody papers, I'll take care of it. I'm your attorney and by that, I'm Aurora's attorney, too. I'm deeply sorry I wasn't in town. If I had been, this debacle never would've happened. Lilith was clear about her wishes but her attorney was the only one who knew."

Gabe nodded, shaking the attorney's hand. "Thanks for getting in touch with me so fast."

"Here's everything you need—passport, birth certificate, school records, shot records, everything." Damien handed Gabe a flash drive. "I'll have the house packed up and everything sent to you."

As he turned to go, Gabe stopped and thought for a moment. "Can you wait on that? She—Aurora—might want to go there one more time, but I don't think that time is now."

Damien nodded. "Sure, let me know when and I'll send you the keys. Lilith owned the condo, so there's no hurry." The attorney waved to Aurora, shook Gabe's hand again and turned away.

Gabe got into the car and put the key in the ignition. Before starting the vehicle, he sat still for a moment, eyes closed.

Jill put her hand on his arm, offering her tireless support.

With a deep breath, he turned to face the child sitting in the seat behind Jill. The gray eyes were wide beneath the fringe of soft dark hair but her expression had relaxed, more curious with a tinge of sadness than flat out terrified. Gabe couldn't believe this beautiful little being was his child but resolutely pushed aside the marveling for now.

"We can go back to your house when you're ready or Damien can pack it all up for you. Nothing needs to be decided today. For now, though, how about we find a store and buy a few things until we can take a real shopping trip?" Gabe's gut was in knots, his heart pounding.

He felt unsure and out of his league, but heaven knew the newly motherless child being taken by strangers had to feel much worse.

The girl made a face and wiggled in the seat, tugging at the neck of her dress. "T-shirts and jeans, please—this awful dress is going in the trash."

Gabe laughed, turning to start the car, meeting Jill's smile with one of his own.

They would make this okay.

* * *

His head was spinning, his thoughts coming from all directions crashing together. Nothing made sense. In the space of less than twenty-four hours he'd gone from dedicated fireman turned carefree tropical fisherman to the father of a nine-year-old girl.

There was so much anger at Lilith—anger with no place to go. Lilith had kept his own daughter a secret from him and then gotten herself killed in that car wreck, leaving the child motherless and at the mercy of strangers.

After settling Jillian and Rory—the girl had informed them she was never called Aurora—in their hotel room, the adjoining door partially open, Gabe sat on the bed in his room. He leaned forward, elbows on his knees, and ran his hands through his hair, back and forth. Repeating the motion several times, he realized he was desperately wishing he could talk to Charlie.

Where had that come from? He'd only talked face-to-face with the woman once. Granted it was after several weeks of talking in the dark about everything and nothing, thus creating a bond of sorts, but still.

He wished he had her number, then it occurred to him that he did have her number—he had only to open The Painted Parrot files and look it up.

He could text and hope she'd reply. Tugging his phone free from his pocket, Gabe accessed the property's files and searched 'Charlie', hoping that was the name her reservation was under.

His search turned up four Charlies, one current tenant. "Bingo." He saved the number to his contacts and opened a text.

He texted a lame-sounding "Hello from Gabe—text me?" knowing the number showed up anonymous and not wanting her to ignore it.

Rather than sit and stare at it, willing Charlie to reply, he dropped the phone onto the floral patterned bedspread and paced the small room, his thoughts returning to the little girl in the next room.

He'd found a strip mall containing several stores, and followed them around, carrying bags while Jill helped Rory buy a week's worth of clothes and whatever else was immediately needed.

They could shop properly later—Rory would need furniture for her room and so much more. The seemingly endless list of things that came to mind made Gabe's addled brain spin even more.

Right now, he desperately needed to get back to the island to try and regain some equilibrium; he couldn't take a deep enough breath to think straight until he'd returned to his island, to the shore.

Their flight first thing tomorrow morning wasn't soon enough for his liking, but he'd deal—he couldn't ask a pregnant lady and a freshly traumatized nine-year-old girl to rush and fly out tonight. They needed to rest—he'd pace.

****Chapter Eighteen****

CHARLIE WAS SURPRISED yet not when she dug out her chiming phone from under the couch cushions where it'd fallen some time before and found a minutes-old text from Gabe.

She felt the connection of a new and deepening friendship with the man who'd been a voice in the night these past few weeks.

Pushing her sleep-wild hair back, she saved the number and texted him back, "All's well?"

While she waited for his reply, she sat up in the couch corner where she'd taken refuge hours ago and rubbed her face, barely noticing the skin made tight from tears that had been shed and dried during sleep. She was accustomed to tears all the time—asleep or awake.

It almost seemed like meeting Gabe face-to-face was part of her vivid dream world.

Her phone chimed again. "Can I call?"

She smiled, already looking forward to hearing his voice as she replied.

"Of course." She'd hardly hit send before her phone rang and he was on the line.

"Hello, there."

* * *

At the sound of her voice, Gabe felt tension begin leave his shoulders, his body responding to their connection.

"How are you, Charlie?" he sat against the headboard of the hotel bed, ceasing the pacing he'd been doing for hours.

"Tell me everything."

He did just that, told her everything that'd happened in the past twenty-four hours, letting her be there for him as he'd been for her over the past weeks.

"So I'll be back on the island tomorrow, brand new daughter in tow." Gabe leaned his head back and closed his eyes, focusing on Charlie's voice.

"Mercy."

"Enough about me. How are you?"

Charlie made a *ppfftt* noise into the phone. "I'm the same as I always am. This is big stuff for you—and for Rory."

"Yeah. She seems sad and scared but okay. I'm hoping the island will work its magic on us both."

"Like it's doing for me," Charlie agreed softly.

They sat in a companionable silence for a few minutes, on opposite sides of the world.

"When we were interrupted last night, we were talking about our families. Tell me about your parents." Gabe pushed off his shoes and settled back more comfortably into the pile he'd made of hotel pillows.

Charlie understood his need for random conversation and complied. "Okay, um, my Dad died in 9/11, Mom a few months later. No siblings or extended family, just me left."

"I'm sorry, Charlie. That was a dark, tough time for many of us."

"Where were you?" she asked, catching on that 9/11 was personal for him, too.

"Fighting fires from Marine One at first, then helping anywhere we could in the days following." He paused a beat. "What a fresh hell."

"I'm sorry you had to go through that. When did you leave the city for the island?"

"My last night in the city was the same night I met Rory's mother. One night, no last names, few words. And now a motherless nine-year-old child." Gabe's self-disgust was evident.

"You don't seem like a one night stand kind of guy," Charlie said, sensing he was about to tell more of the story.

"First and last time, that one. In either my defense or proclamation of guilt, that night I was beyond drunk and reeling from the horror of those few days. My buddy Ray had bowed out a couple years before that and ran a bar we'd all gathered at. He says he looked around at our rag tag bunch, all shell shocked and stupefied and locked the door. Locking out the world and locking us in together—safe, if not sound." Gabe's words trailed off.

"Smart man, that Ray," Charlie said softly.

As much as she liked talking with him, her concentration was fading fast. "You have to catch a plane in a few hours, try to rest, Gabe."

"I'll see you soon, Charlie," he replied, ending the call and remaining motionless.

He shoved the memories back into the hole they'd come from, not in any mood to remember the night that had changed his life—both then and now.

Just as he started to drop off into a fitful sleep, a soft knock came at the partially open adjoining door. So soft, Gabe wasn't sure he'd actually heard it.

He stepped to the door and opened it further.

Rory stood there, looking impossibly tiny clad in sky blue pajamas with frolicking puppies on them, her dark hair falling over her shoulders.

Her cheeks wet with tears, she put her arms around his waist and sobbed. Gabe looked about wildly, searching for someone better suited to this than him. Someone like the girl's mother or fath—oh, boy.

He glanced into the darkened room beyond, seeing that Jill slept deeply, exhausted from the trip.

Putting his arm around the small shoulders, he drew the girl into his room, backing up until he sat on the edge of the bed.

Rory pushed herself into his arms, burying her face in his neck and holding on tight. Her sobs made Gabe irrationally want to wring Lilith's neck for causing this—their—child such pain.

"What can I do, little one?" Gabe stroked her back gently as the sobs slowed to hiccups.

As she looked at him, her dark lashes spiky with tears, Gabe felt a flutter then a tipping sensation as his heart fell.

This was his child, his daughter. He knew very little about her beyond that fact, but right that moment he became hers forever.

"M-my stuff. I can't go without my stuff."

Gabe realized he'd been hasty in trying to whisk her away from the ugliness of the Baxters. He'd planned to bring her back to the home she'd shared with her mother when they both felt steadier. Belatedly, he saw that Rory wouldn't be steadier with nothing familiar in her new island home.

"Okay, then, we call Damien in the morning and we go get your stuff."

"Just like that?" her voice was incredulous, like she wasn't used to someone actually listening to her lately.

"Just like that. How about we go buy another suitcase, you can fill it up to take to the island and we'll have Damien box up the rest and send it to us later?"

Rory nodded, wiping the tears from her face.

Gabe lifted the girl and laid her on the bed, pulling back the covers so she could crawl inside. Exhaustion was stamped all over the little face as she sank back against the pillows. She chewed her lip and took a deep, shuddery breath. "I never had a Daddy before."

"That's okay, I've never had a little girl before. We'll learn together." Gabe smiled, tucking the covers around her.

"You're nice. Why did Mommy never tell me I had a nice Daddy?" Her eyes heavy with both sleep and confusion, Rory tried to make sense of the scrambled world she now lived in.

Gabe held up his hands with a shrug, "I've no idea, Rory. And, for the record, I never, ever would have left you, had I known." The little girl nodded, seeming to believe him. He hoped so.

"You'll be right here?" she whispered as sleep claimed her.

"Right here, little one." He stroked the hair back from her face, thinking it'd be a few days before he made it back to his island—and maybe that would be okay.

As he lay awake atop the covers, the small warm body close to his side, Gabe finally had a moment to think things through.

While he was glad he'd charged into the Baxter's stone cold world and rescued this girl, perhaps a whirlwind turn around back to the island wasn't the best idea.

The island was home, it was healing—for him.

For Rory, her whole world was brand new and strange. She was lost. She needed some of her things, she needed to say goodbye to her home.

They'd take tomorrow—today, now—to do that, put Jill on the next flight back to Nash and then, later this evening, they'd make the two-hour drive to his family home to relax for a few days. Why didn't he think of that before?

Taking Rory to his family home, to the B&B where his parents lived their solid, comforting life, where his sister and her family thrived, would be the perfect way to show the girl she was not alone in the world any longer as well as bolster himself at the same time.

****Chapter Nineteen****

WHILE TIME MIGHT NOT heal grief—she refused to believe healing ever happens when you lose your one true love—it does often allow you to slowly begin to think of things besides the overwhelming loss.

Early mornings before sunrise found her sitting atop the table or counter, Billy Joel on the iPod speakers, papers scattered, pen in hand, another pen tangled in her hair, computer at the ready as she made notes and researched her project. The rest of the days were still a wild card, but the mornings were slowly becoming a habit that was bringing a reluctant Charlie back to the land of the living.

Then it came.

The dream that made what had happened the night she'd lost Jack come into clear focus.

The dream during which Charlie left the cottage and walked into the sea.

* * *

"Jake! Turn loose of me, ya mangy mutt!" Nash shoved the dog's head from the leg of his cargo shorts.

Jake tugged harder. "Damn it, dog, that's dangerously close there—leave off!" Nash frowned, never having seen such behavior from the sidekick they all loved.

"You missing Arch, are you?" He squatted down to rub the dog's head in both hands. Jake barked and ran a few feet up the beach and back again. Repeating the action, the dog disappeared into the darkness ahead, barking furiously. He returned to tug on Nash's shorts again.

"Have you lost your mind, dog?" Nash pulled his pants free as it dawned on him that maybe Jake's out of character antics were a Lassie move of sorts.

Changing tactics, he called out, "Jake! What is it, Jake?" Following the dog's lead into the darkness, Nash heard screaming above the barking of the dog and the sounds of the sea.

Breaking into a run, he nearly tripped over Jake, standing in the water, barking furiously into the darkness. Nash shone his flashlight then promptly dropped it as he waded into the water. He grabbed the screaming woman tightly just as the water hit him waist-high. She fought him, screaming "Jack! Jack! Somebody do something!"

Nash's arms were iron-tight around the woman, his years as a firefighter kicking in as he hefted her into his arms and made his way back to shore. Standing her on the sand, he kept his arms around her as she fought him. He could see she wasn't coherent, her eyes wild and unfocused, her body fighting to run into the sea. The piercing screams had ebbed into uncontrollable sobs as she chanted, "Jack. No, Jack!" over and over. From his experience, he knew no amount of reassurance would help her right now, so he held on, murmuring nonsensical sounds as she crumpled to the sand.

Thankfully help came soon, for Jake had 'Lassied' his way to the bar where Matteo had been closing up, dragging the man down the beach. While the chef called paramedics, Nash held onto the woman—now sobbing quietly, "It's too late. Too late. Oh no, no... Jack." She struggled against his grip briefly, her hand reaching out to the sea, then her head fell forward and she went frighteningly limp.

****Chapter Twenty****

"SHE'S AMAZING, GABE." Tally tucked her arm through her brother's as they walked along the New England shore. Ahead, her three boys flanked Rory, each trying to best the other in getting her attention.

"I've known her less than 36 hours and she's already my hero." Gabe nodded. Shell-shocked that he was a father, it somehow felt right.

"How did she sleep last night?"

"She curled up next to me and cried herself to sleep. Cried a few times in her sleep." He rubbed a hand over his chest.

Tally made a sound of sympathy, squeezing his arm. "Like they say, having a child is letting your heart walk around outside your body. Out where you can't protect it."

"Damn right. Think she's going to be okay?"

"It'll take time, of course. Just listen to her and to yourself, I think you'll both be fine. You call me anytime." Tally hugged his side as they sat to watch the kids and the ocean waves.

"It's good to be here. Good for Rory to see she's not alone in the world."

"Being spoiled by Mom is good for that," Tally laughed.

Sheila Montgomery had embraced her new grandchild with the same warmth and affection she lavished on the other four. Rory had immediately relaxed in her presence, even slipping out of Gabe's room early this morning to join her in the kitchen. When he'd come down, she'd been chatting with Sheila and two of the boys, a stack of pancakes in front of her.

As the group returned to the B&B, Rory left her cousins and came to Gabe's side, slipping her hand in his. He didn't know if he'd ever get used to the tripping feeling his heart made when she looked up at him with those eyes just like his own. Tally smiled encouragingly at her brother and, calling out for her trio to wait up, she jogged ahead.

Turning to face the sea, Gabe sat down on the sand. The little girl, still holding his hand, stood beside him. Smiling at her, he gestured to the sea with his free hand, "This family—your family—has lived by the sea for a long, long time. I love it so much that even when I moved away, I found a place by the sea, on an island. I'd like to take you there, where it's warm and sunny all the time. I have friends there I think you'll like; there are lots of kids, too."

Rory nodded, but her lower lip trembled. She looked from him to the sea and back again, tears rolling down her face. Crawling into his lap, she buried her face in his shirt. Her little body curled into him took Gabe's breath away as he wrapped his arms around her. He stroked her back as she sobbed, looking out to the waves for comfort, which came, and solutions, which did not. There was so much to say, yet so little to say. He couldn't bring her mother back and he couldn't give her back the life she'd had. The best he could do was show up and offer her the world he did have and hope it would be enough.

They spent the rest of the day immersed in life at the B&B. Gabe joined Tally's husband and their father in taking care of things about the place, while Rory played with her cousins—sometimes drifting off to swing alone until one of the boys would find her.

The little girl showed up at Gabe's side often, not saying a word, just clinging to him for a few minutes. Having sought his mother's wisdom after the first time she did that, Gabe simply stopped what he was doing and knelt to her level.

Sometimes she just hugged him tightly and ran back to play, other times she sat quietly on his knee, leaning against his chest, lip quivering, and still other times she buried her face and cried. Holding her as she cried into his neck, for the first time in many, many years, he found his rock-solid control shaky at best.

While Sebastian and granddad took the three boys fishing, Rory opted to stay behind and make cookies with her grandmother. Gabe settled on a quilt out in the yard with Tally and his tiny new niece, quietly talking over B&B business, their parents' health, as well as catching up in general. Rory joined them, curling into a ball between her aunt and her father, both of them drifting off to sleep in the sunshine.

A few days spent just like that gave Gabe the encouragement he needed to begin his life as a single father. Thankfully, he had his family here and his friends and community on the island to offer his little girl.

As Gabe and Rory boarded the boat from the big island to home, his phone rang with Nash's ringtone.

"Hey, Nash-Man, almost home." Gabe answered the call with a grin. A grin that faded instantly.

"She did *what*?!?"

Chapter Twenty-One

SHE WOKE IN BITS and pieces, as if she were inching closer and closer from far away. She felt sluggish and heavy, every body part was weighed down, even her eyelids.

Hearing his voice, the panic she'd first felt calmed and she relaxed. Once relaxed, her eyes opened easily. She blinked several times to clear her blurry vision, her eyes feeling both sticky and dry. There's a name for that, but it wouldn't come to mind at the moment.

Feeling so weary, her eyes drifted closed again, listening to his voice and floating.

Gabe paused in reading out loud and stood, leaning over the bed, gently brushing back her ever unruly hair.

"Charlie?"

She slowly opened her eyes again, blinked a few times and smiled weakly. "I'd know that voice anywhere."

Gabe was taken aback. Her face lit up, like she was delighted to see him.

He shook his head slightly as if to clear it and smiled back at her.

Charlie winced as she took two tries to push herself up in the bed. "I'm so stiff and sore. What happened?"

Gabe raised the head of the bed further as she sat up and pushed back her hair, automatically seeking a hair band from her wrist.

Finding nothing there but the plastic hospital bracelet and IV tubes, she frowned. "I'm really thirsty, could I have some water?" Her voice was more husky than usual.

Gabe poured a glass from the pitcher on the bedside table, offering it to her with a straw.

Charlie drank deeply, emptying the cup.

"What happened to me?" she asked again, her voice sounding more like her normal husky tone.

"Well, what do you remember last?" he asked, unobtrusively pressing the nurse button as he took the cup from her

"So thirsty and so tired," she murmured, putting a head to her forehead, moving her legs about restlessly.

Gabe moved to straighten the pillows behind her, nudging her to lie back.

"Hmm, I think the last thing I remember is getting ready to go to lunch at Panera. I can't...I can't remember exactly who I was meeting." Charlie yawned and, once resettled, her eyes drifted closed.

He froze in the act of smoothing the covers over her, his hands pausing near her shoulders.

"Getting ready to go to lunch at Panera?" he repeated, his gaze on her face. "Charlie?" She'd drifted off to sleep, a real sleep, not a traumatized coma.

Gabe sat down heavily in the chair next to Charlie's bed where he'd spent a lot of time recently.

Has she forgotten the last several weeks of her life? he wondered, unsure of what that meant for her, for him, for their friendship. But, he argued with himself, she'd clearly known him.

He tried to dismiss the prickles of unease at his neck, but experience had taught him better than to do so.

As Charlie slept deeply, Gabe stepped to the doorway when the nurse responded. Lani, the day nurse for much of Charlie's stay in the island hospital, regarded him with concern, his expression causing her to touch his arm in both question and as a steadying move.

"Gabe, what is it? Is she awake?" Lani walked past him to her patient, examining her closely for any changes and taking vital signs. "She's resting easily," Lani said, turning to Gabe questioningly.

"She woke up," Gabe said, gesturing for the nurse to return to the doorway.

"She asked me what happened and I asked her what she remembered last. She said the last thing she remembers is getting ready for lunch at Panera—that was over two and a half months ago."

Lani frowned in concern, then nodded. "While alarming, I know, it's not uncommon for patients that experience deep trauma to bury their memories. It's too early to say she's done that, though, Gabe. She may say the same thing next time she wakes, she may not. She many not even recall that she woke up at all. Page me if she wakes again. In the meantime, I'll let the doctor know she woke and we'll see what he thinks. Likely he'll be by in short order. Gabe?"

Lani waited for him to look at her, smiling reassuringly. "It's important that you stay calm while we see what's going on, okay?"

The man had hardly left Charlie's side in the nearly ten days she'd been there. On top of that, Gabe had read and talked to her almost constantly, his voice hoarse with the effort.

Between him, their friends and her children, Charlie had not been left alone for one minute. She'd have all the support she needed, especially if she was finally waking up for them.

Lani patted Gabe's arm again and left to call Dr. Taggart.

Gabe pulled out his phone and called Troy and Cassidy, although he knew Cassidy to be on her way at that moment. Staying in a hotel room close by the hospital, she'd finally settled into a groove of sorts over the last nine days while her mother lay in an inexplicable coma.

After nearly running herself into the ground staying by Charlie's side, she'd listened to Gabe explain—yet again—how he wasn't a stranger and along with her brother and him, they'd made a schedule of sorts, ensuring someone was always by Charlie's side, leaving the other two able to leave and rest, tend to life from time to time.

Gabe paced the floor in the hall as he called both the kids and texted Jill, leaving Charlie's door open so he could see when she woke again.

* * *

This time Charlie's eyes opened more easily and, after just a few blinks, she focused on the man in the chair next to her bed. His brow was furrowed in concentration, his dark blond hair curling at the collar of his open-necked white shirt.

At the sight of him, she felt steadier and safe.

Sensing a change, Gabe looked up from his laptop and smiled at her, silently reminding himself to go slowly.

"Hey." He set the computer aside and stood.

Charlie grimaced as she cleared her throat, causing him to move quickly to pour a glass half full of water and hold it out for her to drink from the straw.

She drank deeply and smiled her thanks, finding the button to raise the bed to sit up a bit more, readjusting her pillows.

She patted the side of the bed, motioning for him to sit beside her. He sat, back to the door, and took her out-stretched hand in his.

She cleared her throat again before speaking.

"Did you know the sentence 'the quick brown fox jumps over the lazy dog' uses every letter in the English alphabet?"

Despite the smudges under them, her eyes danced with merriment, baffling and delighting him at the same time.

Recovering quickly, he replied, "Did you know a group of frogs is called an army?"

She rewarded him with a giggle before sobering and looking him in the eye.

"Okay, I'm stiff and sore but can't find anything hospital-worthy wrong with me, so to speak. Why am I here, what happened?"

With her free hand, Charlie pushed back her hair with a slight frown, looking again for a hair band to secure it.

Gabe noticed and made a mental note to ask Cassidy to get some for her.

"What do you remember last?" he asked, holding his breath for her answer.

"I told you, getting ready to go to lunch at Panera. I'm not sure who I was meeting. Did I have a car accident or something?" Charlie frowned in puzzlement as she tried to remember. She knew it wasn't uncommon for accident victims to not remember the actual accident, so she wasn't particularly worried.

"You did, but you're well on the mend now," Gabe said carefully, sidestepping any specific answer.

Unobtrusively pushing the button for the nurse, he looked closely at her face.

She seemed good, color was coming back to her face, she kept sitting up straighter instead of reclining. While he'd like to ask more questions, he was a bit unsettled at her unfamiliar upbeat mood and wasn't sure where to go from here.

Just as he pressed the call button, Cassidy came through the door like a whirlwind, her hair seemingly everywhere like her mother's only blond instead of chestnut.

The girl dropped the bags she carried beside the chair and smiled brightly at her mother. "Mom! It is so good to see you awake!"

Gabe moved out of the way for Cassidy to hug her mother, pushing back Charlie's hair and reaching to her wrist to hand her an elastic. The shared habit would've amused Gabe if he hadn't seen Charlie's panic stricken expression over her daughter's shoulder. He reached out a hand to Cassidy, stilling her movements, his eyes on Charlie.

"Charlie?" he said quietly, recognizing the fear in her expression. The last time he'd seen a look like that on Charlie's face was when she'd awakened screaming from a nightmare.

"Mom?" The fledgling nurse in Cassidy had her stepping back and looking into her mother's eyes, her hand on Charlie's wrist seeking her pulse. "Mom, it's okay." Cassidy frowned slightly.

Charlie reached a hand out to Gabe, who moved quickly to her other side to take it. Puzzled and more than a little worried, he gripped her hand in return and, following her lead, held firm.

"Can—ahem—can you get me some—some fresh water? I'm terribly thirsty and it's tasting a little stale." Charlie forced a smile that belied her death-grip on his hand.

Cassidy looked at her mother again with a frown but picked up the pitcher and said, "Sure thing, be right back."

She gave Gabe what he took to be a warning glance as she left the room.

"Charlie?"

Her breath came uneven and shaky and Gabe feared a panic attack was imminent. He pushed the nurse call button again with his free hand then took Charlie's other hand.

"What's wrong, Charlie?" He kept his voice calm and soothing, if there was one thing he knew, it was how to bring her out of what she called a freak-out moment.

Her wide and frightened eyes met his puzzled and worried ones.

"Just look at me and tell me what you can." His slight smile was reassuring, his grip on her hands grounding.

"She called me Mom, and—and—" Charlie stopped, trying to draw a full breath, feeling her throat close and panic loom.

"Charlie, breathe, c'mon." Gabe looked at the door briefly, wondering where the hell Lani was.

"I—I Don't. Know. Who. She. Is." Charlie whispered, biting off each word with emphasis, her eyes on his. She took a deep breath followed by another one.

"Cassidy?" Gabe couldn't help his incredulous tone.

"That girl is a stranger to me. I've no idea who she is." Charlie's eyes were wide and frightened.

The room door opened as Cassidy returned, followed closely by Lani and Dr. Taggart.

"Hello, Charlie. It's good to see you awake." Dr. Taggart smiled and shook her free hand, gesturing to Gabe that he was fine where he stood. "I'm Tom Taggart, I've been watching out for you while you've been here. I understand you have some questions for us." The tall doctor looked Charlie over, glancing at the IV and the machines as he rested his fingers on her wrist and looked into her eyes.

"Hello, Doctor. What happened to me?" Charlie forced herself to breathe evenly and remain calm, her fingers gripping Gabe's hard enough to make him hiss.

She sent him a look of apology and loosened her grip a bit, but didn't let go.

Gabe winked in reassurance, stroking her fingers with his thumb.

"Why don't you tell me what you remember last and we'll go from there?" The doctor showed no sign of concern as he finished his cursory examination and stood back. His body language displayed only curiosity, setting Charlie at ease a bit.

"As I told—" Charlie paused and closed her eyes, forcing herself to breathe in and out.

"Take your time, Charlie," Dr. Taggart said calmly, writing on his clipboard and handing it to the nurse, who quietly left the room.

After another breath and clearing her throat again, Charlie said, "The last thing I remember before waking up here is that I was getting ready to go to Panera for lunch. I know I was meeting someone, but I don't recall offhand who that was. I remember getting dressed, I remember being annoyed I couldn't find my green scarf—then I woke up here." She looked at Gabe, then at the doctor and Cassidy in turn. "Is somebody going to tell me what happened? Why am I here?"

Dr. Taggart patted her hand. "You had an episode and passed out. You came to us and you're doing great, we've just been waiting for you to wake up."

Charlie narrowed her eyes at him. "How long? How long have you been waiting for me to wake up?"

"Ten days," the doctor replied

"Ten days?" Charlie was shocked.

"First of all, welcome back," the doctor's smile was warm.

"Now, let me check on a neurology consult I've asked for, Charlie. We also need to get you started with some basic PT to warm those muscles back up. I'll be back shortly." Dr. Taggart left the room, leaving Charlie with her mouth agape, looking to Gabe.

Cassidy's intuition plus nurse training had her looking at Gabe, patting Charlie's hand and following the doctor out. "I'll be right back, Mom."

Charlie waited for the door to close behind her daughter before she sat up straighter, tugging on Gabe's hand, pulling him closer.

"Tell me the truth, don't you dare follow their 'protect her from herself' path. It's bullshit. I need to be able to count on you." Her dark blue eyes were worried yet clear, her voice low yet strong.

This was the Charlie Gabe knew was in there all along. This Charlie was taking charge. Right now, though, he was more than a little worried himself.

"We need to go slow, Charlie, okay?" he said.

"I'm more than a little freaked out that I've been lying here for ten days for no clear reason. I'm a LOT freaked out that that beautiful girl calls me Mom and I have no earthly idea who she is." Charlie's voice broke just a little before she hissed quietly, "What kind of mother can't remember her own child?"

"Hey, hey, you've been through a lot, let's take it slow." Gabe's thumb stroked hers.

"Do me a favor and get rid of them for a little while...please? I need to think. I'm resting, okay? Please?" Charlie beseeched him, her gaze steady on his.

"A breather is a good idea," Gabe agreed as she settled back into the bed, letting his hand go to pull up the covers and get situated.

When Cassidy returned, she saw her mother's eyes closed and motioned for Gabe to come to the door.

"She'll be fine, let's take it slow. Why don't you go get some breakfast and call your brother, update him?" Gabe fervently hoped his suggestions would not be seen for the getting rid of tactics they were, at least not clearly.

Cassidy hesitated.

Gabe sighed. "Cassidy, you've just seen her reaction to me. I'm no stranger. I've promised I'm not a psycho and provided reliable references, remember?" Gabe gave her a little shove.

"Okay, okay. An hour." The girl pulled her phone from her purse and dialed her brother as she walked away.

Gabe turned back to Charlie, who opened one eye and warily looked around.

She sat up, moving her legs experimentally, taking stock of the IV and readjusting her tumbled hair. Her fiddles with that hair made him grin, every time.

She took a deep breath, crossed her legs carefully and patted the bed. "Come, sit, please?"

He obliged, sitting and turning to face her. He reached out his hand and Charlie gripped it with a sigh.

"I—It will be okay, I know...but right now? I'm terrified." Tears flooded her eyes and lingered on her dark lashes, threatening to fall.

Gabe's heart twisted. "Just rest, relax, Charlie. We'll figure it all out soon."

"I have to let some of this out, so I can hold it together when— what was her name—returns. Whether I remember her or not, I'm obviously her mother and mothers don't just fall apart," Charlie said, bowing her head, her voice trailing off to a whisper.

"I know my name is Charlie Reilly. I know I live near St. Louis. I know I was going to lunch at Panera ten days ago. I haven't thought much past that yet, everything is so jumbled together in my head." She paused for a deep breath, looking up at him.

His gaze was kind, encouraging her.

Inside, he was shocked, she kept saying "going to lunch ten days ago"—did she not remember the island, the last two and half months? How could she remember him, if that was the case?

Gabe tamped down his own flare of panic and managed to keep his expression encouraging amid her scrutiny.

She licked her dry lips, briefly wondering if there was chapstick around. Chewing the edge of said lips, she said, "I know you, I feel like I do, anyway. I feel like I've known your voice for a long time— but I can't remember your name." She paused, closing her eyes. "I'm fighting so very hard against the urge to scream, to freak out. I'm sorry for laying it all on you, for asking you to be my confidant, but I don't know what else to do."

Before Gabe could speak again, Cassidy came through the door, her brother on her heels. Charlie quickly rubbed her hands over her face and smiled, her smile faltering a bit as she saw Troy because she had a feeling she should know him, but didn't.

"Mom, so glad to see you awake!" the young man hugged her and gently kissed her cheek.

Upon the kids' arrival, Gabe had stood, remaining next to the bed. Charlie reached for his hand without looking at him, her eyes on the young adults as they bantered back and forth, unpacking odds and ends from the bags Cassidy had brought in.

The expression on her face was stricken, despite her determination.

"Mom?" Troy sat on the edge of the bed. "What's wrong?' He patted her hand. "Are you feeling okay, considering?"

Charlie was saved from answering by the return of Nurse Lani and an unfamiliar doctor.

"Charlie, this is Dr. Carlisle, our neurologist. He'd like to spend some time talking with you, if that's okay." Lani's smile was reassuring; she was good at her job.

"Okay." Charlie nodded.

"It's best if Charlie and I talk alone just for a bit." The doctor looked at Cassidy, Troy and Gabe.

Charlie's eyes flew to Gabe, her grip on his hand tightening.

Gabe was torn, knowing the doctor needed to do his thing yet not wanting to leave Charlie alone. As if reading his mind, Charlie nodded her head, releasing his hand reluctantly.

"Shoo, all of you, the sooner you go, the sooner you come back."

Lani held the door as the kids went out, looking back at their mother over their shoulders. Charlie smiled at them, wiggling her fingers in a wave.

Troy and Cassidy relaxed at the familiar wave and went down to the waiting room at the end of the corridor. Gabe followed them, giving Charlie a wink on his way out.

*   *   *

As they sat in the waiting room, Cassidy said, "I'm worried, I don't feel like Mom is quite herself."

"Cass, she's been through the wringer on top of being asleep for ten days, of course she's not herself." Troy rolled his eyes. "Let's just see, okay?" He rubbed his sister's shoulders as they waited.

Gabe paced the floor, looking out the wide windows that over-looked the big island.

Relief at Charlie's waking had already given way to a worry that gnawed at him, deep inside. Did she remember Jack? Did she remember losing Jack? Those questions burned in his mind, not because he was jealous but because he was afraid for her.

Mulling all of this over, he walked to the other side of the wait-ing room and leaned against the windows. He took the time to call Jillian, agreeing that they would hold off on their usual afternoon visit until further word from him.

He talked to Rory, still feeling the prick of pride and amazement that she was his. He hoped that feeling wouldn't ever go away. After telling her to text him a joke later, he put the phone back in his pocket, just as the doctor emerged from Charlie's room.

Dr. Carlisle approached the trio, pulling up a chair to sit facing Troy and Cassidy. Gabe joined them, sitting on the edge of his seat.

"In cases like Charlie's, we're essentially flying blind," the doctor began, "We really have no way of knowing the effects until Charlie knows them and can tell us about them. We do have a few screening tools to help guide us. Physically she checks out so far. I just sent her down for a few tests and we'll have her up and about today. She needs to take it slow, as she'll be weak. We'll have her eating light foods that won't shock her stomach, if that goes well, she can eat at her own pace. That's the easy stuff."

Dr. Carlisle paused and looked at each of them in turn.

"Charlie's memory is fractured right now. As you heard her say, the last thing she remembers is getting ready for lunch—she assumes that was ten days ago. From what you've told me, Cassidy, that actually happened over two and a half months ago. She doesn't remember the episode that happened at the restaurant, she doesn't remember being on the island for these past weeks, nor does she remember the incident that brought her here."

The doctor paused again, focusing on Troy and Cassidy. "This next part is going to be hard."

Cassidy grabbed her brother's hand on one side and Gabe's on the other.

"From what I can tell at this time, she does not recognize either of you and she doesn't remember her husband, or the fact that he is dead."

Cassidy gasped, covering her mouth with her hands.

"What??" Troy stood abruptly and began to pace the floor.

Gabe sat quietly, letting them process things as they needed to.

"She knows you, Gabe, although she admits that she needed to be reminded of your name. You're familiar to her, she said, especially your voice." Dr. Carlisle smiled encouragingly at him. "She's going to need you."

The doctor looked back at the kids. "It's important that we give Charlie a chance to remember things on her own, even if that takes a while. For today, I'd like you to write down as much as you possibly can about the loss of your father and what's happened in Charlie's life since then. Write an exhaustive account for me and for the psychologist I'm consulting with this afternoon, okay? Bring in pictures of people in her life, your father, her best friend, coworkers. We need to know as much as we can in order to help Charlie."

Dr. Carlisle reached out to pat Cassidy's shoulder gently. "Cassidy, she's awake and she's physically healthy; the emotional trauma will take longer—in fact, we've no idea how long—but Charlie seems like a strong person to me. Baby steps." The doctor shook hands with each of them, promising to touch base with them later in the day.

Cassidy sat motionless, tears streaming down her face. "She doesn't know us. She doesn't remember Dad. Oh God, Troy, she must feel so lost and alone!"

Troy knelt in front of his sister, taking her hands in his. "But she's not alone, Cassie, okay? She has us, she has Gabe, she has

Trudy—somebody needs to call Trudy—and she has her doctors and therapists."

Troy stood, helping his sister to her feet. "Right now, we've got to take some time and write this history for the doctor, that's imperative. You'll write what you know, Gabe?" Troy turned to him.

Gabe nodded. "I've paper in the room."

"Since she's gone for tests right now, let's go get my laptop and find a place to do this." Troy pulled his sister along.

"We can't leave her alone with nobody waiting for her in the room," Cassidy protested.

Gabe inclined his head. "I'll be there."

Cassidy turned on him. "Why is it you she remembers and not her husband or children?" She wasn't hateful or mean, just genuinely puzzled, confused and, yes, hurt.

Gabe shrugged, holding his empty hands out, palms up.

Troy took his sister's hand and tugged again. "Let's go."

She let herself be pulled along, saying to Gabe, "I'm sorry. I am glad she does recognize someone, at least."

Gabe waited as they left, taking a moment to stand in front of the windows, the sun blazing outside, the air cool inside.

He agreed with Cassidy, how alone Charlie must feel.

He straightened his shoulders and said to himself, "Well, then you'll be right there, Gabriel ol' boy." And turned to go back to Charlie's room to wait for her return.

*   *   *

As she was wheeled back to her room, Charlie fought to stay awake, exhaustion weighing heavily on her body and spirit. There was so much she needed to do; she needed a computer so she could learn about what was going on with her, she needed a shower, food—oh, and to remember her children.

A tear leaked from her closed eyes as she settled back into her bed, Lani already at her bedside. Charlie quickly wiped it away and struggled to sit upright.

"I know you're tired, but how about a shower and some food then maybe a nap before the afternoon consults?" Lani smiled, handing her a list of food options to choose from.

Charlie made a face and said, "I may not know much today, but I know this is not my menu of choice."

Gabe laughed from the doorway. "I promise you decent food once your stomach is ready, okay?"

Charlie stuck her tongue out at him, chose soup from the list and agreed to the shower.

Lani left, saying she'd send in a nurse aide in to help her shower and dress in the yoga pants and a t-shirt waiting in her closet, thoughtfully provided by Cassidy as they'd waited for Charlie to wake up.

"Gabe?" She spoke quietly, the exhaustion and fear showing in her expression as well as her voice.

"Hmm?" He moved to stand beside the bed, his heart twisting at how sad and lonely she looked. She reached out her hand, and he grasped it with a smile. "You're a trooper, Charlie."

"I'm a survivor," she agreed, the ghost of a smile flitting across her face before she frowned. "Gabe, promise to tell me the truth?"

Gabe nodded, hoping to hell and back that he wouldn't regret it. He knew what she was going to ask and he fervently prayed every good Catholic boy's prayer he could think of for strength.

Charlie took a deep breath to steady herself and said, "I have a husband, I must. But...you're not him, are you?"

Even expecting questions about Jack, the effect of this one surprised him. He felt as if she'd punched him solidly in the gut, leaving him breathless on the ground.

He swallowed hard and shook his head, his eyes never leaving her face. "No, Charlie, I'm not."

Her expression was a dagger in his chest, as her eyes welled up with tears that she bravely fought, dashing them away with her free hand.

"I wanted it to be so, but I just knew in my heart..." she trailed off on a deep shuddering breath.

Gabe stroked her fingers to calm both her and himself as he bit his tongue, letting her ask what she would.

"Your voice is the only thing in the world I recognize right now. I knew you immediately, with no confusion, yet I don't even know my own ch-children. I don't question our connection, yet somehow I still feel alone." She gave him a watery smile, squeezing his hand.

"The truth, Gabe, you promised. I feel him, I know he exists. Why isn't he here? This is clearly a gigantic crisis in my life so where is he?"

Gabe stood motionless, her hand gripping his like the lifeline he was for her.

"He hasn't been in your life for a while, Charlie." The words of the party line they'd agreed to tell her tasted terrible in his mouth. Truth but not truth and it killed him a little inside to have to say it. However, after having been witness to the destruction losing Jack had left in its wake, he knew Charlie wasn't ready to face those details or she'd have remembered on her own. The traumatized mind was a fragile thing.

Charlie persisted, "Why isn't he here? Why do I feel a yawning black hole edged with a strange, distant sadness when I think about him? Why do I feel the beginnings of a damn panic attack when I think his name—which I did not remember on my own." She pressed him, forcing him to look into her eyes again. "Why, Gabe?"

Gabe cleared his throat uneasily. "You're going to talk about that with the therapist."

Charlie made a sound of disgust and yanked her hand from his. "You're supposed to be on my side, Gabe, mine." Her eyes sparked with fury, her sensitive emotions boiling over.

He leaned forward, spearing her gaze with his own and taking her chin gently in his hand. "Charlie, I'm right here, I'll not leave you. I swear to you we'll talk about it anytime you need to—after the therapist gives us a green light or you remember on your own, whichever comes first. Just know that you're right about our connection."

This was the only answer he could safely give her.

Charlie's eyes were both angry and confused, twisting the dagger she'd landed in his chest even further. She was finally asking him to help her—and he had to refuse.

*   *   *

Before she could press him further, the nurse's aide—Fiona, her name tag read—bustled in to help Charlie shower. Smiling and efficient, she inadvertently ended their conversation briskly, focused on the job at hand.

Without sparing him a glance, Charlie tossed back her hair and carefully walked to the shower on her own. "Feels like I have sea legs," she laughed to Fiona as the aide closed the door behind them.

Gabe walked to the window, scrubbing his hands over his face and letting out a deep breath. This was as tough as anything he'd faced with Charlie thus far, yet tougher on her to be sure.

While he waited, he took the time to jot down a few notes about Charlie's time on the island for the consultation. He was not sharing their nightly talks or the details of her dreams, just how he knew she battled with nightmares from time to time.

To withhold all the information about her dreams would be to hinder her healing process, but the deep details weren't needed he thought grimly—feeling the need to protect her as much as he possibly could.

His heart twisted again to think that Charlie was going to have to learn about the loss of her husband all over again whenever her memory allowed it.

Gabe decided to pull the doctor aside for a one-on-one talk and ask him specifically what to do. Charlie didn't deserve evasive maneuvers that would cause her to lose faith in him—or in herself.

No matter what, as soon as he could, he would answer her questions without tap dancing around the truth.

He'd answer them and shelter her as she dealt with the fallout.

****Chapter Twenty-Two****

ONCE CHARLIE REGAINED some physical strength, she was a dynamo, hating to be confined and always looking for something to do.

Lacking focus for her beloved reading, she burned through crossword puzzles, kicked all of their asses at Scrabble, and begged for yet one more round of Mario Kart.

She walked as much as her body and therapists would allow, visiting other patients and chatting with their families in her circles of the hospital floor.

The afternoons were spent outside the building, laughing herself silly with Gabe as they ate picnic lunches Jillian packed—complete with Rory's specialty brownies. He brought Rory by most afternoons and they played croquet or tossed a frisbee.

Today, however, she was alone for the first time in many days.

Gabe had reluctantly gone home the night before, needing to spend time with Rory, promising to bring her back with him this afternoon.

She'd managed to convince both kids to leave her for a few days, to go all the way back to their homes and take time to pay some attention their lives and get some solid rest. Neither of them had been inclined to agree to her urging, and it had taken the better part of the previous afternoon to convince them.

She smiled now, thinking about it. Even though she had no memory of them—not even a stirring—they were people she could like. That much she knew. Cassidy, yes, she was a pretty girl, but more notably, she was determined and smart. The questions she'd asked Charlie, Gabe and the doctors had all been thoughtful and intelligent. And Troy, while quieter than his sister, was just as determined and smart—preferring to chime in only when what he wanted to know hadn't yet been addressed. Charlie had looked up several times yesterday to find him staring at her, his expression tender yet confused. She imagined it was much as he'd looked as a little boy.

Sitting in the chair by the window, her mind wondered about things she had no answers for. Thus far, her memory remained stubbornly the same despite all efforts to nudge it in therapy. No new memories surfaced, no flashbacks hovered.

So far she knew she loved pasta and chocolate milk—but not together. She knew she didn't like many vegetables but loved fresh bread and fresh fruit.

Troy had laughed at her request for strawberries, saying she'd never liked them before. That was puzzling but she took it in stride, knowing such things were bound to happen.

Charlie was thrilled when she realized she did remember Gabe's daughter Rory and the story of how he'd found her a few weeks ago.

While Cassidy and Troy were pleased for their mother's sake, she could tell it hurt them that a stranger, his child and friends were the only people in their mother's memory.

Her heart was strangely silent when it came to her children. This brought her no shortage of anxiety, if she lingered on the thoughts for long—which she was doing right now.

Disheartened and lonely, Charlie let her guard down for a bit as she clasped her knees to her chest and looked out the window, lost in thought. No matter how much company she had, she still felt so alone. Would that ever change? Would she ever remember her life, those who loved her, those she loved?

Today's therapy sessions had been a bit disconcerting. In the morning therapy session, she'd recognized not one person in the pictures they'd shown her. She knew the pictures to be both real ones of people in her life and some random ones as well, some celebrities or TV stars. She couldn't name one.

She considered that maybe she needed to let it be; move on and start a new life instead of trying so hard to remember her old life. She'd voiced this thought to Jenna, her therapist, who'd responded that it was too early to give up, but that taking it slow didn't hurt anything.

In the afternoon PT session, she'd been forced to stop and ordered to rest the remainder of the day due to a cramp in her calf muscle. Both the disappointing therapy session plus the injury added up to an exhausting time on any given day, and on a not-so-good one, they were overwhelming her resolve.

Scolding herself for the self-pity just in time, Charlie heard Rory's chatter in the hall. Sitting up straight, she smiled at the dark-haired sprite as the girl skipped into the room a few steps ahead of her father and Jillian.

*   *   *

Gabe met Charlie's eyes and his heart clenched.

She'd been crying.

Damn it all, he knew better than to leave her side, but he also knew he'd needed to be by Rory's side as well. Rock and a hard place.

Leaning in to kiss her cheek, he whispered, "I missed you," bringing a smile to her face.

Jillian hugged her and set a bag on the table.

"Picnic fare today. Gabe said you really enjoyed it the last time."

"I don't think there's been a bite I haven't enjoyed." Charlie smiled, appreciative of Jillian's unfailing ability to take care of everyone around her despite being hugely pregnant and practically running the The Painted Parrot these days.

Rory chattered on about the duckling family she'd seen while they unpacked the food and enjoyed the meal together, opting to stay inside as Dr. Taggart was due to come by anytime.

The doctor showed up just as the picnic had been cleared away. Jillian nudged Rory out the door amid hugs and promises of a joke via text soon.

Closing the room door behind them, Gabe shook his head, an incredulous expression on his face. "Nine-year-old girls never stop talking—or is it just mine?"

The doctor laughed as he took the chair just vacated across from Charlie. "Well, Charlie, you're doing superbly. I think it's time we talk about letting you out of here. You're in great physical shape and the rest is as good as we can make it." Dr. Taggart smiled reassuringly as Gabe took Charlie's hand.

"Out of here?" Charlie echoed, her grip on his hand tight.

"I know it's a scary thought, but you're ready to live life outside of this hospital."

The doctor told her how therapies could easily be continued outpatient; she would be released from PT in a day or two most likely anyway. While she was doing very well physically, he told her it was the opinion of her medical team that it would be best if she stayed where things were familiar. Rather than going back to St. Louis with Troy and Cassidy, the team felt strongly that remaining in the islands for a while was likely for the best, where she could ease back into life before actively trying to remember her past.

Gabe listened to the doctor with her and when the man left, promising to check back in the following morning, he sat down, pulling the chair close so their knees touched.

Her face was worried as she chewed the corner of her lip and twined her fingers in her hair. Gabe waited patiently for her to speak, knowing her mind was racing.

Charlie was so determined and focused, but he could tell that the news of losing her newly established groove had shaken her.

"You heard what he said," she said, meeting his gaze.

"I did."

"I know one thing and that's that I'm not going to live with these kids—even here in the islands. They have their own lives. I'm getting to know them, I accept them as my children, but they're strangers to me, Gabe. My life is full of nothing but strangers. I can—I am—dealing with that but I need to do it on my own terms, not worrying about what others think or would like me to do."

Gabe chuckled and Charlie frowned. "That's funny?" she demanded.

"No, no." He held up his hands in defense. "That's YOU, Charlie. It's nice to hear you being you, that's all." He ducked her swat to his head.

"In all seriousness, what are you thinking? Let's talk it out." Gabe leaned forward, letting his hands hang between his knees.

Charlie straightened, resolute. "I've already decided I will not go with the kids. They're not going to like it, but my mind is made up. I'd like to go back to the island, stay there awhile. The kids can visit, keep in touch, whatever, but I don't want them to live with me there."

Gabe nodded. "I understand. It's only been a week since you woke up. They're still strangers. As much as you want to love them, that's a fact. However, you can't shut them out forever."

"I know. I just need some time, Gabe." She took a deep breath. "You know they aren't going to take it well at all. They're determined to take care of me." Charlie had to smile at how they'd tried so hard to take charge yesterday. "In therapy today, Jenna said it was up to me when I go home or explore places I used to go and so forth. The thing is, I don't even know what 'home' is right now. I'd like a little more time—I'd like to be stronger before I try to pick things up. So," she took a deep breath, a sip of water. "If it's possible, I'd like to go back with you."

Gabe thought she was quite possibly one of the bravest people he'd ever met, to go at this feeling so alone, yet determined to go forth.

He nodded. "Okay. Come home with me. You can have the cabin as long as you need it and there'll always be another one for Cassidy and Troy when they visit. If we're booked, I'll figure something out."

For the next half-hour, Gabe told her of the plan he'd been talking about with Jill, knowing Charlie would be dismissed from the hospital long before she was ready to live alone and suspecting she'd want to stay on the island. He told her the references he'd asked for and already looked into for her therapies—assuring her he'd not taken charge but merely made inquiries to be certain she could find what she needed there.

Charlie listened, touched at the lengths he was willing to go to help her. When he was finished, she thought for a moment, then agreed.

She was going back to The Painted Parrot—same place she'd been before the incident but a different cottage. A new cottage where any remembering she did would come naturally.

He promised to see to it that her plan to continue regaining her physical strength and then start "field trips" to help jog her memory happened as she wanted it to happen.

Charlie was relieved to have a plan in place, relieved to be in control yet also cared for. She'd be looked after yet be in charge of her life and have all her own space she wanted. She was beginning to think she really wanted quite a bit.

"Charlie, Troy and Cassidy are going to protest, really protest. They aren't children. They're going to say I'm a stranger. They're going to say it's crazy that you'd run off with a stranger and send them back to the States." Gabe wanted her to be ready for any response.

"Gabe, everyone is a stranger to me. Except you. They know that by now, like it or not. I've given their possible responses some thought. I hope they'll respect my wishes, but I am an adult, despite my problems of the moment. I'm growing to like the two of them, I am. But, I still don't know them, I can't bring myself to trust them."

"Let's get some sleep, okay?" Gabe held out his hand and helped her stand. Charlie stood, keeping a loose hold on his hand as they walked the few steps to the bed. Having gotten ready for bed earlier, she settled in.

Gabe pulled up the covers and tucked them around her, his hands coming to rest on her shoulders, his eyes meeting hers.

"Charlie, again I promise you with every fiber of my being that I will do whatever you need, when you need it. I know you feel alone, but I swear to you that's not the case. You're never going to be alone as long as I've anything to say about it." His voice was soft yet deliberate. "You're going to kick ass and take names, lady."

As he had every night since she arrived at the hospital, Gabe read to her as she drifted off to sleep. Since she'd woken from her coma, she'd wanted him to continue. The way Gabe saw it, it was the least he could do.

* * *

"Come home with me." Gabe's voice from the night before echoed in her head as Charlie awoke early the next morning, having slept restlessly during the night.

Gabe had suffered the same fate, for she'd kept a grip on his hand most of the night even as she'd fidgeted and mumbled. He wondered if she simply stressed about the day ahead or if her mind was forcing her to remember things bit by bit.

She pushed back her hair, freeing his hand, and sat up cross-legged on the bed, facing him. Gabe flexed his hand a few times, scrubbed his hands over his face and through his hair.

"Morning, sunshine." His voice was morning raspy yet tender; she looked so lost and worried.

Charlie considered him thoughtfully, then nodded and started to rise and get ready for the day.

Gabe returned her gaze steadily for a moment, nodded back and moved out of her way.

While she showered, he freshened up and changed clothes in the hospital's guest bathroom at the end of the hall. Dressed, his bag packed, he sat on the bench in the guest suite and called Jill to discuss further details of what needed to be done.

"The cottage is sparkling clean and ready, I'll stock it today as per your list—plenty of chocolate milk coming up. We're ready," she told him.

Gabe knew he was beyond lucky to have Jill; he'd known she would accept Charlie without question—well, she'd grill him later, anyway.

It would be good to be home, so good.

Gabe heard their voices as he stepped into the hallway and braced himself to champion Charlie's decision.

Her children were not going to accept her desire to send them back home easily, but he'd expected as much. They clearly loved her dearly and to them he was a stranger.

*   *   *

Charlie glanced at him when he stepped just inside the doorway, and leaned there, but she kept her attention on Troy and Cassidy.

It was interesting to the psych junkie inside of her how she liked these two but truly felt no maternal connection whatsoever. It'd been hard to accept them in her space nearly all day every day, for nobody likes strangers hovering when you're feeling vulnerable.

Charlie had been forced to set a few boundaries, sending them back to their lives as much as they'd go, telling them straight out, with kindness yet firmly, that she needed time and space.

Cassidy's face had showed her pain when Charlie had closed the bathroom door to dress by herself, starting the day after she'd awakened, when she'd taken the hair elastics from Cassidy's hand rather than let Cassidy fix her hair. It'd been a learning experience for them all.

These moments and others went through her mind as Charlie listened to them talk, saying nothing from where she sat cross-legged in the middle of the neatly made bed.

The kids went back and forth, trying to explain how they planned to help her, how being at home would be best and finally how Gabe was a stranger.

Gabe caught her eye and winked in solidarity.

He wanted to stand by her, to offer her his hand, but knew this needed to be between her and her kids.

She looked wonderfully strong and healthy sitting there dressed in capris and a tee that Jillian had helped her pick out online a few days ago, when she'd mentioned needing some new things of her own to wear. Her hair was pulled up into that adorably messy, complicated knot that suited her so well.

*   *   *

Troy realized Gabe was in the room and whirled on him with a glare. "You put her up to this. You're taking advantage of a woman with no memory of her life!" He stabbed a finger an inch away from Gabe's chest for emphasis.

Gabe lifted his open hands out to the side. "Your mother is an adult with opinions of her own."

Cassidy stared, looking back and forth from Gabe to Charlie. "We made such a huge mistake in letting him in here, Troy. We should've told them he was a stranger." She spat the word at him.

It stung as intended, but the sting was eased by Charlie's dark blue eyes meeting his as she smiled.

He'd stand in the damn fiery gates of hell for that smile.

"Mom, seriously, can't we stay here with you? Daddy wouldn't want you to be all alone so far away from us, especially in the shape you're in." Cassidy delivered what she thought would be the piercing blow, tears streaming down her face as she beseeched her mother.

Charlie patted the bed in front of her, encouraging Cassidy to sit down and gestured to Troy to sit in the chair next to her.

"Okay, I've sat here and heard you out, both of you. It's my turn." Her voice, clear and strong, brooked no argument.

She folded her hands in her lap and looked at each of them in turn. "First of all, do not, and I mean do NOT, direct your anger at Gabe. This is my decision and mine alone."

"But, Mom—" Cassidy began, stopping short as Charlie held up her hand.

"My turn," she said firmly, patting Cassidy's leg but returning her hands to her lap. "You two have been beyond amazing this past week, in what memory I do have of you. I'm honored to be your friend, to know that I am your mother, I truly am. What I know of who I am, in just a few short days, I know I don't want to hurt anyone—much less you two." Charlie's hand went to her hair, twisting a stray curl around her finger.

This was a new habit that Gabe would've found cute if he didn't know it belied her calm exterior, hiding turbulent feelings.

She took a deep breath, let it out slowly. "That being said, you're still mostly strangers to me—as nearly every person in this world is, at this point." Charlie tried to put it as nicely as she could, but these two needed to see it from her perspective.

Cassidy burst into fresh tears, Troy's expression was wounded. Charlie's face saddened at their pain but Gabe could see there was a distinct element of distance there.

"So you'd leave us orphans?!?" Cassidy sobbed, Troy stood up to embrace his sister, over her head, his expression pained.

Charlie sighed. "There's nothing easy about any of this for any of us," she said gently. "But you have to realize that before I can be what you want or need, I have to know who I am."

"But how can you learn who you are from thousands of miles away from home?" Troy was trying hard to understand.

"Honestly? At this moment, I have no home. Home is a familiar place—and nothing is familiar. Who I am needs to come from me and me alone," Charlie replied.

"Isn't being around familiar things part of the treatment process for regaining your memory?" Troy asked, sitting back in the chair, his sister calming down.

"It is and it isn't. It could be more harm than good if I'm not ready for it. I don't feel ready for it just yet and my medical team agrees—you heard them. Not to belabor the point, but again, nothing is familiar right now."

For the first time since the discussion started, Charlie faltered a little, her resolve still strong but her emotions beginning fray. "Please, please try not to take this personally, but I have to think about what I feel is best for me right now."

Troy and Cassidy looked at each other for a moment and, to her and Jack's credit, they knew they had to help her as best they could.

"If it's what she wants." Cassidy nodded to her brother and they looked at Charlie with twin sad expressions.

She gave them both a slight smile.

"Okay. But I have a ton of questions for you, mister." Troy turned to Gabe, where he'd stood through it all, waiting.

"Fire away," Gabe invited.

For the next few minutes, Gabe answered the kids' questions about anything and everything they could think of, with many of those answers being "I don't know; we'll have to see."

When the doctor came in, they were as ready as they could be.

Troy felt the need to ask his own questions, asking his mother's permission before he did so.

Dr. Carlisle assured them that while once familiar places and things could and often did help, it was best done over time rather than immediate immersion. It really was up to Charlie. The doctor told the young adults he would, as he'd been doing thus far, continue to do all he could to help Charlie regain her memory. He said his goodbyes, telling Charlie he was looking forward to seeing her when she visited his office for a follow up soon.

"You have Gabe's numbers, I'll let you know when I get a new cell phone—which will be soon," Charlie began the goodbyes, hoping to be on her own way out of there soon, before she crumpled into an exhausted heap.

"I'm ready to get out of this place, kids." She hugged each of them.

As they clung to her, she pushed back the feeling of being smothered and let them cling for a moment before extricating herself gently.

Troy shook Gabe's hand, meeting his gaze head on. "Thank you, for whatever it is you are to her. She obviously trusts you. I'll call weekly, try to give her space."

Gabe nodded, clasping the young man's hand firmly.

Cassidy hugged him. "I'm sorry, and thank you," she said, fighting back tears as she turned to look at her mother once more. "I love you, Mom. Please come back to us." She turned and left the room quickly, allowing her brother to put his arm around her and lead her to the elevators.

Gabe sighed and moved to Charlie's side. "Intense," was all he said as Charlie took his hands and squeezed.

"It's almost scary how detached I feel," Charlie said thoughtfully. "That should've just killed me, yet I feel confident; I feel like I've taken the first step to finding me."

She looked around the hospital room for a moment and grinned at him. "Let's leave this place in the rear-view mirror, shall we?"

Gabe picked up her bag and his, Charlie carrying the pillow and soft throw Jillian had brought her.

She was both scared and thrilled to be taking the first steps to the rest of her life.

* * *

Gabe loaded their bags into the rental and opened the passenger door for Charlie. Once she was in and settled, she leaned her head back and closed her eyes. The near-silence was a welcoming balm after her time in the hospital, where it was never quiet.

He walked around the vehicle and climbed inside, closing the door. Keys in the ignition, he paused and turned slightly in the seat to face Charlie.

He swore quietly, hating the smudges of exhaustion under her eyes and lines of strain around her mouth that had appeared as the morning wore on.

Eyes still closed, Charlie said, "The quiet is so...quiet out here."

"Hey." Gabe nudged her with his elbow.

"Hmm?"

"Look in the rearview mirror." He grinned as he turned out of the parking lot, leaving her confinement of nearly two weeks behind.

Charlie laughed, some of her spark coming back as she realized she was truly free. Memoryless, but free. "Sayonara!" she called, rolling down the window to wave her arm wildly.

Gabe laughed with her as he drove out of town, to the marina where the boat waited. He was looking forward to being seaside again. The shore was healing, always had been for him and he trusted that it would be for Charlie as well, if she were given the space and time she needed.

He intended to see that she got just that.

Chapter Twenty-Three

THE TWO BEDROOM COTTAGE was open to the ocean breeze, as all the cottages were during the season, wind chimes tinkling as Charlie got out of the truck, waving off Gabe's arm of assistance and walked into the cottage. Gabe gathered their bags and followed.

Sitting down on the couch, Charlie sighed, feeling weary to the bone yet content.

"I have this pleasant cocoon going on right now. I know I don't know much about myself, but at the moment I'm okay with that. How can that be?" she wondered, wrapping her arms around herself loosely.

Gabe emerged from the bedroom where he'd placed her bags and crossed to the other bedroom, dropping his own bag on the bed.

"My theory?" he asked, going to the fridge then moving to sit on the coffee table in front of the couch, handing her a bottle of cold water.

Charlie nodded both her assent and her thanks.

"If you're okay with it, then be okay."

Charlie let her body go boneless in the nest of the couch corner, the stress and tiredness catching up with her. Hospitals are no place to sleep deeply and rest fully. "Good theory," she agreed.

Gabe again noted her heavy eyes, the fatigued smudges beneath them. "You know what? Why don't you go lie down? I'm not leaving you today, so you can rest easy. Rory wants come by with supper as well as to check up on you. She insists she has the best pasta recipe ever." Gabe's eyes rolled up as he mimicked his sassy girl's tone.

Charlie smiled at the mention of Rory. The kid was a spark plug, full of both energy and tenderness at the same time.

He stood and held out his hands to help her up. Charlie let him pull her to feet and walk her to the bedroom door. He kissed her forehead and nudged her inside. "I'll be right out here."

Surprising him, Charlie leaned her forehead on his chest and clung to him for a moment. Her hands rested at his sides, fisted lightly in his t-shirt. He brought his hands up to hug her, reveling in how right she felt in his arms.

"Did you know the rarest type of diamond is green?" She laughed lightly in a punch-drunk way as she moved away and turned into her room.

Gabe shook his head, thinking he needed to brush up on his trivia tidbits if he was going to come close to keeping up.

Charlie shed her clothes for an over-sized navy tee she found on the bed and crawled into the downy bedding, welcoming the cocoon of the dimly lit room with the sounds from the ocean outside the open windows unbroken by the noise of machines or the intrusion of nurses. Knowing Gabe was just outside the open door, she slipped into a deep, dreamless sleep, a restorative rest for both her body and mind.

* * *

As the hours passed, Gabe sat on the front porch, sipping his lemonade. He felt the stresses of the past few weeks melting away, his muscles beginning to relax, fraction by fraction. The sea was soothing, the sun beginning to set.

Hearing laughs close by, Gabe looked up to see his daughter skipping up the slope from the beach, Jill moving much slower behind her. "Hey, Poppet." He set aside his glass to intercept the dark-haired girl's full body hug.

"Hi, Daddy." She grinned. Even after the last few weeks, it still was hard for Gabe to believe this girl with the elfin face and mischievous grin was his child. It was even more amazing that she was so resilient and hadn't had a problem accepting him beyond some shyness now and again as they got to know each other.

Gabe bit back a grin as Jill, now almost 7 months pregnant, collapsed on the step next to him. "Wrangling that kid wearing you out?" he tugged one of Rory's braids with one hand, the other rubbing his friend's back.

"She said he's already grounded at birth after last night's shenanigans." Rory's small hands patted Jill's belly sympathetically.

Jill laughed, her tiredness paling in comparison to the joy of having Gabe home to stay and the laughing girl in front of her to keep perspective. "Mercy, last night was like a rodeo, Cirque du Soleil and a boxing match all at once!"

Gabe laughed out loud, patting her shoulder. "Not much longer now."

"You staying for supper?" He stood, stretching, doubling over as Rory poked his exposed side.

"You need me to?" Jill asked, rubbing her lower back.

"Nope, Rory and I have it under control. Go home, rest." Gabe tossed his truck keys to Jill. "Drive, save a few steps and get the truck outta the way."

Jill pushed herself up, waved and waddled off.

Rory handed her father a take-out bag from The Painted Parrot and, toting the other bag, skipped into the house ahead of him.

*   *   *

Charlie stirred, feeling warm and heavy, half buried in the pillows and cozy covers of the bed. She stretched slowly from her fingertips to her toes, all muscles responding and waking up. The twice daily PT sessions plus her own love of walking about the hospital and the grounds when she could have brought her physical health back nearly up to par. She felt good—really good.

She groaned at how good the full body stretching felt and did it again, pushing back her hair and sitting up, only to flop back against the bank of pillows.

Why do hospitals have such sucky beds? She wondered, idly watching the ceiling fan's slow spin. She sniffed the air appreciatively. Was that food she smelled? All of the sudden she was ravenous.

Charlie climbed from the bed and pulled a pair of bright turquoise yoga pants from the foot of the bed. Skip hopping into them, she opened the door and groaned aloud.

Gabe looked up from setting the table and laughed at her feinted swoon against the door jamb.

"My kingdom for whatever that is." Charlie pulled back her hair, securing it with an elastic she discovered on her wrist where it belonged.

"Milady." he gave an exaggerated bow as he pulled out a chair at the table. Charlie groaned again, her eyes on the pasta dish as she picked up a crusty roll and buttered it, wasting no time biting into the warm goodness.

The sound she made caused Gabe to laugh out loud. "Now I know what speaks to your heart, milady. Bread 'n butter!"

"I thought Rory would be joining us?" Charlie asked, actually missing the girl's exuberant chatter.

"She was here but then decided to go off with the family from the Squid Ink Cottage when they walked by outside. I'm still baffled at how she went from being so clingy to being so independent over the past few weeks."

"I think it's largely due to how you let her do it at her own pace. She learned to trust you and not be afraid," Charlie said, buttering her next bite.

He gestured questioningly to the plates on the table, allowing her to choose what she'd prefer. As he suspected, Charlie pulled the plate of pasta covered with a creamy Alfredo sauce, crispy bacon and pine nuts in front of her and began to eat. She made appreciative sounds from time to time, winking at him over her food.

Gabe followed suit and dug into his steak with matching appreciation. They ate without words for several minutes, pausing only to roll their eyes or drink deeply from the cold tea glasses.

Several minutes later, Charlie leaned back in her chair and raised her glass to Gabe. "Well played, sir. Well played."

Clinking glasses, Gabe, too, sat back comfortably, his legs stretched out to the side of the table. "That was a meal," he agreed heartily, setting aside his tea glass and pouring himself a cup of coffee.

"Thank you from the very bottom of my starving belly." She smiled, feeling truly relaxed for the first time in—well, she wasn't sure how long, exactly.

Gabe saluted her with his coffee cup as he sipped it slowly.

"I don't know how long it's been since I had a meal like that. Of course, being that I only remember the last week of my life..." Charlie shrugged and laughed.

Gabe rolled his eyes at her. "Sassy wench," he teased. "The chefs at the Painted Parrot are good ones. Matteo is creative and loves to experiment while we depend on Bev for traditional favorites. Matteo is young and reckless; he has a plane and loves to fly..." Gabe stopped suddenly as Charlie went pale, her eyes wide and unfocused.

"Charlie? Charlie, listen to my voice. Just breathe. That's it, just breathe in and out. You're okay." Gabe kept his voice calm and low, wanting to touch her but knowing not to. His experience with shell shock gave him a lot to fall back on in this situation and, for a change, he was thankful for that.

Charlie took a shuddering breath and, steadying her shaking hands, took a long drink from her glass. "I-I don't—." She drank deeply again then put her face in hands, sitting as still as a stone.

"Hey, no need to think about it right now, unless you really want to. It can wait." Gabe reached out and took her hand.

She nodded, feeling steadier by the minute. Both of them expected such episodes to happen, not that it made them any easier to deal with.

"I do love the beach," she said suddenly, with a note of surprise in her voice.

"Yeah?"

"Yeah, I really do. Who knew?" Charlie laughed, thrilled to be certain about something. She paused for a moment, then said, "We did it," she said softly, meeting his gaze a bit shyly.

"Hmm?" His eyebrow raised in question.

"We did it. We weathered my first episode they warned us about." She tightened her grip in a squeeze then released his hand. "You said something about dessert?" She pointed at him, a mischievous gleam in her eye, the momentary lapse apparently quickly dismissed.

"I did. You feel like getting out for a walk on the beach? Matteo makes a kick ass hot fudge cake I'm partial to."

Charlie considered his question and nodded, she did feel like getting out. "I think I do. Let me change."

She was back in minutes, a pair of white sandals in her hand.

Gabe gave a low whistle and a wink, admiring the sea green sundress she'd chosen.

Her hair was smoothed and caught loosely at her neck, a few strands free to frame her face. He'd thought she was beautiful before the incident, but free from her burden of grief, she dazzled him.

She gave him a bright smile he recognized as carefree and happy. And even though he knew forgetting her life wasn't a good thing, he couldn't help but be grateful for her relief—however short lived it may be.

They strolled in a companionable silence, watching the lowering sun set the sea ablaze. As the blue of the night crept up the sky, the lights from The Painted Parrot spilled out onto the sand, music heard faintly as they drew closer.

"You sure it's not too soon for company?" Gabe had a momentary pang of worry that the lively bar would be too much for her first night out.

"I'm positive. I feel good." She picked up a stick of driftwood to draw aimless squiggles in the damp sand at the water's edge. "And that is the extent of my drawing ability." She laughed, tossing the stick into the sea and whirling around to walk backwards in front of him.

"Hey, did you know that giraffes have purple tongues—that way their tongues are protected from sunburn while they eat the leaves off tall trees?" Her laugh wrapped around his heart and squeezed as he laughed with her. That warm squeeze was becoming a familiar sensation.

"I can't remember my own children, but I can remember the color of giraffe tongues." Charlie rolled her eyes, walking close to his side as they approached the bar.

Before they stepped into the light, Gabe leaned down and picked up a tiny pink shell. Handing it to Charlie, he folded her hand around it. "Did you know that shells found at sunset have especially good luck?"

She stroked her thumb over the tiny shell, slipping it into her pocket. "I'll treasure it; Lord knows I need good luck."

"Daddy! Charlie!" Rory ran out of the bar and into Gabe's legs with every ounce of her energy.

"Oof." He caught her in a hug before she knocked him off balance, deeply feeling the novelty of belonging to that "Daddy" shout.

"Jill says Matteo'll have your dessert up in just a sec—I'll bring it to you!" And just like that, she was off again.

Charlie laughed at the incredulous expression that seemed always on his face when Rory was present.

Sidestepping his usual greeting of the masses, Gabe guided Charlie to a table by the rail. As people called out, he waved but stayed his course along the edge of the bar floor.

"They expect you to make your rounds; don't avoid them on my account, Gabe. Meet me at the bar." With a little nudge, she brushed past him and joined Jill where she sat at the bar while Nash manned the taps.

Gabe shook his head, yet again impressed by her bravery, and began winding his way through the crowd. As he greeted and chatted, he pulled out his phone and added a few folks to the next day's charter, conspiratorially whispered details about hidden coves to couples and held out his hands in exaggerated fish size guesstimates to kids and adults alike. He was clearly in his element, his laugh loud, his winks abundant.

When Rory popped up at his side during one such fishing story, he swung her into his arms and raised his voice for attention. "Folks, I have something incredible to share with y'all tonight!" Rory grinned a little shyly at his wink, one arm around his neck, her head touching his.

"Some of you already know, but I've been remiss in making an official toast-worthy announcement. Raise a glass, my friends, raise a glass to celebrate that this beautiful princess has come to live with us here on the island—welcome to paradise, my daughter, Rory!"

As glasses were clinked and voices raised in cheers, the little girl smiled and waved, calling out, "Here's to living in paradise with my Daddy!" obviously enjoying the spotlight.

The rest of evening was filled with laughter. Gabe joined Nash behind the bar, serving drinks and cracking jokes as the music played, customers danced and paradise lived up to its name.

He watched Charlie lean in close to Jill's ear and whisper something that sent them both into a fit of giggles, watched her play hand games with Rory, winked back at her when she caught his eye.

It was like she was simultaneously a trusted friend and yet an intriguing stranger. The shadows were gone from her eyes, her laugh was quick and musical, she looked like she belonged right here. With him.

He certainly felt like she did.

*   *   *

They left the bar in full swing, waving to Matteo, who'd agreed to serve as closing night manager a few nights a week.

Charlie nudged Gabe to walk along the shore, nearly ankle deep in the water. She carried her shoes, the skirt to her dress falling just at her knee, well above the water.

The slight suction feeling of the sand on her feet as the water pulled back had an odd sort of grounding feeling. Her contentment eclipsed the constant disquiet that lingered in the corner of her mind, leaving her lighthearted and smiling.

Gabe walked along beside her while Rory frolicked in the moonlight several yards ahead, her dark hair streaming behind her, Jake gamboling alongside.

"It's hard to believe I've missed nine years with her." Gabe watched the girl with regret in his eyes.

"It is hard to believe she's only been with you a short time," Charlie agreed, swinging her arms slightly, the sea breeze soaking deep into her soul.

"She started calling me Daddy last week." He smiled at the memory. "I was behind the bar, talking stuff over with Nash and she ran up, calling 'Hey, Daddy...' telling me something about a shell she'd found. I almost embarrassed myself by serving a drink mixed totally wrong, but luckily I managed to save it," he said with a wry grin, looking out to the sea where a few boat lights bobbed in the moonlight. "She's called me Daddy every day since then."

"I wish you hadn't spent so much time away from her, at the hospital with me—not that I don't appreciate it." Charlie hastened to amend what she felt sounded like an accusation.

Gabe took her hand in his, holding it loosely as they walked.

"I talked to her about it the first day you were there. I saw her every day and she was beside herself helping Jillian with the baby's nursery. You know she was at the hospital plenty. She wanted me to help you. Whatever Lilith might have been, she raised a remarkable girl."

Charlie stepped out of the water. "Let's sit here a bit." She smoothed her dress under her and sat on the sand, her toes in the damp sand at the water's edge.

Gabe called out, "Rory, stay close," and sat beside her, both of them gazing out at the starry sky.

Charlie turned to look at him, his profile cast in the moonlight. "You know you don't have to stay at the cottage with me, Gabe. I'm physically well and you need to pick up life with Rory and your business, your friends." She tucked a wayward curl behind her ear.

"I know. I just thought that maybe the first night in a new place you might rest better knowing you've company nearby. And maybe I'd worry less, seeing you settled."

"Uh-huh, truth comes out does it?" Charlie laughed, poking his side. "Okay, tonight only," she agreed on a shriek as the dog ran close, shaking water all over the both of them and a delighted, bedraggled Rory tackled her dad from behind, sending him toppling over into the shallow water.

"You asked for it, kid." Gabe stood with the wriggling girl under one arm, walked knee deep into the sea and dropped her. He turned and ran before she could grab his legs and make him fall. Her shrieks and sputters were rewarded with licks and nudges from her faithful companion as Gabe collapsed next to Charlie, the sounds a balm to his new daddy heart.

"I think that qualifies as child abuse, Rory," Nash laughed as he and Jillian strolled up.

"You two should see how slow you're moving, it's comical." Gabe pointed at Jillian then had to move of the way quickly as she held onto Nash for balance and aimed a well-placed kick.

"You want to come home with us, Princess? I've a need for your brownies tonight plus I want to go shopping in the morning and Nash says I can't go alone." Jillian winced slightly, one hand on her lower back, the other resting on Nash's forearm for balance.

Gabe held up one finger at his daughter. "One condition, oh Princess."

Rory cocked her head in question, one hand rubbing Jake's head, the other hand propped on her hip. "Yes, milord?" She curtsied prettily, batting her dark eyelashes, her eyes sparking with mirth.

"Sassy brat." Gabe stuck out his tongue, still holding his finger up. "One condition." He repeated. "I want brownies—still warm brownies—delivered to Charlie's door."

Rory gave him a thumbs-up. "Sure thing, Daddy-o."

Nash waved in farewell as they turned to make their way back up the beach, moving at Jillian's snail pace, the girl and her dog running circles around the both of them as she chattered.

* * *

After Rory had gone off with Nash and Jillian, they made their way back to the cottage, Charlie asking Gabe questions about the his charter service after he mentioned he'd be back on the boat the following morning.

When getting water from the fridge, Charlie laughed at the chocolate milk bottles she'd found waiting for her. Gabe raised his hands, palms out. "Gotta support your habits."

"I don't even know my habits." She shrugged as they settled in on the couch. They passed awhile in companionable silence, he with his laptop, her with her Kindle.

Looking up from his computer, he saw that Charlie had laid aside her reading, slid down into the couch corner and fallen fast asleep.

He decided she wouldn't rest well there and nudged her gently. "Go to bed, Sleeping Beauty."

Her dark blue eyes opened and she yawned. "Okay." Charlie did just that, waving a hand to him over her head as she closed the bedroom door behind her.

So far, so good, Gabe thought, putting away the laptop and heading for the small second bedroom. Having slept in awkward positions and amid hospital noises for too many nights, he was looking forward to a decent night's sleep. Showered and clad in gym shorts and a fresh t-shirt, he was asleep in minutes, leaving his bedroom door open should Charlie need him during the night.

Before his alarm went off in the wee hours before dawn, Gabe woke from a sound sleep to full alert. He lay still, trying to figure out what had wakened him. No sounds came as minutes passed and he chalked it up to the unfamiliar bed plus the first deep sleep in weeks.

Just as he turned over and drifted back off, he heard Charlie's voice. He was out of his room and into hers before the next sound came, moving quietly but quickly.

She appeared to be asleep but was whimpering softly, tears on her face. Gabe's heart sank.

In the weeks since she'd collapsed, there had been hard moments and tough days, but none of them had been about Jack. He strongly suspected that reprieve was over now that Charlie was healthy and had the chance to sleep deeply.

He did as he knew to do and spoke softly to her, "Charlie, it's okay."

She sniffled and sat up, surprising him that she was actually awake and not mid-dream. "I'm okay." She scrubbed her hands over her face and patted the bed.

He sat on the edge of the bed, turning to face her. "Wanna talk about it?" he offered, holding out his hand.

She squeezed his hand then pushed back her hair. "Nothing to talk about, really. I just woke up crying, feeling incredibly sad and alone." Her lip quivered as she shrugged. "I want to know why, but I know it'll just have to come."

"Charlie, you're not alone. You'll never be alone as long as I've got breath, you hear me?" Gabe said earnestly. He hated to hear her say she was alone, she sounded so sad yet so determined .

"You're a good friend, Gabe." She lay back on the pile of pillows, pulling up the covers, already drifting back to sleep.

All tied up in knots, Gabe made some coffee and sat on the porch steps, sipping the coffee and finishing the last of the brownies Rory had brought them the night before.

He scolded himself for considering skipping out on fishing this morn in case Charlie needed him. "You've got to let her live her life, Arch," he muttered, stepping back into the cottage to get dressed and get on with the day.

*   *   *

After attempting to fall back to sleep for an hour or more, Charlie gave up with a sigh. Maybe insomnia was better than waking up crying for no reason she could remember. Making a face, she pulled on a t-shirt and yoga pants and went into the kitchen, realizing she was really hungry.

She fixed a plate of cheese and crackers and sat atop the table, doodling on a crossword puzzle she'd pulled from the newspaper.

Did I always like cheese and crackers? Did I sit on the table? Are crosswords a thing for me?

She couldn't help but wonder at every little thing—*is this the before me or the new me?* She allowed herself to wonder.

How could a loving mother forget her children? A grieving wife not remember her lost husband? It took all she had to think about things and not to give in to a panic attack, but she allowed her thoughts free rein. After a few minutes, feeling the panic rising, Charlie had had enough.

"From this moment on, I'm living the life I have now, right now!" She declared it out loud and grabbed a legal pad to make a list—she needed some things from town.

* * *

A quick knock came at the door as Gabe stepped inside—the morning sun rising over the sea behind him.

He was amused to see her sitting atop the table. It appeared that some things don't change.

Charlie pointed to the fresh brewed coffee pot with her pen as she muttered to herself and scribbled on the paper.

"Hi. Could someone take me to town soon?" she asked him as she opened a container of cookies and pushed them towards him. "I've thought of a few things I'd like to pick up."

"Sure. Or I can pick things up for you if you don't want to get out." Gabe sipped the coffee gratefully and took a cookie, leaning against the counter.

Charlie shook her head and climbed off the table, taking a bottle of chocolate milk from the fridge. She paced about the room. "I want to go; I need to go. I've decided that living a full life is the best thing I can do right now."

She paused in her pacing and pointed at him. "Before you say it, I know I shouldn't be driving on my own yet—what with the odd blackout moments that happen from time to time—but I can start to carve out a life that'll suit my circumstances well enough. Life is made up of moments that I can't get back. I'm not going to sit around and wait to remember things—it'll either come or it won't."

With a defiant tilt of her chin, she reached up and retwisted her hair into its knot.

Gabe watched her pace and had begun to wonder when she'd breathe between words. This was an interesting side to her; one he hoped wasn't too much effort and wouldn't backfire on her.

Curious, he nodded, sipped more coffee and asked, "What kinds of things?"

"Well, I want a phone—mainly for those therapy appointments and notes and a few odd 'n ends. I know I had one but I can't find it, so I want a new one. And no more wondering about how things used to be; time to be whoever I'm going to be from now on. Oh, and I found my wallet the kids packed. Apparently I've plenty of money for the things I need."

Gabe listened, smiling at her tenacity and inwardly hoping the doctors were right, that letting her live life and remember —or not— as she would was the way to go. What other choice was there, really?

"I'm on afternoon bar duty, and thus free now, so we'll go as soon as I shower."

"Thanks, I'll be ready." Her smile, full of hope and free of shadows, made his heart do that squeeze thing. Yet he couldn't help but feel like her happiness was built on shifting sands. Again, what other choice was there?

He dug in his pocket, pulling free a rumpled business card. "Before I forget, here are the first appointments we have set up for your therapies. Day after tomorrow." He handed her a card with the PT and psych appointment times listed. Dr. Carlisle had felt that she shouldn't waste time getting her therapy routine started.

Charlie dropped the card on the table and walked with him to the porch, leaning on the rail to admire the morning view as the sea sparkled in the morning sun.

"Thanks for being here, Gabe. I bet not many people would take on a woman who doesn't know who she is. And one that won't go back to her family."

Gabe reached over to tuck a wayward strand of hair behind her ear. "We're friends, Charlie. I care about you. You're the bravest person I've ever met, and that's saying a lot."

She shook off the moment and gave him a shove. "Go shower, I'm a woman on a shopping mission."

Chapter Twenty-Four

GABE TOOK CHARLIE shopping for the things on her list, enjoying how animated and strong she seemed. Gone were the dark smudges, the haunted look in her dark blue eyes. Instead she glowed with health from inside out, her eyes clear and sparkling.

He suspected this Charlie was much like she'd been before her world had been shattered, before she'd lost her husband.

While Charlie lay in the hospital those nine days, Gabe had heard the story of the accident that had taken Jack from her and the story of her breakdown a few months later from Troy and Cassidy. Nash had also told him about the night Charlie had walked into the sea. With every detail, he was amazed that she was still standing after such blows to her world.

Gabe held the moments he'd shared with her in the dark close to his heart, knowing she might never remember them and actually hoping she'd be spared such memories.

By her request, he fielded calls from Troy and Cassidy. He assured them that their mother was fine, just not ready to talk with them, but that emailing her would be good.

At first, Cassidy grew irate with him, again accusing him of being a stranger taking advantage of her mother. Troy made veiled references to Charlie's bank account, letting Gabe know he was watching things carefully.

Gabe didn't take offense to any of it; he'd have been surprised if they hadn't reacted as such. Personally, he was hoping to convince Charlie to at least talk to them soon—or he was certain they'd show up at the door. After a few times, both kids were cordial and undemanding of him, simply asking after their mother.

* * *

Charlie filled her days, pulling out her papers, looking over her books and, surprisingly, reconnecting with her work.

She was relieved to easily refresh her memory of most of what she'd been working on, although she wondered what kind of mom remembered her writing but not her own children. Still, the thought of the kids and her former life didn't disturb her—she actually felt oddly disconnected when it came to those things.

She spent the days getting to know Gabe, Rory, Nash, and Jill, helping out at the bar, and taking long beach walks. She spent nighttime hours online, researching or writing articles on various subjects involving kids and learning—which was apparently something she knew about.

Gabe was always close, still sleeping in the second bedroom, a cot nearby for Rory.

Charlie refrained from further research about memory loss and treatment plans, considering it enough for now that she went to see her therapist twice a week. Generally the therapist simply listened to her talk about her days and what she hoped for the future. She advised Charlie of her options in treatments and exercises they could employ in attempts to jog her memory. Charlie had asked that they wait awhile before attempting such.

There'd been no more blackouts or nightmares, which both relieved and puzzled her. Shouldn't she *want* to remember?

* * *

She mentioned this to Gabe one evening. Charlie rarely talked about anything deep, preferring their easy friendship and lighthearted days.

This time she sighed, setting aside her crossword puzzle.

"How can I be content not remembering anything about who I am, Gabe? Of not knowing what my life was like? What kind of person doesn't want to remember?" She leaned against the porch post, half-turned to face him, her face barely visible in the waning light.

"Charlie, I think it's safe to say most people would be reluctant to open up what feels like Pandora's Box." Gabe reached out and took her hand in his.

She nodded, watching Rory and Jake run past, the night setting in. "What an apt description, Pandora's Box."

She fell silent, leaving her hand in his a moment longer before she pulled back her hair and sat up straighter. "So, I want to take up a hobby. Maybe I've done it before and that's why I want to do it, I don't know."

"You could ask the kids," Gabe suggested, hoping it wouldn't backfire on him.

"I want to make pottery," Charlie said happily, pointedly ignoring his nudge for her to talk to Troy and Cassidy.

"Pottery? You want to paint mugs and little animal figures?" Gabe asked, rather incredulously.

"No, silly; I want to create pottery. I want the clay, the wheel, the kiln, the whole shebang," Charlie laughed, the moment of self-reflection gone—much to Gabe's relief.

He wondered anew what kind of person it made him that he was happy she wasn't remembering? Sure it was a protective measure, but at the same time, he was quite aware of how selfish it was.

"I've been doing my research and I almost have a complete list of things I need, but what I need the most comes from you," Charlie was saying.

Gabe tuned in and said, "Wait, me? What do I know about pottery? Sure, I'll take you to find the stuff and I'll carry it back here, but I'm not sure what else I can do for you."

Charlie looked a bit uncertain as she looked up at him. "I...um...I need a little bit of space for a pottery studio. It can work right here in the cottage, I just need some furniture moved out of the way—like taken out of the house completely."

Charlie's expression was tentative, for she knew she was already costing Gabe income by living there and now she wanted to remodel it?

Gabe watched the play of emotions on her face, enjoying her earnestness and, yes, enjoying her nervousness.

"Okay, we'll move stuff if that's what you want." He nodded.

"Really? Just like that you'll let me mess up this pretty place?" Charlie's face lit up.

Gabe laughed and thought, *If you'll smile like that in my direction every day, I'll rebuild the damn thing from the ground up to your specifications.*

* * *

In the days that followed, Charlie was obsessed with her pottery studio plan, researching further and making a detailed plan to show Gabe. After offering her a rarely used shed to use as her studio, he'd said he'd come by after Rory was settled tonight to look over her plans.

Printing out her plans so they could more easily look them over, she realized she was hungry—supper had been hours ago and she hadn't been all that hungry then.

Her kitchen was rarely used beyond microwaving the meals that Gabe and Jill insisted on keeping her freezer stocked with and heating water in the kettle for her nightly mugs of hot chocolate.

Charlie had to admit that since her odd blackout when cooking the ravioli, she might've been avoiding doing much in the kitchen. Her supply of chocolate milk was low, she wasn't in the mood for crackers and cheese, so Charlie resolutely marched to the stove and started the oven to heating. She took a glass container that was marked LASAGNA from the freezer—there was enough for two in case Gabe arrived hungry—and set it on the stove.

While she waited for the oven to heat, Charlie sat on the kitchen counter and allowed herself to consider things she normally pushed away. Troy and Cassidy both called weekly, Gabe had told her. As she'd requested, he fielded those calls for her. Charlie thought maybe, after the past four weeks, she should think of someone besides herself and talk to them.

It occurred to her that email or texting might be easier at first and made a mental note to reach out to them. She'd gotten that new phone last week but had yet to fire it up and use it. She shrugged and hopped down from the counter, putting the lasagna dish in the oven. The timer set, she went out on the porch, the doors open as always. She sighed as she settled into the hammock, her full-speed ahead pace catching up with her for a moment, her eyes drifted shut to the soothing sounds of the sea.

It felt so good to just be, she thought, as she slipped into a light sleep.

The dream—or was it a memory?—came almost as soon as Charlie's eyes had closed, as if it'd been hovering at the edge of her consciousness, waiting.

A door closed with a bang, a man laughed, the rumble of his voice vibrating against her skin as he kissed his way down her neck. Her own laugh, her arms wrapped around broad shoulders clad in a blue oxford shirt. Her senses swirled with the feel of his arms around her, the sound of his rumbling chuckle, the rasp of his short beard against her skin, the smell of him—always a mixture of fresh soap and just pure man.

Charlie felt as if she were on a spinning ride, faster and faster, then flying off into space, alone— falling, reaching out and finding nothing to hold on to.

*   *   *

"Take it easy, Charlie."

She struggled to wake up, arms holding her gently as an eerie scream faded away.

"Wha-What was that?" Charlie pushed herself up from the hammock, balancing unsteadily on the edge as Gabe knelt in front of her, his eyes wide, his heart racing right along with hers.

"What was that scream, Gabe?" Charlie wasn't quite oriented just yet, struggling to place the terrifying sound in case help was needed.

Gabe scrubbed his hand over his face. "Charlie, honey, that scream came from you. You were dreaming." His voice was predictably gentle and warm.

She took several shaky breaths then a steadier one, and realized the oven timer was wailing.

"The food!" She pushed past Gabe as he stood and caught her.

"I already got the food out of the oven when I got here. I could smell it was done." The timer continued to beep as Charlie stood in Gabe's loose embrace, regaining her balance and her equilibrium.

"Okay now?" he asked softly, his hands on her shoulders, his eyes on hers.

Charlie nodded, moving to go inside and stop that infernal beeping. She pushed the button and silence fell in the cottage. Shoving back her hair, she turned to the counter where Gabe leaned, waiting.

"I was dreaming."

Gabe nodded. "Yeah, you were. Wanna tell me about it?" Her forlorn expression made him want to hit something in frustration. Between her and Rory, he was certain his heart couldn't take much more, yet it kept right on showing up.

She breathed deeply, gathering her thoughts. "Well, what I recall doesn't make a lot of sense. Surprise." Her mouth twisted wryly. "I heard laughing, both mine and a man's. I felt so loved and so safe one minute, then I was spinning, falling through space alone, freezing and terrified the next minute." Charlie shuddered, her hands over her face.

Gabe could hardly stand it, having seen similar expressions and reactions from her grieving before her memory loss. He'd illogically hoped not to see such again, for his own sake as well as hers.

"No details?" He was reluctant to ask questions but knew they were part of the process he'd committed to going through with her.

"Oh, Gabe…" She leaned on the counter, her face in her hands. "It was so overwhelmingly wonderful then shockingly terrifying, all in the span of a few seconds"

Gabe stepped close and reached out to stroke her arm. "Knowing you're going to remember things doesn't make it any easier when it happens," he said softly, aching with her pain.

Charlie turned her face into his shoulder, her muffled voice saying, "No, no it's not." Pushing away, she rubbed her face a few times and looked up, squaring her shoulders and pushing her hair back. "However it is progress, and that's something I'm supposed to be in favor of."

And just like that, Charlie was once again strong and composed.

Gabe didn't know whether to be glad she was able to handle things in such a way or to be frustrated that she was doing, as she'd called it when they'd first started talking, "the pull up the mask thing."

She took two forks from the blue jar she'd bought at the antique store last week and placed on the counter. Little touches like that were making the cottage Charlie's home. Handing him a fork, she placed the lasagna dish on the counter between them, waving her own fork at him to eat as she turned and took two bottles of water from the fridge.

Gabe grinned; her way of doing things was so simply Charlie. Why bother with plates when you could eat out of the dish?

The ease with which Gabe and Charlie ate in silence, with the exception of a few appreciative murmurs for the cheesy deliciousness in front of them, spoke volumes about their deepening friendship. Charlie knew the bond connecting the two of them was strong, going back farther than she was able to remember, but she could feel the security and peace it brought her.

They finished the food, leaving the dish to soak in the sink, and Charlie spread out the pages that outlined her pottery studio plans on the table. They talked and made notes, coming up with a detailed plan and list of supplies.

As Charlie entered the last of the information into the computer, Gabe yawned, and she looked up at him with realization. "Gabe, I'm so sorry! You've got to get some sleep—go, go!"

She shooed him with her hands as she stood. Gabe laughed but agreed; morning came early for a fisherman. He waved a hand behind him as he left the cottage, part of him wanting to nudge her to get some sleep as well, the other part not wanting to be a nag—especially when he knew she didn't sleep much.

*   *   *

Charlie did, in fact, get ready for bed, the feeling of bone-deep fatigue new to her. She'd been full of energy, sleeping in short, hard bursts when she did sleep, but now she felt drained and exhausted.

She shrugged off the questions hovering at the edge of her mind for another time-briefly wondering if that 'another time' was going to come back and bite her sooner rather than later.

She snuggled into the welcoming depths of the covers, newly purchased in her favored shades of blue, the room windows slightly open to let in the fresh, cool night air.

Recently, she'd learned she was a fresh air junkie, liking to leave windows and doors open as much as possible. Gabe told her she'd

been that way before and, somehow, this little tidbit was comforting. She fell asleep quickly, the night air stirring the curtains and
whispering over the covers.

It was as if the dream was waiting for her again, for as soon as
she closed her eyes, the laughter—both his and hers—washed over
her. She felt his arms around her, his mouth nibbling on her neck,
the oxford cloth shirt smooth under her hands and then, in the blink
of an eye, she was spinning out into space—alone and terrified.

Charlie awoke, sitting straight up in bed sobbing as if her heart
would break. By the way she was feeling in that moment, she was
sure it already had—time and again.

Chapter Twenty-Five

THE DREAM VANISHED after that night, not that Charlie slept much. She still dreamed, but only in fragments she hardly remembered upon waking.

The days passed in a blur of activity as she found a groove of her own in the tropical world. The nights passed in a haze of writing and pottery, sleep happening only when her body forced the issue.

She emailed her children and tentatively started a routine of touching base with them once a week via email—phone calls were too hard, as she felt her lack of much to say would hurt their feelings further. At least with email, she could take time in composing something.

In her heart, she still felt no different; there was no glimmer of recognition, but Charlie knew she had to take steps to begin to nudge her memory about some things. Her children topped that list. Her husband was a close second.

And that was another roadblock. Charlie knew her husband was dead—that much they'd had to tell her. How else to explain a loving husband being absent while his wife faced such a crisis? It also helped explain the dreams she'd had. While that fact made her sad—she was human after all—it didn't register on a heart level. With no memory of the man, how could she mourn her loss?

At first, she'd simply set that aside but now it began to bother her. Her husband. She wasn't sure what—if anything—she wanted to do about her feelings, the vague and incoherent questions that were floating around in her mind, just out of reach.

At Charlie's session that day, her therapist, Jenna, had reminded her she could take her time but that sometimes actively trying to remember could be a good thing, although often a roller coaster ride along the way. Jenna had said there were pictures and details in her files that she could share bit by bit when Charlie was ready. She did advise that Charlie not actively try to jog her memory alone, since the blackouts she'd had were unpredictable.

Charlie had left that session pondering her options; the thoughts weighing heavier than she'd expected and she was quiet almost the entire ride home.

Gabe had remained silent, putting Billy Joel on the truck radio and offering her his hand when driving allowed. She'd looked at him and smiled slightly, eyes troubled but her hand joining his on the truck's console.

"My port in the storm," she'd said softly, returning her unseeing gaze to the side window.

His chest ached, every fiber of his being wanting to offer her platitudes and promises, but he'd simply stroked her hand and driven her home.

*   *   *

Troy and his sister sat together at their usual table in their favorite diner. This diner had been a Thursday night family ritual for as long as both could remember. They'd continued, just the two of them, since just after their father had died.

Cassidy sighed, meeting her brother's questioning glance and shrugging. "I just don't know what to do anymore. I thought Mom would be home long before now. Hell, I never thought she'd leave like she has."

Troy's face wore an expression of sympathy and grief. "This is much harder than I expected. I want her to do what she needs to do, but I feel cut off completely."

Cassidy sipped her coffee and nodded. "Although the emails have been nice. They're a little formal but it's better than no contact at all. I just wish she'd let us call or visit."

Troy fingered the saucer in front of him, stirring his coffee slowly. "Well, I was thinking maybe we'd ask her to come home to visit, even just for a day. From what I've read, it could jog her memory or it could have no effect at all. I know it's her decision, but I don't think it hurts to ask."

It was hard to lose your father and your mother in the span of one year, especially when your mother and sister needed you to be on deck, taking care of things.

"I was thinking more about asking her if she'd let us come and visit her. That way she wouldn't be subjected to the baptism by fire of home unless she wants to be—and we could still get some time with her." Cassidy was hopeful about this and Troy couldn't blame her one bit.

"Okay, let's ask her—both of us—via email. Ask her if we can come to see her. On her terms. I don't want to make her feel guilty, but I know in my heart she doesn't want to just ignore us indefinitely," Cassidy suggested.

Troy nodded his agreement, remembering. "She sure used to love Christmas. I wonder if any of that will still be present, even if she doesn't remember it. I'd love to talk with her about things she's remembering—she was such a blank slate, there has to be something. Then again, according to what she's said so far, she wouldn't know if something was a memory or just a new thing. Scary stuff. I should feel more for her than for us. It's just hard."

The two ordered their supper and turned the subject to their jobs and date lives, desperately trying to keep the family that seemed to be dwindling far too rapidly connected and afloat.

* * *

"Hey, Charlie!" Rory called as she skipped into the pottery shed where Charlie was leaning over a bowl, glaze dripping from the ladle. Jake took the moment to flop on the porch and rest, his partner-in-crime's nine-year-old exuberance a trial for the middle-aged dog.

"Hey, yourself," Charlie replied, finishing her glaze job and setting the ladle aside.

"What color will this one be?" Rory asked, knowing from recent experience that the color of the wet glaze wasn't always the finished color once the piece was fired.

"I call it Blue Jazz." Charlie took off the apron and went to the sink to wash her hands. "The whole thing is deep blue and the top drizzle is kind of a darker turquoise with a bit of a sparkle to it."

"Ooohhh, that'll be pretty." Rory skipped around the table and back out the door. "C'mon!"

"A change of clothes and I'm ready to go," Charlie called out. "Meet you down there."

While at the bar the night before, Gabe had told her what a serious oversight it was that she'd lived on this island all these weeks and had yet to venture out on the boat to explore with him. Laughing, she'd agreed to an outing today. Rory, having been all over the place with Gabe since she'd come to live there, was eager to show off her favorite spots.

Charlie made a face at her clay spattered reflection in the mirror and opted for a quick shower. Minutes later, dressed in turquoise capris and a white tank with a royal blue anchor on the front, she made quick work of pulling up her still-wet hair into a messy knot and headed down the beach.

*　*　*

Gabe looked up from the helm of the boat, amused at the scene before him—Charlie walking along, Rory skipping around her in circles with Jake frolicking somewhere in the middle.

He didn't know how they weren't tripping over each other. He stowed the packed cooler and checked the life jackets under the seat, standing up and pushing his shades to the top of his head.

"It's a beautiful day for a boat ride." Charlie's smile was bright.

"It's always a beautiful day for a boat ride," Rory replied, grinning at her father.

"You're a quick study, Poppet." He laughed, ruffling her hair and reaching out a hand to help Charlie board.

"I've got paradise, food, drink and beautiful women—what more could a man ask for?" He winked at Charlie and pointed to the benches. "You can sit there or stand with me, whatever suits you."

Within minutes they'd left the shore behind, headed out into the open sea. Rory and the dog sprawled on a bench seat while Charlie stood beside him, her body slightly touching his, shoulder to hip, her gaze on the open sea.

Gabe throttled down, pointing out dolphins jumping off to their right, water droplets falling like sparkly diamonds. "As you might remember, to our west is what we call the mainland—about 90 minutes by boat. The big island is where the airport is. That's also where Matteo is from."

Charlie rolled her eyes. "As I might remember?"

He laughed.

"To our east we have several more islands, most undeveloped and uninhabited except for one, and it's all military support. Otherwise, it's us and the big blue sea." Gabe expertly steered the boat east, pointing to a shoreline coming up.

"That's Shelter Cove, technically uninhabited and uncharted but to locals it's a lesser known spot for getting away. We don't bring tourists here, by unspoken agreement. It's big enough that you rarely run into anyone else, especially if you know your way around. I come here often."

"And he knows his way around," Rory said from Gabe's other side. "He showed me Shelter Cover the first week I was here. I have lots of hiding spots." The little girl's cheeks were flushed with the sun, her eyes full of love as she leaned against his leg.

Gabe responded with a one-armed hug as he steered the boat around the island into a cove where the water calmed.

*   *   *

Once anchored, they gathered the picnic supplies and headed for lush shade several feet off the beach. Gabe took the cooler while Charlie carried the blankets, Rory bringing up the rear with a bag while the dog, as usual, ran circles around her.

The picnic food was delicious—cold fried chicken and potato salad with brownies for dessert. The lemonade was poured into ice filled glasses and held against sun-warmed cheeks as they left the world behind and enjoyed the afternoon.

While her father and Charlie finished eating and gazed out at the few clouds in the sky, Rory dashed off to explore, her walkie talkie in her pocket and Jake at her side.

"That kid is exhausting—wonderfully so, but damn." Gabe flopped back on the blanket, an arm over his eyes.

"I don't think they ever stop talking at her age," Charlie laughed. "I remember thinking Cassidy would surely keel over from talking without breathing, but she—" her voice stopped mid-sentence.

"Yeah?" he prompted quietly.

"Yeah." Charlie's eyes were wide, her hand over her mouth. "I don't remember anything specific, just that I thought that at some time. Nice to know the mother in me is still there."

He reached up and took her hand from her mouth and brought it down to rest with his between them.

"That was nice—a memory without any drama." Her voice was quiet but steady.

They sat quietly for a few moments, the sun warm on their faces, Rory's voice faint in the distance as she called to the dog.

"Let's talk about you for a change—a guy like you single, there must be a story here." Charlie stretched out beside him, shades over her eyes, her shoulder resting against him.

Caught off-guard, he was thankful an arm was still over his face, concealing his expression.

"Past history now." He knew better than to hope that'd be the end of it; he hadn't lived on this planet with women all this time and learned nothing.

"Oh, come on, Gabe. You know all kinds of things about me, probably things nobody else knows—not even me." At the truth of that statement, her light laugh turned into a giggle and everyone knows giggles multiply at an insane pace.

He chuckled, lifting his arm to watch her. Warmth curled low in his belly at the sight, her hair pulling loose from its knot, the sun catching it in sparks of copper.

"Ever been married?" She laid aside her shades and rested her hand on his arm where it lay between them.

Replacing the arm over his eyes, he resigned himself to the conversation. "My marriage was yet another casualty of 9/11."

"I'm sorry."

"Me, too. It was a tough time. Just couldn't be there for each other then I wanted to—needed to—leave the city behind and she didn't."

Shocking him, she leaned over and kissed his cheek softly. "Her loss."

"Let's explore." He pushed up to stand, tugging her with him.

They followed the direction Rory had taken, checking in with her and arranging to meet at a rock formation she wanted to show Charlie.

Gabe kept Charlie's hand in his as they walked along the shore, the cove keeping the waves calm and lapping at their feet. They talked about the pottery studio, about Matteo's newest recipe venture, stuff that made up their daily life on the island, both of them content to live in the moment.

Charlie's laugh rang out as he again demonstrated Jillian's waddle walk when she brought up the nursery she and Rory had just finished helping Jill decorate.

"She's gonna kill you for doing that over and over. Once she can chase you without fear of toppling over, that is."

The afternoon waned into evening as they caught up with Rory and explored the ancient rock formations in the middle of the island. Returning to the boat, it was a spectacular sunset ride towards home.

Gabe watched Charlie lean her head close to Rory's as they both reclined on the beach seat, admiring the view. As Rory drifted off to sleep against Charlie's side, Charlie's eyes met his.

He quieted the boat engine, letting them float along in the evening's golden light.

"She's really going to be okay, isn't she?" He said quietly, his gaze on his little girl's sleeping face. Charlie nodded, laying Rory over on the seat and moving to his side. "I really think she is."

They leaned against the railing, shoulder to hip, as the setting sun touched the sea, lighting it on fire. Charlie turned and gently kissed his cheek once, twice, nibbling at the edge of his lips. He shifted to face her and his breath caught as she leaned her body against his, her head resting against his chest. He set his hands lightly at her hips. This was her move and he couldn't stop her if he wanted to. She kissed his neck lightly, her hands on his chest, fists slightly curled into his shirt. Lifting her head, she nibbled her way across his lips, deepening the kiss as she slipped her tongue inside his mouth and thus slowly tore him apart. He responded with restrained fervor, his tongue dancing with hers as his arms slipped around her waist to hold her to him. She nearly brought him to his knees when she slipped a hand under the back of his t-shirt, inside the band of his cargo shorts, cupping his hip and holding him close.

His lips lit a fire along her jawline and behind her ear where he paused, leaning his head against hers. His voice was ragged, "Charlie—"

She tipped his head back with a hand under his chin and placed her fingers over his mouth.

Before she could speak, Rory's voice came in the gathering darkness, "Why are we stopped, Daddy?"

"Well, Poppet, while you were snoozing, we watched the sun set." With just a quick clearing, his voice was remarkably clear, earning him an impressed arched eyebrow from Charlie as she moved aside to make room for Rory between them.

He winked at her and started the boat, making quick work of the stretch of sea between them and the shore.

"I'm starving. Let's go have hot fudge cake." Rory hopped out of the boat with the lines in hand, already a pro.

"You two go on, I think I'm going to make an early night of it," Charlie said.

She promised Rory they could make mugs in the pottery studio the next day and the girl ran on ahead, calling out in the twilight, "C'mon, Daddy, I might eat it all!"

Gabe jumped off the boat, double-checking Rory's tie off before he turned to face Charlie.

Before he could speak, she covered his lips with her fingers again and whispered, "See you after closing?"

He nodded, kissing her fingers before she dropped them and turned to walk up the beach towards her cottage, looking back to give him a wave of her fingers.

Well, then.

* * *

She was waiting for him on the porch steps at 2am, an empty chocolate milk bottle between her bare feet, her hair falling free in riotous curls about her shoulders. He sat down beside her, shoulder to hip.

Where they went next had to be up to her. He knew what he wanted, had likely wanted for a long time and simply denied even the thought amid her grief and chaos. But it had to be her call.

Her hand on his shoulder for balance, she stood and moved to stand on the steps below him, positioning her body between his knees. He met her gaze straight on, bringing his hands to rest on her hips. His mouth went dry as he realized that, under his hands, she was clad only in her favored over-sized navy tee.

She quirked an eyebrow at his astonishment and simply brought her mouth to his, arms going around him, a hand slipping inside the band of his cargo shorts to rest at the top edge of his hip again.

She kissed him slowly and gently, yet so thoroughly he forgot to breathe.

"I have one request." She whispered over eyelids and cheeks before returning to his mouth.

"My kingdom…" He dragged in a breath, his hands tightening on her hips.

"No words." She kissed along his jawline, his short beard prickling her lips, one hand on his chest, the other still cupping his hip.

He nodded, taking her head in his hands to tilt it just so and devouring her mouth slowly but completely, his tongue dancing with hers.

She stepped back and drew him to his feet, pulling him up the steps and into the cottage. The lights were off except for a small tabletop lamp but she didn't stop, drawing him along behind her into the bedroom. The moon gave off just enough light that he could see her. She motioned to his clothes with an airy wave of her hand, dazzling him with her sultry smile as he moved to comply with her wishes, tossing it all aside.

He heard her breath catch as she looked at him in the moonlight and he smiled, stepping closer, his hands sliding up under the t-shirt and sweeping it off her in one motion. God help him, she was beautiful.

Before he could move, she pushed him back onto the bed and straddled him, inches away from driving him over the brink into mindlessness.

Leaning forward to kiss him, pouring all of her passion into him, she moaned when his hands cupped her breasts, his thumbs stroking her peaked nipples.

He understood she wasn't going to wait, that she was going to take and take some more. He gasped out loud as she shifted her hips and sheathed him in one motion. She rose above him, riding him, their bodies one. She cried out his name, holding tightly to his shoulders.

It was then that he lost his mind. He held her close and rolled her beneath him, pouring his heart into her, knowing he gave her the ability to shatter it beyond repair.

* * *

She woke slowly, knowing exactly where she was and whose arms she was wrapped in. Snuggling deeper, she nipped his neck with her teeth, then soothed with tiny flicks of her tongue.

His chuckle rumbled beneath her lips as he shifted to his side, stroking his fingers over her face.

"I wish time would stand still," she whispered, resting her hand on his chest, fingers brushing the hairs there.

Wordlessly he brought his hips against hers and, in one fluid motion, had her pinned beneath him again.

"Oh, my," she breathed, opening her legs wider and settling into the rhythm he set.

Together they created a magical bubble where time did stop, where the world outside the room was left to spin without them for now.

* * *

As dawn began to streak the sky, he slipped from the bed where she slept soundly, tucking the covers around her.

He was shamelessly relieved that she didn't wake as he dressed — he had no idea what to say after such a night. Logically, he knew to take her cue, see what her reaction was. That was damn hard to do, feeling like this. So much he wanted to say, so much he wanted to ask. Yet not.

At his cottage, he showered and was back out the door to the boat, coffee in hand, in a matter of minutes. He didn't have his sidekick this morning, as Rory had stayed with Jillian and planned go to town with her this morning. Rory volunteered as sidekick to save Jill from Nash's constant, hovering presence.

154   DANA TANARO BRITT

On the JohnB, Nash put them out to sea and they rode along in companionable silence for a time, working in tandem seamlessly.

"So." Nash leaned against the railing, the boat idling as he sipped coffee and watched the sun fully rise in the sky.

"Hmm?" Gabe stowed gear and picked up his own coffee mug, raising it to the rising sun.

"Something on your mind, Arch?" Nash knew his friend well and had noticed Gabe starting to speak but changing his mind several times this morning. He'd also pulled out his phone to send a text—something he never did this time of day.

Gabe sipped his coffee, rubbed a hand over his jaw. "It's both wonderful and worrisome that I've just left Charlie's bed."

To his credit, Nash didn't drop his coffee but did drop his jaw. "Oh man. Arch."

"You can't say anything I haven't already said to myself. It was her move and there was no discussion. I have no earthly idea what she's thinking." Gabe set the cup aside and throttled the boat on to the next spot.

Nash clapped his friend's shoulder before he turned to gear up. "I just don't want you hurt, Arch."

Gabe nodded, his eyes on the sea, a grin threatening at the corner of his mouth.

"It was good?" his friend grinned, unable to help himself.

Gabe laughed. "We don't kiss and tell, Nashman, but I will say aye, it was good.."

With an ease borne of long hours working together, they finished the fishing run and headed back to the shore. Nash manned the wheel while Gabe leaned against the rail.

"Brother, question for ya."

Nash merely looked his way and waited.

"Is it cowardly to just let it roll? Especially when that's clearly what she wants?" Gabe dropped his shades to hang around his neck, dragging his hands through his hair.

Nash shook his head. "We always give the lady what she wants. That being said, this one has some serious power to mortally wound you, my man. Falling for a damsel in distress that could wake up and toss you aside in a blink is a potential FDNY-style 10-66."

Gabe couldn't deny the truth of Nash's words. "Frankly, I'm scared shitless. I have a million questions, most of which she can't even answer. Yet by no power on this planet would I turn away from her."

"You'll be there for her, and you know I'm here for you." Nash looked his friend square in the eyes for a long, hard moment. "For both of you."

With that, he tossed the lines out to where Rory hopped about on the shore like a jumping bean, and the rest of the day began.

****Chapter Twenty-Six****

THE KALEIDOSCOPE of emotions zinging through her body and soul fueled Charlie into a frenzy of motion. Determined to steer clear of analyzing anything, she spent the day in the pottery shed, throwing clay to the cranked up beat of 80s tunes, losing herself in her creations and relishing the physical work.

After several hours, she wiped the sweat from her brow with a forearm and sat up straight, arching her back and rotating her neck. She moved the piece from her wheel and put it, along with two others, into the electric kiln for drying.

"There." She'd completed most of a set of nesting boxes for Rory and started on a deep mug for Jillian's soon-to-be-pressing need for coffee during sleepless nights with a newborn.

It felt incredibly good to work on a project after sitting about the hospital feeling useless. She had her writing and the pottery and, with the baby coming soon, she hoped to convince Gabe to let her take over some of Jillian's duties about the island.

She was making a life here, a really good life.

* * *

The afternoon sun had just begun to wane when Charlie noticed she was starving. It'd become habit to have supper at the bar and enjoy her friends' company of an evening; tonight would be no different. She knew Gabe was on deck at the bar, having been witness to the schedule discussion a few days ago while painting at Jill's.

Aside from an early morning text that said simply "Good morning, beautiful"—one she didn't see until she'd finished in the clay—she hadn't seen him since he'd left her bed.

She had to admit that there was now a new flutter of anticipation inside her at the thought of Gabe. She embraced it and shoved away any trifling worries about her lost memory. She knew she wasn't married or involved, that was enough.

Riding the high that'd propelled her all day, she showered quickly, left her hair down to finish drying in the evening air and headed down the beach, the light and music beckoning her in the waning light.

*   *   *

Every fiber of his being went on instant alert when she stepped into the bar. She took his breath away, not only because she was beautiful—her hair curling and catching the light like little licks of flame—but because she was Charlie. Gabe inclined his head in a private salute at her tiny-just-for-him smile; her bottom lip caught in her teeth as she blushed.

He hadn't had a clue what to expect when he saw her again, but, from what he could tell so far, she hadn't any regrets—and for that he was beyond thankful.

Nash's elbow to his ribs brought him back to the drink he was mixing as she made her way to the bar. He bantered with the customer as he served the drink and, taking a gamble, he walked around the bar to Charlie's side as she settled on seat next to Jill.

He leaned in and kissed her cheek, his whisper tickling her ear, "Your place or mine?"

Over Charlie's shoulder, he saw Jill's eyes widen. He gave her a wink, then met Charlie's eyes, holding her gaze for a moment before he returned to his station behind the bar.

The night passed as most island nights at The Painted Parrot full of laughter and banter, drinks flowing, music playing. He was relieved to see that nothing had changed; she laughed and acted just as she had before last night. Well, nothing had changed in a bad way—those new heated looks she kept giving him had his blood well on the way to boiling.

Rory popped in amid a bunch of tourist kids and island kids, passing out water bottles to her friends as she excitedly told him about the empty sea turtle nests they'd found down the beach and asked if they could hit Matteo up for cookies. At his nod, she was gone in a flash, leaving him staring after her yet again.

"How are we gonna survive this Daddy thing?" Gabe's voice was incredulous as the activity lulled and they leaned against the bar in front of the Jill and Charlie.

Nash laughed. "At least mine won't arrive walking and talking like a Tasmanian devil." They paused to consider the now sparkling girl in comparison to the sad child that had come to them just a few short months ago. That sad little girl didn't leave Gabe's side for weeks, bonding him to her like glue.

"Big bad firemen brought to their knees by a little girl. As it should be." Jill nodded. "Have you given any thought to school prep yet, Gabe?" She rubbed her side with a grimace.

"Not really. I'm gonna talk to her about it soon, see what her thoughts are. Hey, Nashman, take your woman home before she delivers in my bar."

Nash put up both hands and walked around the bar to assist his wife down from her perch. "Don't have to tell me twice."

Jill pointed a finger at Charlie, "Don't forget Girl's Night Out coming up." She looked from Charlie to where Gabe was laughing with a customer down the bar. "A-HEM, you so have stuff to share."

Charlie stuck her tongue out, waving them away. "Go. Rest and stuff."

The couple left the bar slowly, Jill smiling in response to her husband's low voiced suggestions as to how they could spend the rest of their evening.

With just a few scattered customers easily taken care of by Jane, Gabe wiped down the bar and leaned in front of Charlie. His gray eyes met her dark blue ones, speaking words he couldn't—or didn't dare—say out loud.

"So, what did you do today?" He reached out and tucked a curl behind her ear, letting his fingers tangle in her hair when she leaned her cheek into his hand for a beat or two.

"The pottery shed got a good workout. I'm feeling the effects of throwing clay most of the day. It felt so good to be doing things. I didn't see your text until I headed over here." Her smile did something odd to his insides, something new, something he wanted to keep around.

"I just didn't want you to think I left you without thought this morning. You were sleeping so soundly, I couldn't bring myself to wake you—and don't think I didn't want to." He wiggled his eyebrows and growled quietly, sending her into giggles.

Relief shot through him as he realized she wasn't going to pretend things hadn't changed. He'd been figuratively holding his breath all day, not knowing what to think or how to take his feelings. Gabe tossed down his towel as Matteo rounded the corner between the restaurant and bar. They exchanged nods as the chef went and spoke to Jane. Perks of both having good friends and being the boss, when you want to give up closing duties, you can.

"Walk you home?" He held out his hand to help her down from the bar stool, her touch sending a shiver up his arm.

"Rory?" She asked, as they left the bar.

"She's watching a movie with Katie and the kids. They'll take bring her home later and she'll find us."

By unspoken agreement, they walked hand in hand down to the water's edge, Charlie pausing to slip off her shoes. He held out his other hand for her to loop the straps over his fingers, the act of carrying her shoes giving him a ridiculous thrill.

*   *   *

Splashing lightly in the waves, Charlie walked close to his side holding his hand and arm against her, his heat making her tingle all over.

"I know there seems like so much to say, but at the same time, I feel as if words will tarnish the magic."

He squeezed her hand slightly in agreement as they turned to walk up the beach to her cottage, the fairy lights from the porch welcoming them.

He dropped her shoes on the porch and slowly backed her up against the wall, letting his body touch hers from head to toe, his hands braced on the wall just above her shoulders. He kissed her forehead and let his lips travel down her cheek to her neck, his tongue wreaking all kinds of havoc on her breathing.

Her legs going weak, she let him hold her up, her arms slipping around to grip his shoulders, the knee he'd nudged between her legs supporting her as he brought his mouth to hers. She truly thought she'd float up and out into space, she felt so light, so free.

He lifted her against him and carried her to the hammock, lowering her to sit in the soft fabric sling. Eyes on hers, he nudged her to sit back into the hammock as he knelt on the porch between her knees. He kept her gaze, his eyes dark, lids heavy with desire, as he slid his hands along her thighs, pushing her dress up to her waist.

When she stilled his hands with hers, needing a moment to breathe, he leaned in and dropped his mouth to her collarbone kissing his way across and back again. She dropped her head back and tangled her hands in his hair, the wavy strands springy and soft, as he brought his hands up to unbutton the front of her dress. Laying the fabric open, the sea breeze prickling her skin, he bent his head to her.

She ceased to breathe and, yet again, time stood still.

*   *   *

Tugging the hammock blanket over her, Gabe grinned at her unconscious state—apparently she had a penchant for falling asleep almost immediately after sex. He was glad to see her sleeping, after all the sleepless nights he knew she'd suffered. That fact alone made him want to tuck her in with him every night if it meant she'd be able to sleep like this. Loath as he was to leave her though, Rory didn't need to wake up alone.

He dressed, debating waking her to go inside instead of leaving her asleep on the porch, he turned to find her watching him, her eyes shimmering in the barely there glow of the fairy lights. She mesmerized him, just looking at her all flushed from being with him made him want to never leave her side.

"Hey." He shrugged into his shirt and, leaving it open, crossed to hold out a hand to her. "Let me tuck you in inside?"

She shook her head. "I'm good right here."

She stuck a foot out and nudged his leg, putting the hammock in motion. He briefly wondered if she had any idea how many nights over the past few weeks she'd spent in a hammock just like that one. Shrugging off the thought, he kissed her forehead and leaned there for a moment, soaking up the smell of orange blossoms and warm woman that was Charlie.

"Rory doesn't need to wake to an empty cottage, or I'd not leave you. You know that, right?"

"I know that." Charlie caressed his jaw lightly, grinning as she let her foot slide up his leg. "Temptress," he growled against her neck, pinning her down and biting playfully as she giggled helplessly.

She shoved at him. "Go, get some sleep before Rory pops up."

He groaned. "No amount of sleep is enough. That kid is a firecracker."

Her laugh followed him, wrapping those ribbons of warmth around his heart as he stepped out into the darkness.

*   *   *

Far from sleepy anymore, Charlie rocked in the hammock, letting her mind drift from pottery designs to her children's emails about visiting plans. She supposed she needed to give them some kind of answer soon; she just didn't have one to give right now.

She also supposed she should start giving more time to trying to remember things about her past, but was that really necessary? If she was happy now, was it vital to try and remember who she was before? She realized she was living in denial and probably on borrowed time. But what harm was there in that? What if she never remembered, couldn't they just live this life? It could be a very good life, she knew. Maybe diving into her writing would take her mind off things for a while.

****Chapter Twenty-Seven****

"SERENA TOLD ME school starts soon." Rory didn't meet Gabe's eyes as she swirled syrup around the pancakes on her plate, the anxiety hidden behind her pretended nonchalance clearly visible to Gabe's ever-increasing Daddy radar.

"It does." He nodded, sitting back in his chair. "Do you want to go?"

Rory looked at him in surprise. "I have a choice?"

Her quizzical look made him laugh. "Yes, you have a choice. It's your life that's been turned upside down. I think what you do next is up to you."

In recent weeks, Gabe had talked at length with his sister and his mother and had decided to truly leave the school decision up to his daughter. Tally homeschooled her boys and had given him tons of information on options when Rory had been glued to his side with no sign of being ready to part from him.

"I don't want to be away from you." The quaver in her small voice turned his heart inside out. He didn't see grief or fear in her very often these days, but from time to time she'd still suddenly cling to his side for hours at a time or crawl into his bed at night and cry herself to sleep.

Gabe pushed back his chair and motioned to his lap. Rory climbed up and snuggled against his chest, a place she'd become comfortable early on.

"Poppet, you don't have to be away from me for one second you don't want to be." He stroked her hair, his other arm holding her close.

"I can't just leave school and come to find you when I want to, though." She sniffled, close to tears.

"That's true, but who says you have to go to school?"

"I don't?" Rory's head popped up and connected with his chin, the jar causing him to see stars.

"Ouch! Oops, sorry, Daddy!" She rubbed both the spot on her head and the one on his chin ruefully as she looked up at him.

Gabe rubbed his jaw against the sting and smiled. "Nope, you don't. I've done a lot of reading and talking to Aunt Tally and Grandma. I've learned there are a lot of options besides school. For one thing, I think you're learning all the time. For another thing, like Aunt Tessa and your cousins, lots of people homeschool."

Rory's jaw dropped, her expression hopeful. "You mean I don't have to leave you? I don't have go to school?"

"Not if you don't want to." He'd read things about homeschooling and even unschooling that resonated with him and had been hoping for a way to bring up not sending her to school.

"So what will I do instead?" She hopped off his lap and carried both their plates to the sink. "You're in the wood shop today, right?" She rinsed the plates and wiped off the table while he finished his coffee.

"I thought you'd do mostly what you already do around here—you're learning tons and you're a huge part of our operation. I can put you on the schedule or you can pop in where you want to help like you do now. You already read tons of books and we talk about all sorts of things, right?" Gabe set his coffee cup in the sink. "And, yes, wood shop for a few hours for me today. Santa's elf's gotta get busy."

Rory considered what he'd said as she stuck a book, snacks and a notebook into her ever-present backpack.

"If there's anything you want to do, anywhere you want to go, you've only to tell me, Poppet. Anytime. We can make a weekly plan if you want; I know you like lists. We're making our way together now." Gabe tipped her chin up so she'd look at him. "You're not a visitor here, you know. You belong. You're not just part of my world, you are my world."

He was pretty sure the smile that lit her face could fuel his soul for the rest of his life, if his heart didn't burst first.

Hugging her small shoulders, he said, "So, what's your agenda this morning?"

"I gotta check on Jill, cause..." Rory widened her eyes, pantomiming a huge belly sticking out.

Gabe laughed out loud at her antics. "Let me know how you find things."

"Will do, Daddy-o." She hugged his waist, called Jake and dashed out the door.

While he often felt anger at Lilith for her decision to keep Rory from him all these years, he also felt gratitude at the care she'd taken with their daughter in the nine short years she was with her. The kid was nothing short of incredible.

His phone chimed a text from Charlie and, reading it, he laughed out loud.

Naked picture warning it said, followed by a picture of her bare foot.

Way to start the day, he mused, texting back a picture of his middle finger, laughing all the way to the shop.

* * *

The two enjoyed a light-hearted text exchange from time to time throughout the day, both of them buried in their work—Charlie writing and Gabe making toys for the FDNY holiday toy program.

Gabe had just texted her to come by Nash and Jill's instead of the bar for supper, as they wanted to talk shop and juggle the schedule to free Jill up for her impending motherhood. Charlie hoped she could convince Gabe she was more than feeling up to taking on some of Jill's duties.

After wrapping up her writing for the day, she checked her email, hating how it made her feel defensive and unsure to do so—knowing the kids worried, no matter what she said to them. She decided to reply later, needing to ask Gabe a couple more things about them before she tried to inquire about their lives. She'd make notes from what Gabe said and hopefully remember some details from now on.

Replying to Gabe's text that she'd see him there within the hour, Charlie headed for the shower to unkink muscles spent sitting much of the day. She was eager for company after the quiet day. She wondered if that was a new Charlie thing or an old Charlie thing. Was she an introvert, extrovert or in-between?

The outdoor shower was inviting, the light filtered by the deep foliage around it, the hot water a balm. Charlie tied her hair up out of the way and stepped into the spray. Just like that, in the blink of an eye, she heard children laughing and splashing. Her heart soared with joy in the moment only to wilt with disappointment when it faded just as quickly. *Oh, my babies.* She felt sad yet also happy as she realized that one fleeting memory had been enough to bring back some feeling of motherhood. More scenes from that sunny day flashed through her mind, as if she was watching a highlight reel starring her children.

*   *   *

"Your job is to sit and look pretty," Nash sternly told his wife after steering her to a chair for the third time. She stuck her tongue out at him, but sighed in relief and accepted the glass of lemonade from Rory. Gabe unpacked the food Matteo had sent over while Rory set the table and Nash poured drinks.

"Charlie was on her way, wonder what's keeping her?" Gabe mused, checking his phone and finding no new texts after the one she'd sent over an hour ago.

Nash met his look and tipped his head toward the door, turning to distract his wife and Rory by trying—yet again—to bet on when this baby would appear.

"Be right back," Gabe tossed over his shoulder, neither girl nor woman paying him any mind.

He made short work of the distance to her cottage and stepped inside.

"Hey, Charlie, let's eat," he called out, glancing about the empty room. He checked the other rooms quickly, tamping down a tiny frisson of alarm that prickled at the back of his neck. The pottery shed, that thought soothed him a bit—maybe she'd gotten absorbed in a new project. Then he saw her—a lone figure sitting at the water's edge. He breathed a sigh of relief that he'd found her, yet his stomach knotted in dread. The list of possibilities that could cause her pain was long and none of them good, in his opinion.

Forcing himself not to run, he went to her side and sat down.

She sat cross-legged, drawing in the damp sand. As the tide washed away her words, she drew them again. Her face was drawn, but she didn't appear to be in crisis from what he could tell.

"Oh, hey." She looked at him, startled, her eyes unfocused.

"Hey, yourself." He laid a hand on her arm, rubbing gently to soothe himself as much as her.

She leaned into him slightly and resumed doodling in the sand. He read her words before the water washed them away.

Troy. Cassidy.

As was his habit, he waited for her to be ready to tell him what was on her mind. He was relieved she seemed sad but not devastated.

"I had clear memories of the kids when they were little." She blew out a breath. "Not just a fragment or a vague feeling, but the first full-fledged memories that I can still recall in detail after it's over."

"Tell me?"

She nodded, chewing her lip as she continued to write her children's names over and over in the sand.

"They were playing in the surf, a beach much like this one. Laughing and tumbling over with every wave. Jack lifting them back to their feet. Little bitty bodies, big belly laughs." She drew a deep, shuddery breath and gave him a tiny smile. "It's given me a connection I didn't have before."

She laid her ahead against his shoulder, letting the sea wash away the names in the sand. "How can a memory both mend and break my heart?" Her voice was barely audible above the waves.

He leaned his cheek against her head, knowing she didn't expect him to answer.

"So, what's for supper?" She stood and held out her hands to pull him up.

"No idea." He rolled with her change of subject, grasping her hands with a mischievous grin and pulling, toppling them both onto the sand.

She shrieked before breaking into laughter and kissing him. Sobering, she touched his face, ran her fingers through his hair.

"These first real remembered memories are a treasure. I'm torn between hoping for more yet wanting things to stay the same."

He twirled a stray curl around his finger as she lay sprawled a top him. "I can promise you one thing will stay the same—me."

"My anchor. Because of you, I'm able to be whatever me I find right now." She nodded, resting her forehead on his.

Narrowly avoiding the waves, they stood up and headed for Nash's, dusting off the sand.

They found food waiting on the porch table and Nash playing Go Fish with Rory while Jillian slept in the hammock.

Gabe waved a hand in Jill's direction. "Surely soon?" This waiting game was making him antsy, never mind said baby's parents.

"Jill said if not this week, she's gonna evict him," Rory informed them as she put away the card game. "I'm gonna go get us some dessert."

"Make sure it includes my chocolate cake fix, Poppet," Gabe called after her.

"Do I look new here?" Rory skipped backwards, waving her arms for emphasis before she turned and ran full tilt for the restaurant.

Nash burst out laughing. "Wonder where she got that?" he referred to the comment they often heard Matteo spout when addressing kitchen mistakes made by his assistants.

As they ate and talk turned to the schedule for the days ahead, Charlie spoke up, "Let me help, guys. I live here; I want to do my part."

Gabe looked at Nash, who shrugged and nodded, leaving the decision to him.

"Okay. You see the schedule, what do you want to do?" he pointed at the computer screen. "I have Matteo and Jane on closing duties from now on, excepting the odd time Nash or I feel the need to be around. That's a big, permanent change. A perk of being the boss."

"Especially now that we're adding 'Daddy' to our resumes." Nash's grin was a little less cocky and sure as his gaze fell on his sleeping wife, her belly rippling as the baby tumbled about.

"All will be well, Nash, women have been giving birth just fine for centuries," Charlie patted his hand as she looked over the screen.

"How about I open the bar and do the cottage rentals in Jill's place? I'd like the action and it won't take me long to learn the ropes."

Gabe rolled his shoulders, frowning a little.

"Out with it, Skipper." Charlie nudged his leg with her foot.

"Are you sure you want to take all that on? Why not just help out where you want when you want rather than schedule you?" He was concerned that the pressure would stifle her healing process, remembering how she'd so badly wanted to hide out when she first arrived on the island. He wasn't about to bring that up, though.

Charlie crossed her arms. "That's not helping, that's catering to me in a lady of the manor style—letting me dabble." She air-quoted the word with a grimace. Charlie stuck her tongue out at the laughing men, pulling the laptop over and typing in the changes. "I want to open four days a week to start with, then run the supper hour a couple of days once I find a groove and you both see it will work. I can also oversee the cottages."

"I can keep the books, Arch." Jill reached out her arms for her husband's help in hauling her bulk out of the hammock. Nash moved quickly to oblige her, bracing his legs as she stood and leaned heavily against him.

His uncensored "Ooof" earning him a half-serious dark look from his wife.

"Oh, hey, I keep meaning to ask—where'd the nickname Arch come from?" Charlie pushed aside the computer.

Nash and Gabe exchanged a look.

Jill put her hand on Nash's arm. "The Melbourne Road fire. It was an ugly one, an apartment building engulfed in flames, people screaming, and firefighters missing." She reached out to touch Gabe's arm, too, as if to reassure herself they were both right there.

Nash picked up the story. "It was wildly out of control, but finally everyone, dead and alive, was accounted for—except Gabe and a little girl. The captain of another unit was calling it, refusing to let anyone go back in, the roof was caving. Just as I pushed past the guy to head inside, Gabe came walking out of the flames, the little girl coughing in his arms. I'll never forget the sight—flames so many stories high behind him, he looked like an avenging angel... thus Archangel."

Gabe gripped his friend's shoulder. "Archangel my ass. So many losses that day—six residents, two of our guys."

Charlie's hand was over her mouth, her eyes wide.

Jill hugged both men and moved the conversation on, knowing neither man wanted to dwell on it. "I can keep the books, I'm not helpless."

Gabe rolled his eyes. "And why would you keep the books? We added that to Jane's list, she's adamant about it."

Surprising them all, Jill didn't protest again. "Okay. I'm going to bed." She waddled into the house.

Nash and Gabe exchanged shrugs, having learned that nothing was predictable with women—even less so during pregnancy.

"Good night," Charlie called as she moved to pick up the food remains.

Nash stopped her. "I'll get it. You two get out of here. I'll send Rory on when she comes back."

"Call me," Gabe said with a meaningful glance in the direction Jill had gone.

"Don't doubt it, Arch." Nash swallowed audibly, his gaze following suit.

* * *

Hand in hand, Charlie and Gabe walked toward the beach.

Once out of sight of Nash and Jill's porch, Charlie turned and nudged him into the shadows against a tree. She twined the fingers of both hands in his and kissed him thoroughly, resting her hips against him.

Gabe chuckled deep in his throat, letting his head fall back as her lips played over his throat.

"I've been thinking." She pulled him forward to resume walking.

He cleared his throat with a "Hmm?" and struggled to clear his mind as well. Her kisses were potent stuff—coupled with her sudden topic changes, he was feeling rather dizzy .

She swung their hands between them and stopped to sit on a waist high rock at the top of the beach. He stood between her knees, leaning forward to brace his hands on the rock on both sides of her.

"It occurred to me that I'm not being fair to you." Her words trailed off.

"Charlie, I'm a big boy." He kissed her mouth once then again. "I can handle whatever you dish out." His mouth nuzzled her ear. "And, I must say, I do like what you've been dishing out." This last part came out on a growl as he buried his face in her neck.

Charlie couldn't help but giggle, bracing her hands on his chest to hold him at bay.

Before she could continue, Jake ran up between Gabe's legs, Rory close behind.

"Chocolate cake!" She waved a bag, leaning against the two of them, her eyes heavy with the lateness of the hour.

Gabe looked at the girl and back to Charlie, twisting his mouth ruefully, the moment tucked away for now.

"Let's walk Charlie home and get you to bed, Poppet." He kissed Rory's upturned nose and took her hand.

Charlie slid down from the rock and took Rory's other hand, the girl between them as they walked to her cottage.

Rory chanted softly, "One two, buckle my shoe..." and in the blink of an eye, Charlie held another child's hand in hers and another man walked beside her. The memory was crystal clear yet gone so fast that Charlie was motionless, stunned.

"What's wrong, Charlie?" Rory looked at her quizzically, then looked at her father.

"Rory, remember how I told you about how Charlie doesn't remember some things?" Gabe spoke carefully, taking Charlie's hands in his.

Rory nodded. "Uh huh, you said I shouldn't worry but to come and get you if Charlie acted funny."

"Good girl. I think this is one of those times. Let's get her home." Gabe worked to reassure his daughter and help Charlie at the same time.

"I'm okay." Her voice was quiet but strong as she squeezed his hands and looked down at Rory. "I'm fine, kiddo."

Rory smiled, grabbed a second wind and ran along the path ahead of them with the dog.

"A flashback?" He searched her face for clues to how she was feeling. She nodded, chewing the corner of her bottom lip.

"One minute Rory was singing, the next minute it was Cassidy's hand in mine...and Jack walking beside me." Charlie's eyes were on Rory and the dog as they approached her porch.

Her reaction to Jack coming so readily to mind twice in one day after weeks of nothing about him seemed oddly low-key. Gabe rubbed his neck, running a hand through his hair.

At the steps, she turned, kissing the top of Rory's head, barely sparing him a glance. "Go to bed, kiddo. You and I get to take over for Jill starting tomorrow."

Gabe scooped up the girl and climbed past Charlie, settling Rory into the hammock with Jake at her side. The girl was asleep before he could cover them both with the blanket. He took a moment to brush back her hair before turning back to Charlie. He took her hand, went inside the cottage and sat down on the couch, pulling her onto his lap. Ghost or no ghost and however beloved, he wasn't leaving Charlie at the mercy of the dead if he could help it. Not anymore.

Wordlessly, he wrapped his arms around her, tucked her head against his chest and waited. As the minutes passed, he felt her body relax into his as she let sleep claim her. He settled deeper into the couch, letting his head rest back against the cushions.

****Chapter Twenty-Eight****

JILL FINALLY WENT INTO LABOR and birthed an adorable boy right as a last minute week-long wedding party joined in on the already frenzied final hurrah of the busy season, effectively keeping all of them hopping.

Charlie learned the ropes quickly and could work the bar or tend to tenant needs as well as any of them, settling into the island life like she'd always been there.

One afternoon amid the frenzy, Gabe stopped by Jill's porch. He carefully plucked the sleeping baby from her arms and settled into the other rocker. "Let's do some male bonding, Zane Gabriel."

Jill took advantage of the moment, holding up a finger and disappearing inside. She came back out a few minutes later, her short hair damp, wearing fresh clothes and carrying two glasses of lemonade. She settled into the other rocker with a sigh, propping her feet on the porch railing.

"Okay, spit it out. You've far too much going on to be sitting here rocking my baby—although it is great therapy and he is pretty cute."

His head was against the back of the rocker, his eyes closed, the baby snuggly on his chest.

"It's been weeks since she's had any flashbacks that I know of. She's dropped back to seeing Jenna twice a month instead of weekly.

She says she has no need to pursue memories that don't want to come forth. Am I wrong in supporting her instead of encouraging her to try and remember?"

"Honestly, Arch, I've wondered the same thing. I know you're giving her a safe place both physically and emotionally, but I do wonder if this magic bubble is going to burst badly for her at some point." Jill replied thoughtfully.

He rubbed his temple with one hand. "I'm scared for her, Jilly." He shifted the baby to his shoulder, nuzzling the downy soft cheek.

"I look at her sometimes and I can't breathe for the fear that her peace will suddenly all be gone in a single moment—and there's nothing I can do about it. And, yes, that what I have with her will be gone with it."

Jill moved to hug his shoulders and take the now wriggling baby. "You're going to have to trust her, trust what the two of you are building to be stronger than anything else. It will get her—and you—through. That being said, I think maybe it's time you consider pushing her just a little—get her to talk to the kids, at least." Jill put the whimpering baby to her breast as Gabe turned down the steps.

"I know, but it's hard when it could all be gone in a blink—she could remember everything and walk away from me—or she could forget all of this. I've never felt more helpless in my life—not even during 9/11 or Melbourne Road." He held up his hands and let them fall.

"Just be there, Gabe, keep showing up." Jill blew him a kiss as he waved and jogged off.

* * *

"Let's play hooky and sneak off to that back room in your pottery shed," he growled, sending her into giggles as she held him close. They leaned against her porch railing as the evening sun put on a spectacular show as it dipped into the sea, colors exploding in vibrant shades of pink and orange before fading into purple and blue.

"It's against the Girl's Night Out code to ditch your friends for a guy," Charlie gave Gabe a shove in the direction of the bar. He drooped, grasping his chest. "That wounds me, Charlie." Dramatically blowing him a kiss, she picked up her picnic basket and headed down the beach.

*   *   *

"Mercy, I thought I'd never get here," Katie flopped on the blanket next to Jane, the box of decadent chocolate éclairs she'd made already in Charlie's hands.

"Babysitter run late?" Jill asked, filling four glasses with ice cold pink bubbly. Girl's Night Out meant frilly, fizzy drinks or beer in bottles—sometimes both, whatever suited them in the moment.

"Something like that." Katie evaded the question, causing the other three to raise their eyebrows in unison.

"Oh, come on, I don't want to talk about my kids' father tonight. I declare this GNO an escapist one tonight—drinks, food, jokes. No more, no less."

All four clinked their glasses high and drank deeply, Jill quick on the refills and Charlie opening the pizza box with a flourish.

"Instead let's talk about Charlie sleeping with Gabe." Jill teased, ducking Charlie's arm, the other two's mouths dropping open.

"I knew it! Twas only a matter of time." Jane boasted, nibbling at her slice of pizza.

Charlie pushed Jane's leg with her foot, "How could you possibly know that?"

"Oh, come on, Charlie! Who wouldn't tap that handsome hunk, and him at your beck and call day in and day out?" Katie snapped her fingers in illustration.

Charlie opened her mouth to protest, but instead nodded. "He is handsome, isn't he?" At her friends' shouts of laughter and the barrage of questions, she merely raised her glass in salute and drank it down.

The talk turned to Sheriff Luke's new haircut, their laughter ringing down the beach as the sun set into the sea, the twilight a comforting blanket of blue.

*   *   *

On her way to the bar the next afternoon, Charlie stood and admired the view, smiling as Gabe's arms came around her and he nibbled at her neck.

"No can do; you've got company, remember?" Charlie leaned into him.

"Rory is pretty excited about the boxes of her stuff Damien brought." Gabe acknowledged as they walked the short distance to the restaurant. "Looks like moving day at our place; she might need her own cottage."

In the restaurant, they joined Nash and Jillian along with the visiting attorney, Damien Sharp. Damien had been part of Nash and Gabe's firefighting team for a short time that had included 9/11, so they had a few stories together. "I think Adam still holds the title of most embarrassing moment," Nash laughed. The trio of men sobered, thinking of Adam, who lay in a permanent vegetative state after suffering catastrophic injuries in the Melbourne Road fire.

Clinking their bottles in a wordless toast, they sat in silence for a few moments. Charlie gave Jill a questioning look to which she mouthed, "Later."

Just then Rory popped in asking if she could unpack boxes with a few friends' help. Gabe shrugged a why not, and she was gone in a flash.

"She's thriving, Arch." Damien pointed his fork at Gabe as the girl whirlwind ran out of the restaurant, the mood once again light.

Gabe nodded. "She is. The first few weeks she was glued to my side 24/7. I had to ask permission to shower or pee and she'd be just outside the door waiting. When I tripped over her sleeping across my doorway, I put a cot in my room. It's still there, but she's not used it in weeks."

Jill put in, "Now she's a Tasmanian devil, all over the island all day long. Yesterday she rocked this baby and folded laundry while I took a quick shower. She was gone before I could hardly thank her."

Nash laughed, spearing a fried pickle with his fork. "Zane needs to grow up and marry her—what's nine years difference?"

"You have any more trouble out of the Baxters?" Gabe asked Damien as Jane stepped up to refill drinks.

"They complain every few weeks, I handle it. I've told them that if Rory wants to see them, you'll let us know." Damien sat back, nodding at the coffeepot Jane held up.

Gabe nodded. "From what Rory has said, she hardly knows them. Lilith took her to see them once or twice a year for about six years, then not at all. Poor kid was terrified when they picked her up."

"I'm sorry for being out of touch when it happened—I would have never let them have her." Damien's expression was rueful.

Gabe waved the apology off. "All is well now, that's all that matters."

"So we've got you in the Sea Glass Cottage, Damien. Here's the key, not that anyone closes, much less locks, doors around here. I just came from there myself, so things should be in order for you." Charlie handed the key to the attorney.

"Just give one of us a holler if you need anything." Nash put in, taking the baby from Jill so she could finish eating.

Tired from the day's travel, Damien decided to call it a night, making plans to join the guys on the sea early the next morning.

Watching the man leave the restaurant, Nash met Gabe's eyes, the slight frown matching his. "All these years he's barely stayed in touch. Never visited. He's got something on his mind."

"Something," Gabe agreed, leaning back in his chair, playing with the back of Charlie's hair. "So you prepped Sea Glass for Damien?"

Charlie nodded, pushing away her empty pasta plate and sitting back. "Mmhmm. Just checked to be sure it was clean and ready, you know. They always do a great job. Twas odd, though, I had a weird sense of deja vu while in there—like I'd been there before, but also like something was trying to surface."

Jill exchanged glances with Gabe then spoke carefully, "You *have* been in there before, Charlie. That was the cottage you stayed in when you first came here."

"Ah, so that's where I was when I lost my memory?"

Gabe tensed, but she didn't seem disturbed, merely curious. He nodded and waited for the next question with more than a little dread.

"Maybe you'll tell me about it later?" She'd never asked before, but now Charlie seemed to want more details.

"Sure he will, just ask," Jill answered for him, seeing how the question left Gabe swallowing hard.

"I don't know about you guys, but I'm ready to call it a night." Nash stood, baby in one arm, holding out the other hand to tug Jill to her feet.

Gabe and Charlie followed suit, parting ways with the trio just outside the bar. Gabe answered his walkie talkie to hear Rory tell him she was going to sleep in the hammock on Charlie's porch while she waited for them.

By unspoken agreement, they made their way to Charlie's cottage instead of walking by the sea. Once there, they saw that Rory was indeed sound asleep in the hammock, Jake snuggled by her side.

Charlie tucked a blanket around them both and followed Gabe inside, the door standing open as always.

Charlie excused herself a moment, Gabe making himself comfortable on the couch. He figured she'd want to talk after the comments about the Sea Glass Cottage.

While he waited, Gabe pulled an envelope Jill had given him earlier from his pocket and opened it. He read the pages through and let them drop to the coffee table with a muttered curse, striding out to the porch where his daughter slept.

*   *   *

Charlie found him kneeling by Rory's side, his eyes intent on her face. "Gabe?"

Wordlessly, he turned and wrapped his arms around her. The little girl slept on while her father held tightly to Charlie.

Confused, Charlie sat next to him and held on, stroking his back rhythmically, dropping light kisses in his hair from time to time. Several minutes passed with his face buried in her neck, his arms tight. After a while, he sat back, scrubbing both hands over his face and leaving them there for a few beats.

"She's sick, Charlie," he whispered brokenly, fisting his hands against his eyes until his knuckles went white.

"What do you mean she's sick? Look at her, Gabe. She's a picture for perfect health." Charlie took his hands in hers, looking into his face, his expression heartbreaking.

Rory stirred in her sleep, wrapping her arms about Jake and murmuring nonsensical words.

Looking at his child, Gabe realized that never in his life had he ever been so terrifyingly helpless—not when fire rained all around him, not Charlie's grief—nothing had rendered him at such a loss. It was truly the most horrifying feeling he'd ever experienced. He took one of Rory's hands in his, in sleep her fingers curling around his trustingly. He met Charlie's gaze, her eyes filled with compassion and puzzlement.

He opened his mouth, shrugged and closed it. His throat felt as if it were made of ground glass as he tried again to speak.

"Let me get you a drink, okay?" Charlie squeezed his hands and stood.

"Read the papers." His voice was raspy, as if he'd been screaming— or suppressing screams.

* * *

Charlie was loath to leave him but she needed to understand what was going on. How could Rory be sick? She'd been here for weeks, a glowing testament to island living with her bright eyes and never-flagging energy.

She gathered up the scattered papers, ordering them by page numbers and read the words for herself, sinking to the couch in disbelief and anger. Her fear for Rory, for Gabe warred with her anger at Damien. How could he keep such information from Gabe all these weeks?

She got them both water bottles from the fridge, turning to find Gabe standing in the middle of the room, the papers half crumpled in his hand.

He took a bottle from her and drained half in one gulp. Clearing his throat, he asked, "Will you stay here, stay with her?"

Charlie was startled but nodded. "Sure, of course. What—"

"Please don't leave her for one second." Gabe's gray eyes were stormy, his voice rough, but his touch on her arm was gentle. "Damien has some explaining to do," he ground out, his hands fisting as he turned on his heel and left the cottage in quick strides.

Charlie understood his anger, but feared for his control. She wouldn't leave Rory, but she could call in backup.

* * *

Nash made it to Sea Glass Cottage by the third punch.

He ran in the broken door to find Damien face down, Gabe about to smash his head into the counter.

"Whoa, whoa, whoa, Arch—don't kill him! You'll go to jail and where will that leave Rory?" Nash shouted, using all his strength to grip Gabe's arms and spin him around, bracing himself for a punch as Gabe reeled.

Rory's name brought Gabe crashing to reality and he paused, legs planted wide, the vein in his temple pulsing wildly. He pointed to the papers on the floor, giving Nash a hard stare. "Read those."

He rounded back on Damien, who'd wisely put the counter between them while Gabe had been distracted.

"By all that is fucking holy, WHY?!?" he roared, visibly forcing himself not to leap the counter and plow into the other man again, his knuckles white where he gripped the counter.

Behind him, Nash picked up the half-crumpled papers and skimmed them, shock washing over his face.

"You BASTARD!" Dropping the pages, he stood beside Gabe, rage now radiating from them both.

"It's my job!" Damien cried, his eyes wild as he tried to figure out an escape path around the two men, both in far better shape than he and both fueled by righteous anger.

"It was not your job to lie to Lilith or to keep information from me, Damien. How could you?" The vein in Gabe's temple jumped so hard, Nash was sure his friend would stroke out right there.

Stepping around the counter to push the other man against the sink, Gabe's voice was deceptively calm, "So help me, God in heaven, Damien, if my little girl suffers for this, they will never find your body because I will Feed. It. To. The. Sharks." He jabbed Damien's chest with each word.

Gabe strode out, leaving Nash with the parting words for Damien, "Get your stuff, you're leaving now. You'll go stay at a hotel in town until the morning's boat. Don't you dare fuck with me."

Out on the porch, Nash made a couple of calls and, within minutes, an island deputy was escorting Damien off the property.

Nash's voice was calm, belying his fury. "Don't ever contact me or mine again, Damien. Ever."

* * *

Charlie and Jillian paced the living room of the cottage, Rory still tucked into the hammock and the baby asleep on Charlie's bed.

As they paced, keeping her voice low, Charlie told Jill what they'd learned from the papers.

Jill hissed, "That bastard! He'll be lucky if Gabe and Nash both don't kill him!" Back and forth they paced, ears tuned to the children and for sounds of the men returning.

"I hope Gabe throttles the slimy bastard," Charlie snarled.

"He nearly did." Nash's laugh was wry as he entered the cottage. .

Before Nash could tell them about the confrontation, a sleepy Rory stumbled in the door, Jake at her side. "Where's my Daddy?" she leaned against the closest body, which happened to be Nash's.

Charlie sat on the couch and motioned the little girl over, settling the sleepy child next to her, the dog at their feet. "He's taking care of a few things; you know how it is being the boss man."

Jill went to get the baby, still chewing her lip in concern.

"We'll skip fishing, take the morning to regroup," Nash said quietly as he leaned over to kiss Rory's forehead, his sadness and worry mirrored in Charlie's eyes. Rory sighed and snuggled against Charlie's side, already mostly back to sleep.

"He'll want to cool off before coming back here; he was blazing hot. I'll look after him." Nash assured Charlie as he took the baby's bag from Jill.

Jill hugged Charlie tightly. "I'm so glad they have you," she whispered.

As they left, Charlie tucked a blanket around both herself and Rory and settled in to wait. The long day plus the dramatic evening caught up with her and she drifted off to sleep.

*　*　*

Charlie woke to find Gabe sitting on the coffee table, chin resting in his hands, watching Rory sleep. Exhaustion etched his face in stark relief in the dim light.

She eased Rory from her side onto the couch, patting the spot beside the girl for Jake to hop up. Rory smiled in her sleep, snuggling close to the dog. Charlie smiled at that, then stood and stretched, holding out a hand to Gabe.

He let her pull him along behind her to the bedroom where she tossed back the covers on the bed. She pointed to his shoes imperiously; he obliged and pushed them off. She pulled his t-shirt over his head and tossed it aside, pressing a brief kiss to his chest. She pointed at his cargoes; he raised an eyebrow but pushed them off, too. Gesturing to the bed, she nudged him to get in, pulling the light cover over him. Atop the covers, she piled pillows and curled up next to him. Tired as he was, he made an appreciative sound deep in his throat as her breasts cradled his head.

Charlie laughed softly. "As much as I'd love to get naked and snuggle properly, you need to sleep and not to worry about Rory waltzing in here." She stroked his temple in a light, slow rhythm, brushing back the unruly dark gold strands and smoothing his frown.

The events of the evening and the terror for Rory running through his blood weighed heavily on him. Certain he'd be unable to sleep, he let himself relax against her. It felt good to let it all go for a bit and trust Charlie to keep watch.

* * *

They stood shoulder to shoulder on the beach, watching the morning boat grow smaller and smaller.

"Shark bait," he'd snarled at Damien in reminder as he'd pushed against Nash's restraining hand when the other man passed him to board the boat.

"I assume you called his partner and got all the details?" Nash prodded as they headed back to his cottage to join Charlie and Jill for breakfast.

"Oh yeah, I went to my place after I tried to beat the shit out of a few trees and went a few rounds with Big Al. Made some calls. The doc will call back, but I did get the attorney." Gabe gingerly flexed his bruised knuckles. He gestured to the house, telling it all once would be enough.

Before taking a seat at the table, Gabe motioned to his daughter to join him on the porch. They needed to talk, just the two of them. Charlie gave him an encouraging smile that somehow eased the tautness of his neck just a little.

He sat on the porch steps, turned to face Rory next to him. "You have any idea what's going on?"

She shook her head, her gray eyes wide and worried.

"No worries. Nothing has changed. Okay?"

Rory nodded, her eyes downcast. "Is this about me being sick?" Her small, scared voice had him rubbing his chest as if she'd punched him.

Before he could reply she continued, "Damien told me not to tell you about being sick. He said you might not want me to live with you if you knew."

Gabe struggled mightily to rein in the fury that washed over him. It was a good thing Damien was off island. He lifted her chin with a finger. "Damien was a liar."

"You're not like that." The little girl's smile wobbled a bit as she brushed away tears and hugged his neck.

"Damien wasn't a good guy, but he's not going to bother us again. I don't want you to worry about the things you're going to hear me say in there, we're all in this together. Are you feeling okay? You promise to tell me if you don't?" At her nod, Gabe stood, still holding her.

"You can ask me anything anytime—about this or whatever, okay?" He carried her in, set her down and tapped her nose.

They joined the rest at the table and began to eat and talk, Rory close against his side.

The worst news was that Rory was apparently in a tentative remission from an aggressive, yet curable childhood leukemia. Thanks to a bribe from the Baxters, Damien had edited out that information in the medical records he'd given Gabe. The betrayal of a man they considered a friend—a brother, even— stung both Gabe and Nash. None of it made any sense at all.

As an aside, Gabe told them he'd called the doctor and was waiting for a call back.

The treachery had started two years ago when Lilith had decided she needed to find her daughter's father right after the girl got sick the first time. Remembering where the cab had picked him up that night, she'd gone to Ray's place to track him down. Ray had told her Gabe had long since left town, but he'd given her his name. With that, she went to her private investigator and attorney to find him.

Before Lilith had gone through with contacting Gabe, Rory's illness had gone into remission. Lilith had filed away the information on her daughter's father, intending only to contact him if she had to.

When Lilith died in the car crash, Damien's office had been listed as her next of kin. In their quest to gain full custody of their granddaughter, the Baxters had paid Damien handsomely to not immediately contact the girl's father. In looking up the paperwork while Damien was out of town, his partner had come across the files and put things in motion to contact Gabe. Since their original plan had failed, the Baxters instead bribed Damien to keep their granddaughter's medical information from her father. It was their misguided hope that his apparent inability to care for the girl would weigh in their favor when it came to the custody battle.

When the partner dug further and uncovered the files detailing the deception, he'd immediately written and sent hard copies of the information to Gabe. Information that arrived right on the heels of Damien's visit. Gabe had put the packet aside, assuming it was copies of his paternity papers and all, until that night. He didn't share that Damien had offered him a substantial sum of money to turn the girl over to her grandparents now, saying Gabe didn't need a sick girl, anyway. And he didn't share that she was past due for tests to check her remission. Some things the kid didn't need to know—especially not until he understood what needed to happen next.

As Gabe told them what he'd learned, Charlie's hand on his leg kept him grounded when he wanted to pace and hit things.

Rory had settled into the corner of the room with a coloring book, seeming to be hardly listening. However, when he finished, she spoke up.

"My Mommy's parents keep trying to take me away and they did this even when Mommy was here?"

Gabe nodded, swallowing audibly. This Daddy thing was damned tough.

"I dunno why they want me. They sure weren't nice to us—you're s'posed to be nice to people you want around." She shook her head and kept coloring.

The adults breathed a joint sigh of relief and made noises of agreement.

Since nothing else could be done until the doctor called Gabe back, they agreed to carry on with the day. Nash cleared the dishes and Jill nursed the baby, while Charlie and Gabe headed out to open the bar and tend to tenant needs.

"You coming along or staying here, Poppet?" Gabe forced himself to let her choose as usual when, after all he'd learned, he really wanted her close by his side.

"I'm coming. Matteo said he's doing a new recipe today and Jane is gonna show me how to fold the napkins into boats." The girl packed her backpack and kissed the baby's head.

"I'll come play with him so you can take a shower later," she told Jill as she skipped out the door ahead of Charlie.

Gabe's belly clenched to think she'd not always been so healthy — and might not always be.

*   *   *

Gabe rubbed at his neck for the fiftieth time in as many minutes, unable to ease the tightness that'd taken hold the minute he'd opened the papers last night. He felt caged and was a hair's breadth from telling the next person who ordered a drink to get it their own damn self.

"Fuck this," he muttered, waving a dismissive hand to Jane as she chatted with a couple.

"Later, Boss," she called. She was more than capable of handling things and he had to get out of there. Now.

He texted Jill: *Keep Rory close for the afternoon?*

Sure—you okay? came the reply.

All good. Later. He texted back, yet again grateful for his friends. Now to find Charlie…

*   *   *

Charlie had just thrown a lump of clay onto her wheel and was deeply absorbed in the fluid shape beneath her hands, intent on unwinding after the tense morning.

The score to *The Phantom of the Opera* swelled from the speakers as she closed her eyes and worked the clay. She envisioned the piece in her mind's eye and leaned over the wheel to make it happen.

A shadow fell, causing her to look up. Seeing Gabe standing in the doorway, she stopped the wheel and wiped her hands on the damp towel at her shoulder. His eyes were hidden behind his aviator shades, a muscle jumping in his jaw. After the night they'd had, she was immediately concerned. She scrubbed clay from her hands at the sink and dried them as she went to him.

"Come with me?" His face was impassive, his tone brusque.

"Sure. Everything okay?" She used a remote to turn off the music and lights, closing the door behind them.

"Fine." He took her hand and strode down the beach.

"Where are we going?" she asked, walking faster to keep up, that jumping jaw muscle of his bothering her. In all these weeks she'd rarely seen him angry and never this abrupt with anyone, much less her.

He pointed to the boat as they drew closer. "Going."

"Okay. Should I run and get food to take with us?"

"Going now." Gabe untied the lines and stepped onto the boat, holding out a hand to help her jump aboard.

He fired up the engine and pointed the boat out to sea.

After a few miles, he pulled off his t-shirt, tossed it at her with a grin, the terseness gone just like that, his face relaxing in the sunshine.

She caught the shirt and let it fall to the bench, moving to wrap her arms around his waist. Looking up, she smiled at how the ocean breeze ruffled back his wavy hair, at the sea reflected in his shades.

"I had to get away." He dipped his head to kiss her upturned face, his rueful smile an apology of sorts.

Charlie understood, probably more than even he knew. She kissed him back, deepening the kiss, bringing a hand up to cup his jaw. She turned her body into his, pressing against him from head to toe.

He reached out a hand to idle down the boat, setting them adrift in the sea.

Wordlessly, they undressed each other and came together on their discarded clothes under the afternoon sun.

*   *   *

With the vise of tension that had gripped his neck gone, the wide open sea around them and Charlie asleep in his arms, her legs tangled with his, Gabe could easily believe time had indeed stopped.

He felt this peace every time he was with Charlie, that nothing could take him down as long as she was by his side—or beneath him, as the case may be.

It dawned on him that he hadn't spent any predawn hours in the wood shop making toys since Charlie had begun talking to him, then sleeping with him in the dark hours. She didn't know it, but since 9/11 then the Melbourne Road fire, he'd rarely slept a full night without his own nightmares waking him in a cold sweat. That was where making the toys had come in, a way to fill his mind and his hands in the dark hours rather than risk going back to sleep.

As the afternoon sun prickled his skin, he nudged Charlie gently. "Hey, you're gonna get sunburned in uncomfortable places if we don't cover up."

"I'll take one for the team," she giggled, swinging over to straddle his hips. Raising her face to the sky, she took him on a wild ride on a calm sea.

*   *   *

Much later and more than a little sun-kissed, they shared peanut butter and crackers washed down with cold beer they'd found in the galley below.

"Thanks be to hungry fishermen!" Charlie clinked her bottle to his. She was clad only in his t-shirt; he'd pulled on his shorts, leaving them unbuttoned.

Gabe had motored them around Shelter Island, dropping anchor at the edge of a hidden cove where they watched the sun begin to set. Charlie sat nestled between his legs, leaning back against his chest. His hands rested under the t-shirt, cupping the sides of her bare bottom, thumbs stroking lightly.

After the sun sent up the last blazing flare of the day, night dropped quickly. Gabe kissed her temple and went below to find a blanket, tugging on his shirt as she found her clothes and dressed quickly in the cooling air.

"I haven't felt this calm in a long time." Gabe wrapped the blanket around her. She still smelled of orange blossoms, now sun-kissed and slightly salty. He hugged her and let her go, turning to start the boat.

Charlie settled on the bench for the ride. "We should make a habit of this."

He raised his bottle in agreement, bracing his legs and throttling the boat out into sea.

The trip back was short, full dark just setting in as they tied the boat and hopped ashore.

Charlie stretched and folded the blanket. "I'm going to clean up my abandoned project before it becomes cement. I'll catch up to you?"

"My place?" Gabe was headed to the bar for the evening shift, his favorite time to be behind the bar.

She smiled as she watched him tie off the boat, his windblown hair and sun-golden skin making him the picture of an island bar owner.

"Sure, we'll let poor Rory have her own bed for a change," she called over her shoulder, waving her fingers.

Gabe walked backwards for a few steps, a slight frown on his face as he watched her walk away. He couldn't quite put his finger on it, but something had shifted in the past few minutes. Not bad, not good, just...shifted. He shrugged and jogged down the beach towards the bar.

* * *

After the day spent away from the world in Gabe's arms out on the water, soaking up sunshine, Charlie felt relaxed but also a bit restless all of the sudden.

She'd made her excuses instead of joining him at the bar just yet, giving herself some room to think. She could tell it'd given him pause, but he'd let her go without comment.

Lately she'd been feeling an urge to commit to a life here on the island, to explore what that might mean for her and Gabe—and Rory. To take on a true role in helping run The Painted Parrot, to volunteer in town, to be more than an extended visitor to this world.

Most of the time she could ignore the fact that she had a past life to consider, but lately it felt like she was playing at life instead of truly living it.

While she cleaned up the pottery shed, Charlie was torn between the desire to continue pushing away the memories that had been poking about the edge of her mind and the curious need to remember all she could about who she had been. Could she push them away and go forward with her life, or did she need to try and resolve her past as best she could before choosing her path forward? The same questions were, quite honestly, becoming tiresome.

The recent memories had brought her much good emotion, for the first time she'd wanted to know more. Hiding the depth of her reactions from Gabe, she'd let him believe the memories of the past few days were merely snapshots rather than the pages of her life they actually were. She wasn't just remembering those moments; she was remembering her life bit by bit.

With so many flashbacks happening within such a short period of time, Charlie knew living as if her past didn't exist wasn't going to last. Perhaps it was time to meet it head on before it steamrolled her out of the blue.

Just like that, it was decided. She was going to call Troy and Cassidy this week, spend at least a few minutes trying to go forward with them. Even if Charlie still didn't feel like a mother, as a caring person, she felt a little bad about shutting them out completely. She'd make a start on mending fences, if she could. She was also going to actively try to call forth memories, to open the file and look at the pictures and read the stories about her, to let the images in her mind come, to let the emotions come.

Charlie paced the floor, twisting her hair and chewing her lip. She didn't have to do this alone—Gabe would walk through it all with her or, best of all, she could lose herself in the dark hours with him, keeping the unknowns at bay. He would be whatever she needed him to be, at any cost to himself.

Jill had told her how he'd been there for her in her first weeks on the island—something Gabe hadn't told them until after Charlie's memory loss. Jill hadn't given her many details, but Charlie now knew why she'd known his voice, why his grip on her hand been familiar.

Scrubbing down her tools, she scolded herself. He didn't deserve to be her constant distraction, however good it felt. Her ever-increasing memories would hurt him, and hurting him was the last thing she wanted to do.

Far from ready to face anyone, Charlie took four small sample display trays she'd made as a gift for Katie down from the drying shelf and began to glaze them. Lights blazing, music playing, she got lost in creating a whimsical design that would delight Katie's children and be a fun background for cookies and cake samples.

She wanted a life here; she wanted to come to Gabe whole and strong, having laid her past to rest—whether she actually remembered it all or not.

* * *

Knowing Charlie wouldn't likely see a text anytime soon—she was notorious for leaving her phone unattended for hours—Gabe and Rory walked to find her after leaving the bar around midnight.

As they walked, Gabe was reminded of the odd feeling he'd had all evening, since Charlie had left him at the boat. He shrugged, he'd know soon enough.

"Looks like Charlie isn't here," Rory said from Charlie's porch, the cottage door closed, the windows dimly lit by the porch fairly lights and her habitual tiny lamp on inside.

"Or she's asleep." Gabe went inside, returning to the porch in short order.

"Nope, not asleep," Rory stated the obvious, having dogged his every step.

Gabe gave the girl a playful shove as they walked on to the pottery shed. He breathed a sigh of relief he hadn't realized he was holding at the sight of the brightly lit shed, music spilling from the open windows.

"Hi, Charlie!" Rory burst inside the open door, exhibiting her amazing energy even at past midnight.

"Hey, Rory." Charlie smiled over her shoulder as she placed a freshly glazed tray inside the electric kiln and set the timer.

Gabe's uneasiness eased a bit, seeing her creating, no shadows on her face.

"We brought you supper." Rory pointed to the bag in Gabe's hand.

"I got lost in my project and suddenly here you are," Charlie said to Rory, giving him a look of apology.

She dried her hands and reached out for Rory's hand. "Let's go to your house, shall we?"

Gabe leaned in to kiss her as she took his hand in her other one. She kissed him back appreciatively, laughing at Rory's groan of impatience. "I got a new book to read, let's go!"

* * *

With Rory asleep in her fairy princess room, Jake at her side, Gabe dimmed the cottage lights to a faint glow, the radio playing Van Halen's "Dance the Night Away" and held his hand out to Charlie.

They danced slowly, kissing, touching. Charlie hummed along with the music, every fiber of her being tuned to where Gabe's body touched hers.

Unable to hold back, she poured all her fears and hopes into kissing him with such fervor that Gabe cupped her face in his hands, his eyes searching hers. What he saw there weakened his knees and heated his blood.

They'd take this moment now, in this world they'd created, this bit of paradise that had been free from the fear of the past or worries about the future. She'd cling to the hope that, when all was said and done, they'd be right here—together and whole.

The music faded as he led her to his bed and they did, indeed, dance the night away.

Chapter Twenty-Nine

CHARLIE WAS CERTAIN she'd remember the moment for as long as she lived—the moment her past, present and future came crashing together with the onset of an ominous headache.

As she watched Jillian approach in slow motion, her stricken expression telling Charlie what she was about to say would turn the world upside down; Charlie looked around for Rory, spotting her in the corner folding napkins with Jane.

She instinctively reached out a staying hand in the girl's direction, cuing Jane to keep Rory with her. Jane's hand went to her throat as she nodded, taking in the scene unfolding in front of her, but smoothly keeping Rory's attention.

Charlie came around the bar and met Jillian, pushing out a chair seconds before Jillian's legs gave out. Jill's eyes were wide, her grip on the baby too tight, causing him to fuss.

Jill gripped Charlie's hand painfully and whispered, "They're missing."

Charlie's ears filled with a roar and she shook her head to clear it. "What do you mean missing?"

Jill's hands trembled as she comforted the baby. "The C-Coast Guard just called saying they got a Mayday call from The JohnB three hours ago. They responded to the call but h-haven't found any sign of the boat or-or the guys."

Her words seemed to echo in the nearly empty bar, horror descending like a black cloud, blocking out the sun.

Charlie's hands came up to her head, the headache pulsating against her skull as if it would break through. "Oh, no. Nonononono." She rocked back and forth. "Not now," she whispered. She pushed her hair back and faced Jill. "What's next?"

"We wait. They'll call." Jill's voice broke on a sob. "Charlie, I cannot lose them."

"Look at me. Look at me." Charlie's voice was low and vehement, shocking Jill into focusing on her. "We are not losing them, do you hear me? We are not."

Matteo rounded the corner of the restaurant and came right to the two women. "I have friends in the Coast Guard, the news is out. Listen to me, they will find them. Nash and Gabe are wizards out there, they will be fine." He gripped both women's shoulders, his eyes blazing.

"We'll wait for word here, together," Charlie said.

Jill nodded, settling back in her chair to nurse the baby, both for his comfort and hers.

Matteo went to call in all their back up help, as islanders would flock to The Painted Parrot to stand watch together.

Charlie caught Jane's eye and waved her over, Rory already looking at them worriedly.

"What's wrong, Charlie? Is the baby sick, Jill?" The girl put her hand on the baby with a frown.

Charlie smoothed the girl's hair, tugging Rory to sit on her knee. "You trust me, right?"

Rory's frown deepened. "Sure, Charlie."

"Right now the Coast Guard is trying to find your Daddy and Nash's boat, they're missing." Charlie didn't know how else to break the news but to be straightforward and honest.

"My Daddy is missing?" Rory's voice rose, tears springing to her eyes.

"Look at me, Rory." Charlie gripped the little girl's shoulders and braved the gray eyes so like her father's she couldn't help but send a silent plea. *Hold on, Gabe, please hold on.*

Jill helped out by saying, "Rory, Nash and your daddy have done this before; it's just scary when we don't know where they are right now. But they need us to believe they will be okay."

Rory nodded, scrubbing the tears from her face. "My Daddy will not get lost," she declared, the words stronger than her voice.

"People will be coming. Why don't we set up a kids' corner, Rory?" Jane held out her hand, giving Charlie a watery smile and squeezing Jill's shoulder.

Charlie rubbed her temples and looked around. "Jill, let's move to that corner booth—it'll be more comfortable as people come in and there's room to lay Zane down if need be."

Jill nodded, gripping Charlie's hand. "Are you okay?"

"I'll be better when we get them back." Charlie moved to the roomy booth along the rail.

"I can't believe all this beauty in front of me hides such treachery." Charlie stood next to the booth, gazing out at the sea in a futile effort to see the JohnB.

Jill nodded, silent tears streaming down her face. She took a deep shuddery breath and wiped them away.

Squeezing Jill's shoulder on his way by, Matteo went out to the massive hurricane lantern that hung on a hook just outside the bar. His face was somber as he murmured a prayer and lit the wick inside. He took a moment, head bowed. Straightening, he then fastened the lantern door securely against the breeze, the flame flaring brightly. It would burn ceaselessly until the men were home safe from the sea.

"Tell me what to get from your house; I know the baby needs his bag." Charlie squared her shoulders. Headache or not, she wanted to be moving, to be doing something besides staring at the god-damned unforgiving sea.

Rory at her side, Charlie went to Nash and Jill's cottage to pick up the baby's bag and portable play pen. She added a few more diapers to the bag and slung it over her shoulder.

"I want to get something at my house." Rory tugged her in that direction when they left Jill's.

"Sure." They covered the short distance quickly.

Charlie searched for some headache relief in Gabe's medicine cabinet. As she came out of the bathroom in his bedroom, she found Rory sitting on the bed, tears streaming down her face.

"Oh, honey." Charlie pocketed the pill bottle and took the little girl in her arms.

Rory held a t-shirt of her father's and sobbed against Charlie's chest, her little heart breaking. "I keep texting him and he's not answering. The walkie talkie either."

"Listen to me, kiddo. Your Daddy's not lost, they're going to find him and Nash, I know it. You heard Matteo, they're wizards out there." Charlie hugged Rory tightly, taking her own words to heart. "Now, let's get this stuff back so Zane can be comfortable, okay?"

Rory nodded, pulling on the t-shirt, which covered her from neck to mid-calf.

"Let me pee real quick and we'll be off." Charlie tweaked Rory's nose and stepped back into the bathroom.

Closing the door, she leaned against it, sliding down to sit on the floor. Her head was pounding, her eyes hot and dry. She swallowed the pills with a cup of water, draining the whole cup with a sigh.

"Gabe, you have got to come back to us," she whispered, bracing herself and opening the door.

They returned to the bar to find it filled with people, some islanders, some tourists—all well-wishers who wanted to keep watch for Nash and Gabe's safe return.

Rory hugged Charlie's side until her friends urged her to join them in the kids' corner Jane had set up, complete with movies and craft supplies. Looking so forlorn, Gabe's t-shirt falling off one shoulder, she allowed them to lead her away, Charlie giving her a small smile of reassurance.

Charlie found Jill sitting outside on the terrace, at a table closest to the sea. "I keep thinking if I don't look away, I'm holding a life-line and they'll find their way home."

"Rory put on one of Gabe's shirts; I kinda wanted to do the same." Charlie sat beside her friend, joining her in scanning the horizon closely.

Jill nodded in agreement. "I keep chanting 'Home is the sailor, home from the sea' over and over." She sighed, patting the sleeping baby where he rested in a sling snuggly against her body.

"Has this happened before?" Charlie gratefully accepted the glass of lemonade Jane offered, the other woman was determined to personally see to it that her friends took care of themselves while they waited.

"You two need to eat; Matteo's fixing you an appetizer plate." Jane patted both women's shoulders and disappeared back into the crowd. They nodded, both knowing they'd likely not be able to stomach a bite, but also knowing caring for them and the rest of the crowd was both Jane's and Matteo's way of coping.

Jill nodded, "Once. During a sudden storm a few years ago, they had to radio the Coast Guard. It was a harrowing rescue that ended with them safe but just after, the chopper crashed and a pilot lost his life." She stared out to the sea. "They're going to survive this one, too. They have to."

Charlie's headache had become nearly unbearable despite several medication attempts. She kept having to close her eyes to clear her vision, which wanted to gray at the edges. Putting on her aviator shades seemed to help somewhat; at least that way others wouldn't notice her closed eyes.

* * *

By tacit agreement, Charlie and Jill sat watching the water all afternoon, the Coast Guard calls bringing them no news as the search went on.

Rory joined them often, needing further reassurance that the rescuers wouldn't give up on her daddy and the man she'd come to love as an uncle. The baby played happily in his mother's or Charlie's arms or in his playpen at their side, oblivious to their fears. Jane left her extra helpers to tend the crowd for and sat with them awhile. The three women started several conversations, all trailing off to gaze at the sea.

Katie came in with her three young children, bringing Rory her best friends and plenty of baked goods for all. She slid into the booth beside Jane, her youngest asleep in her arms. "Nothing?"

The other three women shook their heads.

Brought by Matteo, Amos arrived and paused by the lantern, touching the post with his eyes on the sea. He took the cross on a cord from his neck and hung it on the lamp post. When he came to Charlie and Jill, he simply hugged both women, looking them each in the eye for a long moment and took up watch next to them.

Islanders and visitors alike kept vigil, many stopping by the table to offer hugs and words of encouragement that came out trite no matter how well-intentioned. Katie brought in platters of pastries and cookies while Matteo and Jane kept drinks plentiful on the house.

The lantern's flame burned brighter as the evening light began to wane. From time to time, islanders would pause beside its glow, murmuring a prayer, some crossing themselves, others touching the pole briefly.

*   *   *

In hopes of calming her pounding head, Charlie walked out onto the beach and sat on the sand at the edge of the water. She rubbed her temples, the odd feeling of confusion and dazedness a struggle to keep at bay. This helplessness felt vaguely familiar and that was a sensation she did not want to explore further right now.

A few minutes later, Rory found her there and crawled into her lap. Wrapping her arms around the girl, they stared out unseeingly at the stunning sunset.

"Charlie?" Rory tipped up her face to look at her.

"Hmm?"

"What'll happen to me if my Daddy's lost a long time? Will I have to go live with the Baxters?" Her lip quivered, eyes dark with worry. Charlie'd seen those same eyes on Gabe so many times in recent days.

Charlie sent yet another prayer, another thought out to the universe, *Please let him be safe.* She shook her head. "No way will you ever have to go back there, Rory. Your Daddy is going to be found." She hugged the little girl close as Jane crossed the sand down to them.

Wrapping a blanket around Charlie and Rory, she handed them both hot chocolate. "Coast Guard just checked in; no news."

Charlie nodded her thanks, squeezing Jane's hand, and pulled the blanket up almost over their heads, creating a warm, safe space for the two of them inside as they watched the sea under the darkening sky.

*   *   *

The call came at 3am.

The bar was still brightly lit, the vigil candles tended carefully. While the crowd had dwindled, there were still a lot of people on hand waiting for news.

Sheriff Luke had brought in a few cots to make the long night easier. Amos had settled into one of these; Rory and the dog curled up next to him.

Jill lay with her body curled around the baby, talking softly with Charlie sitting on the floor at her side.

The hourly updates had stopped after midnight, the Coast Guard promising to let them know when they had any news.

When Jill's phone rang at 3am, she knocked it to the floor in her haste. Charlie scooped it up and pressed it to Jill's hand with lightning speed.

"Hello?" Jill freed herself from the blanket and sleeping baby to stand, gripping Charlie's hand as she listened to the voice on other end of the line.

"Nash!?" She sank to the nearest chair, her voice shocked and thrilled at the same time. "Where's Gabe? We'll be right there. Oh, I love you so much."

Charlie held her breath, the room silent around them.

"They're safe!" Jill shouted, crying and laughing. "He didn't give any details, just that they're safe and on their way to the hospital now. I could barely hear over the Coast Guard chopper. Thank you all so, so much for being here with us."

In minutes, Jill and Zane, Charlie and Rory were in Luke's police SUV. Lights blazing, he made the trip through town to the hospital as fast as possible.

*   *   *

The story came out in bits and pieces as Nash and Gabe were patched up in the ER, both having suffered cuts and bruises, a wrenched knee for Gabe and a broken forearm for Nash as well as both being dehydrated and exhausted. The JohnB was no more, having sunk after being engulfed in flames due to a fire that had sent the men into the water.

Both men objected to doctor opinions that they stay a few hours for observation, declaring that Jill and Charlie wouldn't let up on their vigil, and home was all they needed. Deputy Luke came to their rescue again, getting them all to the door of their cottages, helping each man inside to their beds—which had all been freshly made thanks to Jane and her capable team.

****Chapter Thirty****

GABE WAS BEYOND GLAD to be settled in bed, clad in gym shorts with his knee raised on pillows. Rory promptly passed out next to him—the girl having not budged from his side since finding him at the hospital.

The entire time he and Nash had battled the seas, Gabe had worried for his daughter—imagining her terror at losing another parent. He'd also worried for Charlie, even though she didn't remember her loss of Jack. To be home with both of them was such a tremendous relief, the exhaustion and stress taking its toll as he struggled to keep his eyes open.

Charlie smoothed the blankets, filled a water bottle for him and generally fussed about until he caught her hand. "Lie down with me?"

She nodded, taking off her shoes and settling in on the other side of Rory. She turned towards him, her arm above the girl's head, hand stroking his face, her foot touching his leg gently. Without another word, he turned his face into her hand and, on a deep sigh, let go into sleep.

*　*　*

It was as if the all-day headache had been a harbinger of what was to come as soon as she let down her guard.

Once the fear for Gabe's safety and the need to take care of Rory and Jill were all over, Charlie's headache had reached epic proportions. She fervently hoped lying here, safely together, would bring healing sleep to them all.

Less than an hour later, her eyes flew open, darting about frantically as she tried to orient herself. Her heart was pounding and her ears were ringing with echoes of unnamed sounds, but the room around her was still and quiet—Gabe and Rory both sleeping deeply.

Her head was pounding so hard, she was sure Gabe would hear it and wake—she could literally see flashes of light with each pound. Charlie bolted from the bed and stumbled into the bathroom, closing the door behind her. Her vision, both blurry and pulsating, her head spinning, she was on the floor—not sure if she'd sat down or fallen there. She could hear her breath coming in harsh gasps and realized she was chanting "Nononono," over and over.

And, just like that, she knew.

*   *   *

Gabe fought his way to consciousness, his body clinging to the healing powers of sleep, but his mind reacting to the sounds he heard.

Turning his head, he saw that Rory slept curled next to his side, the other side of the bed empty.

Charlie. With a groan as every muscle in his body screamed in protest, he pushed himself up and swung his legs over the side of the bed. Once oriented, he realized the sounds that had penetrated his deep sleep were coming from the closed bathroom door. Biting back another groan, he hobbled to the door and turned the knob. The sounds from behind the locked door made his neck tighten in alarm.

"Charlie? Charlie, open the door for me." His voice was raspy, his battered throat protesting its use. Leaning against the door for support, he tried again, "Charlie, honey, let me in. Just open the door, that's all you have to do."

He considered his options—which weren't as many as he'd like, in his current condition. He was pretty much limited to either calling Jill to come and coax Charlie to open the door—making her leave

Nash's side—or waiting her out. Whatever he did would have to be done from the floor if he didn't get back to the bed, as his traitorous body made quite clear that it was done with being upright and not much longer for being awake.

Just as he reached the bed's edge, her voice came from the other side of the door, "Gabe, I'm okay. Get back to bed, I'll be right out."

That had to be enough for now, was his last conscious thought.

*   *   *

From where she sat on the bathroom floor, Charlie was impressed at how strong and sure she'd managed to make her voice sound when Gabe had rattled the locked door.

Clinging to the moment of clarity, she reached up and turned on the water in the sink, hoping to mask any further sounds from her private storm. She sat against the cabinet, her arms wrapped tight around her body to keep from flying apart into a million pieces as memories she'd lost flickered in front of her eyes like an old movie playing in slow motion.

She laughed remembering tiny children and tangled Christmas lights, Cassidy's wild bed head, Troy's thumb sucking habit. She gasped remembering out-of-control sled rides and too-deep swimming pool waters. Oh, there were so many calls of "Look, Momma!"

She moaned, remembering making love with Jack—both tender, midnight moments and hasty-hurry-before-the-kids-catch-us moments—her body always on fire at his touch. She could feel his broad shoulders in her hands, his lips at her neck.

She broke apart with the fresh grief that she'd never hold him in her arms again. His always warm, solid body, his rumbling chuckle, his dark brown eyes all gone from her forever. And how. So many emotions at once made her feel like she was coming apart at the seams as the film slowed, leaving her plastered to the floor, slipping into a dreamless oblivion.

When she woke, her head felt as heavy as Thor's hammer, but the pain had reduced to a low ache. Learning on the sink counter, Charlie ran cool water over a wash cloth and let it rest on her face. The coolness soothed her raw eyes and sensitive cheeks. She must have lain there for hours, by the way her body felt.

Venturing a look in the mirror, she sponged her face again and pulled her hair into a messy knot that was better than the tangled mess springing about everywhere.

She opened the door resolutely, sure of what she needed to do..

* * *

Freshly showered and settled on the couch with his knee propped up, Gabe held his daughter on his good leg while they watched TV. He rubbed his neck as his eyes followed Charlie more than the TV screen, not liking the vibe he was getting from her.

It bothered him that they hadn't had a moment alone; he needed to know she was okay after their ordeal. Losing a husband, even one you didn't remember, then nearly losing the man you loved had to be rocking her to the core.

She felt his gaze and looked up from readying the table. She gave him a small smile and looked away to finish the job at hand.

His neck prickled alarmingly, but he had no choice but to attend to the scene in front of him as Rory jumped up to greet a hobbling Nash and whisk the baby from Jill's arms.

When Charlie had hung up the phone after calling Matteo for food, Jill had called. Despite his discomfort and exhaustion, Nash wanted to see Gabe. She'd suggested they make their way over and they could all eat Matteo's comfort food together.

At the moment, Nash sank slowly into the chair next to Gabe, eying his longtime friend critically. "You look like you battled the ocean and she bitch-slapped you good."

Gabe started to laugh before groaning with the rib splitting pain it brought, risking further pain to hit Nash with a coach pillow.

"Not the worst beating we've taken over the years." Gabe shook his head at the bruises on Nash's face, his arm wrapped in a sling. "Lucky SOBs."

From the kitchen, Jill watched the two of them. "I can't take my eyes off him. I confess I didn't try to keep him home, as I wanted to lay eyes on Gabe for a while, too."

Charlie nodded, her eyes on the food she was setting out.

It was easy for her to stay busy—albeit distracted—as the evening wore on. Food was consumed, the kitchen cleaned, kids kissed and hugged, the detailed story of the accident and rescue left for another day as they talked business and daily life—the focus on reveling in said life.

After the baby had snuggled into his mother's arms to sleep, Rory settled into her fairy princess bed to read the newest April Grace book she'd been waiting for. Finally, Jill coaxed her man home to bed, the two men sharing a long, silent embrace at the door.

*   *   *

Once they were gone, Gabe sagged against the door. "Alone at last. Will you please take me to bed?" His voice was teasing and light, but his color was pale under the sunburned skin.

Charlie helped him to bed, propping his knee and fluffing pillows as he lay back with a groan. Hand on her hip, he pulled her closer and nuzzled her breasts when she leaned over to cover him. Her sharp gasp in response made him frown.

"Charlie?" He reached up to hold her face, his eyes searching.

She forced a smile and brushed the hair from his forehead, letting her hand linger. "Go to sleep."

Exhaustion coupled with pain medication he'd agreed to just for tonight gave him no energy to inquire further. His hand went lax and his eyes drifted closed.

She stood over him for a long moment, committing each feature to memory, remembering how his hair felt in her hands, his growl when he'd burrow into her neck, his gunmetal gray eyes gone smoky with desire, his arms around her as she fell fast asleep after making love, how he'd stood so tall and strong in the bow of the boat with the sun turning his hair copper and gold.

Like treasured snapshots, she gathered these up, one by one, carefully tucking all that was Gabe Montgomery away deep in her heart. Knowing she'd never see him again, Charlie turned and walked away.

****Chapter Thirty-One****

RORY JOSTLED HIM AWAKE as she climbed onto the bed, the morning sun lighting up her face as she peered into his eyes.

"Hi, Daddy. You okay?" The little elfin face sported what had to be the cutest frown he'd ever seen. Eyes that mirrored his own were clouded with worry as he groaned and pushed himself upright.

"Yeah, Poppet, I'm okay." He grimaced at the broad term—hell, even his hair hurt. He seemed mostly functional, that was something.

His phone rang out Jill's ringtone just as he made it halfway to the bathroom. "Hey, get that will you?" He waved in the phone's direction and continued to the bathroom.

When he came out, Rory was standing by the door waiting for him. "Jill says she's on her way over and it's important."

Gabe ruffled Rory's hair on his way by. "Nash okay?"

"She said it's not about Nash so don't worry."

Glancing down, he figured the gym shorts and t-shirt he had on were decent enough and hobbled into the kitchen for coffee. Surprised to find the kitchen empty, he painstakingly made coffee, waiting until he could sit down at the table before asking Rory, "Where's Charlie?"

"I dunno. She wasn't here when I got up." Rory shrugged, engrossed in coloring.

Icy fingers gripped his neck as he asked Rory to bring him his phone. Just as she handed it to him, Jill stepped in the door, Nash right behind her.

"Arch, we need to talk." Nash's voice was roughened by more than just his sea swallowing ordeal, a muscle jumping in his jaw as he made his way to the table and sat down.

"Hey, Rory, you want to go help Jane set up the bar? She has baby Zane up there, too." Jill smoothed the girl's bangs and gave her a little nudge to the door. "They're waiting for you, kiddo."

Gabe looked from Nash to Jill as he returned Rory's careful hug before she dashed off, content to leave him in their capable hands.

Jill poured coffee for them all and sat down next to Gabe, cupping her mug in her hands.

Nash swallowed painfully, his blue eyes bloodshot and sad. "Arch, y'know how the only way to get a stuck band aid off is just to rip the sonofabitch off with a fucking roar? This is like that; no easy way to do it."

Gabe glared at him, irritated and more than a little worried. "Out with it then."

"Charlie left on the morning boat."

"What do you mean she left on the morning boat?" Gabe pushed back his chair and stood, running a hand through his hair.

Disbelieving, he picked up his phone and called Charlie's number, the disconnected message weakening his knees so that he sat back down, hard. "Ouch. Fuck."

"Explain," he bit out to Jill, his eyes flat and flinty.

"Arch, she's a friendly, take it easy," Nash warned tersely.

"Sorry. Explain?" Gabe gentled his tone.

"She left this note for you." Jill pushed the envelope to him.

Leaving it there, Gabe looked at her, waiting.

"After Nash told me, I went to her cottage. That note was taped to the door. I wanted to read it then find a way to protect you from whatever it is. But I didn't." Jill paced the floor, her worry for Gabe making her jittery.

"You saw her leave? You let her leave?" He rounded on Nash, his hands closed into fists.

Nash merely stared him down.

"Matteo called saying she'd come by the kitchen to ask what time the boat would leave. She thanked him and disappeared. When boarding time came, he looked out and saw her board. He was worried, so he called."

"There has to be a reason she left." Gabe checked his phone again for texts or voice mails from her. His hand shook as he repressed the powerful urge to heave the phone across the room. Resigned, he picked up the note and opened the page.

Jill and Nash watched his face tighten and lose color.

"Holy Mary, Mother of God. She remembered everything. She's remembered everything and she's traveling all alone," Gabe whispered, crumpling the paper in his hand.

"She got her memory back?" Jill's voice was incredulous. "Just like that?"

Pushing the crumpled note to Jill, he rested his head in his hands for a few seconds then stood quickly, shoving the chair back against the counter with a bang.

"I need air," he bit out, stalking out the door as fast as his busted up body would allow.

"Let him go." Jill put her hand over Nash's before he could stand up.

She said, "The note says, I quote, 'I remember everything. I have to go. Know that I loved you as best I could. Please forgive me—and forget me.'" Jill closed her eyes, her pain for Gabe and her friend bringing tears to course down her cheeks.

"That's all?!?" Nash was shaking with anger but remained sitting.

Jill nodded, leaning her head against her husband's shoulder.

They stayed that way for a few moments before she stood and brushed the tears from her face. "I'm going to the bar, Rory needs to hear it from me before the news spreads."

Nash nodded. "I'll find him."

"Let him be for a while, Nash? You're both too beat-up to throw punches and that's how the two of you deal with hurt at first." Jill smiled wryly. "Would you please go home and rest?"

"I'll come to the bar, watch my wife and pet our baby," Nash said decisively, giving her a small smile.

Neither of them voiced the choking fear they felt for Gabe.

*   *   *

Inside the wood shop, music blared, effectively obliterating the out-side world. Gabe straddled a stool at the worktable, painstakingly carving details into a jumbo-sized dump truck.

If his body wasn't one big throbbing ache, he'd be having a prize-worthy therapy session with the punching bag in back they called Big Al, but even he knew he'd lose that one right now.

Hours passed unheeded as he finished the truck, set it aside for painting, and moved on to a doll cradle followed by a park-ing garage for small cars. All the while, a bottle of Johnny Walker Blue Label stood to hand for his medicating pleasure. He sipped it straight from the bottle, allowing the burn to seep into every cell, a futile attempt at some kind of balm to ease the hurt and confusion.

She remembered everything—and just left him? The question echoed over and over in his head like a chant. He was going to go after her—just not today.

*   *   *

Nash sat at the bar well into the afternoon, nursing both his phys-ical pain and his worry for Gabe. Jill nudged him home with her and the kids, settling him into his recliner while she nursed Zane in the matching chair. In minutes, the room was quiet as everyone fell asleep, the ocean breeze wafting through the room.

Jill woke after a short time and looked around. Naps were heal-ing in so many ways—they sure needed them all. In her arms, the baby slept the deep sleep of the young and milk drunk. She kissed his sweet face lightly.

Nash was sprawled in his chair with a fretful frown, Rory curled into his side like a kitten. The absence of Charlie was sharp; she'd become family fast, and Jill missed her already. While she felt sorry for Charlie, she was also angry—not just for Gabe's sake, but for her own, too. She'd thought they were better friends than this. That Charlie would have come to her, at least tell her she'd remembered, tell her she was leaving, to take care of Gabe and Rory. Show some kind of feeling.

Even trying to understand the pressure and pain Charlie must have been under at remembering everything, Jill just couldn't believe she'd just left them—with Gabe and Nash hurt, too. At the same time, she thought, they'd known the risks in having Charlie around, but had loved anyway. Wasn't that what love was?

Nash stirred, moving slowly, both because he hurt but also being careful of the little girl curled against him. He met Jill's gaze and wrapped his good arm around Rory with a sigh.

"I'm so sorry." His voice was quiet. He looked at the baby and back to Jill. "At least Zane won't remember nearly losing his old man yesterday, or Charlie leaving us."

Jill nodded, rubbing the baby's tiny back. "I'll not likely forget either anytime soon, though. You missing was just as bad as 9/11 and the Melbourne Road fire—the not knowing, the very real possibility that I'd lost you."

"I know," he replied softly, his gaze on hers.

Carefully sliding out from under Rory with one arm was a challenge, but he did it without waking her. He grinned at Jill in triumph, leaning over her to kiss her and stroke his son's fuzzy head. "You know you're my world, I always find my way home."

She kissed him back fervently. "Good thing I love you despite your shenanigans. Now, go find him and let's patch him up."

* * *

He lay on the floor under Big Al, the bottle clutched in one hand, the other hand over his eyes.

"Oh, Arch." Nash couldn't help but laugh. "You took on Big Al busted up and drunk?"

Gabe squinted between his splayed fingers. "You need to shut your face," he said pointedly.

Nash rolled his eyes and nudged him with his foot. "Or what? Get up, let's get you fed and sobered up, you've Rory to consider."

With a deep, heartfelt groan, Gabe rolled over and pushed himself to his feet, leaning against the punching bag as the world spun.

"Oh, shit. Rory. Is she okay?" Gabe fumbled for the remote to turn off the music and sank onto a stool, rubbing his chest absently.

"She is," Nash affirmed.

"You can say it." Gabe slumped against the table, staring at his hands.

Nash leaned on the table next to the man he considered his brother, shoulders touching. "Nah. Come what may, I know she was worth it."

His friend's understanding almost Gabe's undoing, he dropped his head to his hands with a sigh.

"I'm pissed off at a dead man. And his grieving widow has my heart."

Chapter Thirty-Two

CHARLIE WAS SURE THAT, like Alice, she'd fallen through the Looking Glass; that's about as much sense as the world was making these days.

Shaken to the core by the near miss with Gabe's life plus the slow-motion flood of memories, she'd fled the island. How could she stand another loss after losing Jack? If Gabe hadn't survived, how would she endure that? How could she stay, knowing all she'd left behind here? Knowing she still grieved for her husband?

Her protective flight instinct had kicked in, coupled with the overwhelming need to see her children and make amends for leaving them the way she had. She needed to see them, to grieve her husband afresh. To return to the life she'd abandoned in favor of an island fling. How could she have just left her whole life behind?

That's how she forced herself to think of it during the journey back—she had to rewind life and make amends. She didn't let herself think about the newly recovered memories of the dark days during her first weeks on the island, how she'd immersed herself in grieving for Jack. How the island—how Gabe—had helped her grieve freely. She ignored how being on the island had allowed her to be herself. How Gabe had been her friend then her lover, steadfast and strong.

When her thoughts drifted to Gabe—which they did nearly constantly—and how she'd left him, she made herself remember the hurt she'd caused her children and how she'd tossed aside grieving for Jack like yesterday's newspaper. She forced herself to think about how she'd tossed Jack's memory aside for Gabe's arms. Her memory loss? Pure weakness. She couldn't let herself hurt for Gabe when she shouldn't have loved him in the first place.

*   *   *

The kids had picked up her from the airport and immersed her in their lives in the days that followed. She let them envelop her; the busier she was, the less she thought of Gabe—or so she told herself. Every day one or the other met her for lunch, asked her to see a movie or museum exhibit, came by the house to putter about her garden.

She returned to her tutoring, worked in her garden, went to therapy, visited Jack's grave, took medication to ensure a good night's sleep. And none of it worked.

Through a moving company, she'd arranged for her things from the island to be packed up and shipped.

When she did pause and let her thoughts come unbidden, she felt the loss of Gabe so strongly it took her breath away. It was a whole new grief.

Several times she'd begin to text him from her new phone, just to see how he was, but reminded herself it would only hurt him more to draw out the goodbye.

As hard as she tried to pick up the life she'd had before Jack's death, Charlie could clearly see she wasn't that person anymore—but then, who was she? Was she Jack's wife? How could she be—he wasn't here and never would be again. Troy and Cassidy's mother? Yes, but they're grown and living their own lives. Ms. Charlie the tutor? A good place to be, but tutors were replaceable. Gabe's lover? Ouch, don't go there. Jill's friend? She missed her—and Rory and everyone else in the island world.

Where did the two worlds meet—if at all? And even if she could figure it out, could Gabe ever forgive her? She literally ached with the need to hear his voice, feel his hand grip hers. He'd been her one constant in the turmoil that was her new life—and she'd pushed him away. And now she was adrift.

*   *   *

Paradise blazed brightly in the sunshine, the fishermen returned to the sea, Rory thrived, Zane grew by leaps and bounds, all cottages—except Charlie's—were full all the time, the bar hopped with fun-loving people.

Life was good. So Gabe told himself countless times a day. He dismissed the fact that he wasn't sleeping, that he'd returned to spending his nights in the wood shop as he had before Charlie had come into his life. Only the fact that he now had Rory kept him from drinking himself into a stupor every night.

The day the moving company had come to pack up Charlie's things, he'd asked Jill to keep Rory with her for the night and very deliberately sat on the porch of the cottage with his Johnnie Walker Blue Label bottle, ending the night flat on his back under Big Al—again.

One night, as he sanded down a doll cradle, he thought about how he'd planned to give Charlie some time and then follow, demanding an explanation. Mid-stroke, it dawned on him that she had actually given him an explanation in her brief note. She'd remembered. And it was crystal clear that what she remembered mattered more than what they'd found together. He had to accept that and let her go. As his ever-smashed-up knuckles would attest, there was always his standing date with Big Al.

****Chapter Thirty-Three****

CHARLIE'S FINGERS HOVERED over her phone keys as she tried to gather her courage. She needed to text Jill, to see if he was okay. What if he'd had complications arise after the ordeal at sea? What if…? Once she knew he was okay, she could move on.

Before she could change her mind yet again, Charlie entered the number and sent her message, her trembling fingers causing her to restart the message 3 times:

Hey, Jill, it's Charlie.

She made herself put the phone down, pacing the floor and chewing her lip.

The phone chimed within minutes, Charlie held her breath and opened the message:

Miss you, Charlie.

Jill's simple words brought tears instantly to her eyes.

'I miss you, too. How is he?

Charlie had held thoughts of Gabe at bay for so long, the connection with Jill brought down her mask, tears falling freely.

He's hurting. Rory's very sick.

The bottom dropped out of Charlie's self-absorbed world and, just like that, what she needed to do next was clear.

She texted back: *I'm on my way.*

Jill replied: *Hurry.*

Packing a simple carry-on bag with traveling basics, Charlie was at the airport within the hour. While she waited to board, she called Cassidy. It wasn't an easy conversation as her daughter expressed serious concern for her mother's sanity. Charlie hadn't mentioned the island or Gabe at all since her return, they'd put it neatly in the past. Cassidy reluctantly let her mother end the conversation, making her promise to answer their calls and promise she wasn't running away.

She wasn't running away, Charlie thought, she was running to. She would be there for the friends who had been there for her. She'd be there for the little girl who'd come along and lit up the island, turning her father's world upside down yet setting everything right at the same time. She'd be there for the man who'd made time stand still for her.

* * *

He was begging and begging only felt right on your knees—hell, face down on the floor, but then he couldn't keep his grip on his little girl's hand. So kneeling it was.

When the doctor had told him it didn't look good for Rory, he'd gone into a blind fury that had forced Nash and Luke to push him to the wall outside the room.

"They will kick your ass out of here, Arch! Do you want her to go through one second of this without you?" Nash had bitten out the words one by one, his face against Gabe's, the roughness in his voice breaking through the haze of grief and anger.

Gabe had held up a hand in resignation, his body sagging between the two men for a moment, head bowed on their shoulders. He let them hold him up as he desperately grasped for control.

Luke had spoken quietly, his grip on Gabe's shoulder almost painful, "You're all she's got, man. You gotta show up." Nodding, he'd stood straight, grasping their arms in a brief squeeze, and been quietly fierce since. As another day waned into night, he banished everyone to the waiting room.

Jill hugged him tightly. "Love you." She hadn't told him Charlie was on her way, preferring to let that play out as it needed to.

His mother had simply held him close and kissed his cheek, her familiar touch comforting beyond belief.

"You can stay, Mom."

She'd nodded. "I'll give you some time alone."

He'd pushed the door mostly closed and knelt beside his little girl's bed in the dimly lit room. He begged, making it crystal clear that he'd give his life for hers. He talked softly to her, telling her baby Rory stories he'd read in her mother's letter, reminding her how much her mother had loved her. About Zane's latest tooth and the new fuzzy cowlick that would not lay down. Describing how lost Jake was without her, how he'd taken to staying by Zane's side while he waited for her.

As the night deepened, he'd talked his voice down to a hoarse whisper. And still he talked on.

*   *   *

Charlie rounded the hospital corner to see the waiting room filled with people sitting quietly or talking softly. Jill saw her and came immediately to envelop her in a tight hug.

"I'm so sorry, I—" Charlie began.

"You're here." Jill led her down the hall to the door of Rory's room, nudging her inside.

The sight in front of her both broke her heart and patched those same cracks with love.

Gabe lay on his side in the hospital bed, his arms wrapped around Rory's small body, as if he could share his life force with her.

She went to the other side of the bed and faced him, reaching over the little girl's motionless form to grasp his hand.

His responding grip nearly crushed her fingers as his eyes flew open. Bloodshot and dark charcoal with fatigue and worry, she saw relief in their depths.

With her other hand, she brushed Rory's hair back from her forehead, noticing how hot she was. The child lay still and silent, the only sounds in the room being their breathing and the occasional blip from the machines.

Bringing her gaze back to Gabe, she cleared her throat. "I—"

His features drawn and stark in the dim light, he put two fingers on her lips, silencing her words. He lifted their joined hands and pressed a kiss to the back of hers, closing his eyes for a long moment before meeting her gaze again. That was enough for now.

They turned their attention to Rory, stroking her legs and arms. Gabe retold some of the stories from her babyhood for both her and Charlie's benefit. He reveled in laughing softly with Charlie about many of the Rory-isms and antics that had happened since she'd come to him.

As dawn broke across the sky, the nurse assistant came in and checked Rory's vitals. "Someone will be in to update you soon." She patted Rory's hand and left the room.

*   *   *

Time ticked by and as Rory remained still and silent, Gabe was glad for the comforting presence of his mother and now Charlie.

And now Charlie.

He'd smelled her trademark orange blossom scent before he'd opened his eyes to see her standing across the bed from him during the night. The relief he'd felt paled in comparison to his worry for Rory, but he was glad she was by his side. They had a lot to talk about, but it could wait.

While he kept Rory's little hand in his, Sheila bustled about the room, opening the shades to let in the day's light. Charlie stepped out to ask someone to go for more coffee, returning just as the doctor walked into the room. Gabe stood still, reaching for Charlie's hand as he waited for the man to speak.

The doctor took some time to look at the monitors and place his hand on Rory's forehead. He turned to Gabe, glancing at his clipboard as he cleared his throat.

"Two days ago, I feared a different start to this morning for Rory. Today, I'm cautiously optimistic." He smiled at Gabe's fist pump and shout. "We've a long road to go, but I believe she's turned that corner we were so worried about. We should see more improvement and the strength to wake up a bit before long."

With a handshake and a smile for Gabe, he left the room.

Jill rushed in the door, wide-eyed. "What was that yell about?"

Gabe hugged her tightly, spinning her around. "She's going to make it."

Jill cried with relief, kissing his cheek and going out to share the good news with Nash and the rest of their friends.

Sheila settled back into her chair to resume her knitting. "Why don't you and Charlie get some fresh air for a few minutes?"

"I don't want her to wake up and find me gone," Gabe protested.

"You won't be gone that long, now go." Sheila's gazed speared Charlie. "He hasn't left this room in days; he needs to feel the sunshine and breathe fresh air."

Charlie took his arm and tugged. "She's right. Just a few minutes to recharge a bit so you'll feel more alert when Rory wakes up."

Gabe caressed his daughter's face. "Hang in there, Poppet, you're doing great."

Fresh air and sunshine did sound pretty good. Plus, he needed to tell Charlie that she had to leave again.

*   *   *

They walked around the courtyard in silence, hands linked. Gabe bounced a little on the balls of his feet, stretching his legs and generally loosening up his body. A muscle in his jaw ticked and he kept starting to say something but didn't.

When they came to a weeping willow tree with its curtain of fronds, he tugged her into the quiet green world and nudged her back against the wide tree trunk.

Charlie gasped as he slipped his knee between her legs and pressed his body against her. Hanging one hand on a tree limb next to her head, he reached out to cup her face with the other as he leaned in to lightly touch his lips to hers. At the slight taste of her, he growled and plundered her mouth deeply, like a drowning man reaching for a life rope.

Charlie kissed him back, reveling in how every nerve ending in her body jumped to life, crying out for his touch. She slid both hands into his hair as his lips traveled across her jawline to that spot just beneath her ear. Shivering, she held him tight against her, his warmth soothing and arousing all at the same time. As her knees went weak, the leg he'd nudged between hers and his hands at her hips kept her upright. His mouth still at her neck, he paused, breathing fast and shallow as he tried to catch his breath.

Without lifting his head, he said, "I was going to send you away, but you aren't planning to stay, are you?"

She sighed, her hands curled around his shoulders. "When I heard Rory was sick, I couldn't stay away. I had to see you, see her. But I don't know any more about what to do next than I did when I left. Almost losing you to the sea while I still grieve Jack…I just don't know." Her voice shook as she pressed her lips to his neck as if to soothe the sting of her words.

Gabe pushed himself back slowly, steadying her with his hands until she was standing on her own again. He drew her down to the bench a few feet away, still under the willow tree's sheltering fronds.

"Your note said you'd remembered. Tell me."

Charlie knew what he meant. "Jack—" She stood to pace in front of him, twirling a branch in her fingers. "Jack was a Coast Guard helicopter pilot."

Gabe made a noise of sympathy but waited for more.

"He was lost at sea during a stormy rescue." She returned to sit beside him with a deep sigh. "You can imagine how my mind reacted when I learned you were missing."

Gabe nodded. He wanted to know more about how she'd remembered, more about her life before she came to the island, but he couldn't drag this out any longer. He dragged his hands through his hair and blew out a breath.

"After all you've been through, you just dropped everything to come—I'll remember that always."

Charlie's eyebrows rose. "That sounds suspiciously like a good-bye, Gabe."

He took her hands in his. "If it were just about me, I'd take whatever you can give, no questions asked. I'd risk getting hurt again and again, because you're worth that and more to me. But I can't stand by and watch you hurting yourself by staying just because I want you to and I can't let Rory be hurt by you leaving again. I have to protect the both of you."

She nodded slowly, her vision blurred by tears. She let them fall unchecked; she had nothing to hide from him.

"As it has been since we met, my hand—and my heart—is always open for you, Charlie. If you ever decide to stay, you've only to take hold of it. I'll never let go."

With that, he tipped up her chin, nearly losing it at the shattered expression he'd seen so many times as she'd grieved before her memory loss. Hating that he was the one who'd put it there this time, he turned and walked away, his step as heavy as his heart.

* * *

Before boarding the afternoon boat to leave the island, Charlie walked up the beach to the cottage she'd lived in before her memory loss. She stood at the steps, her chest tight with emotion, her head aching with the wave of memories.

Memories of grieving Jack with every single breath. Of wishing she could walk into the sea. Memories of Gabe's voice in the dark, demanding nothing, offering whatever he could give. Memories of sleeping in the hammock night and day, the lull of the ocean waves numbing her mind, soothing her heart as only the sea can do. Memories of waking from nightmares, screaming Jack's name, to be soothed by Gabe's voice, his embrace.

She walked further down the beach to the other cottage, where she'd come from the hospital to figure out what to do next. The one where she'd accepted her lack of memory—some would call that denial—and begun to make a new life.

The one where she'd made love with Gabe time and again, intending to live in the moment. To stop time. The one she'd begun to call home. Home. Latching on to the word, saying it over and over again, it came to her.

She boarded the afternoon boat with a smile, watching the island grow smaller and smaller. "Home. Of course."

Chapter Thirty-Four

RORY RALLIED AND WAS on the mend in that astonishing way children often are. She was back to her bouncy self and headed home within the month. On her last night at the hospital, Sheila and Jillian declared a girl's night and kicked Gabe out.

"We're gonna do pedicures, Daddy!" Rory hugged his neck, her entire body vibrating with excitement. He kissed her cheek and got out of there fast, before she could beg him to join in the festivities. He'd heard tales of dads with painted toenails and he was pretty sure he'd be a hopelessly willing victim if she thought of it.

Jillian walked him down the hall. "Go, get a good solid night's rest for a change. I had the crew clean the cottage for you and there's food in the fridge. All you have to do is go rest, have a drink and get ready to bring our girl home tomorrow."

Two months of hospital life meant two months of very little sleep, so Gabe wasn't about to argue.

*   *   *

Once back at the cove, far too restless to go to his cottage or to the wood shop, he walked down to the water's edge to feel the soothing pull of the sea as twilight set in.

The Painted Parrot was brightly lit, music drifting down to him. His breathing slowed, the vise grip on his chest eased, and he began to see that his paradise would return in time. Without Charlie, the colors weren't as bright nor the music as sweet, but with Rory and his friends, he'd fake it till he made it.

He was home—parts were missing and he ached for them, for her—but he was home and he would heal.

Just as he turned to head to his cottage in search of a drink and some food, in that order, he was nearly bowled over by Jake. The dog exuberantly ran around his legs, pushing him and yipping joyfully.

He laughed and leaned down to vigorously rub the dog's head with both hands. "Who's a good boy, huh? I missed you, too. But I bet you missed Rory more than you missed me." Straightening, he looked around for Nash, for it was unlikely that Jake was out alone.

The dog barked and ran up towards the cottages, came back and repeated the same dance. Gabe's eyes narrowed, was Jake pulling a Lassie? The dog had only pulled a Lassie twice in his life—once when Rory had gotten her foot stuck in a rock crevice and again when Charlie had walked into the sea. Neither of them was here for Jake to tend. Curious, Gabe followed as the shadows swallowed the black dog.

"Jake! C'mon, Jake, let's go eat!" He called.

Stepping into the shadows of the path between cottages, he heard Jake's bark followed by an answering laugh that stopped him in his tracks. With that laugh, he really was home.

"Hey, Skipper. Did you know there's no reason for the ABC's to be in any particular order?" Her familiar whiskey-laced voice came through the darkness.

He forced himself to walk calmly to the steps of the cottage—the one he'd still not let them rent out to anyone else.

There she sat on the steps, the fairy lights on the porch setting her hair afire in copper bursts as if there were fireflies dancing about in the waves. Light was spilling from the open door of the cottage, Billy Joel's "An Innocent Man" drifting out on the breeze. He looked from the door to Charlie, wondering if his exhaustion had him seeing things.

She smiled at his confusion. A full, genuine smile much like the one she'd given him right in this spot on the night they'd first made love. Inclining her head to the step next to her, she held up a glass and poured from the bottle of Johnnie Walker Blue Label that sat between her bare feet.

He sat down and took the glass, tossing the drink back in one gulp, hissing at the welcome burn. She sipped her own drink and held it loosely between her hands as she leaned on her knees and looked out onto the darkened sands.

"Did you mean it?" She asked, swishing the liquor about in her glass.

"Mean what?" He was further bewildered, if that were possible.

"When I left the hospital last month, you told me your hand would always be open for me, that once I decided to stay, I'd only to grab on."

She sat the glass down and looked at him, her earlier merriment gone, her eyes dark and serious. "Did you mean it?"

Gabe's mouth went bone dry, his breath caught tightly in his chest. In what he felt was slow motion, his eyes on hers, he set the glass down on the porch step and held out his hand.

Without hesitation, she put her hand in his, her lips meeting his at the same time he closed his hand around hers. Never letting go.

"Welcome home, Charlie. Welcome home."

****Epilogue****

AS THE JOHNBTOO bobbed about in the waves, Charlie sighed against Gabe's chest, legs tangled, breathing slowing.

"Hmm." His voice rumbled under her ear, one hand twirling a strand of her hair, the other at her hip, holding her close.

She raised her head to look at him, to run a hand over his cheek, stubbled with dark gold. He waited, his eyes quicksilver in the waning sunlight, a slight smile on his face. Mercy, he was pretty, she thought.

She sat up and pulled her sun dress back down over her head, shrugging at his arched eyebrow. "I can't talk about Jack while naked with you."

He inclined his head and stood to pull on his cargoes, sitting back down against the bench seat and gathering her to him. Her back against his chest, they watched the sun set the sea afire in a blaze of blue, red and gold.

"I've told you how Jack died after a Coast Guard rescue mission, how I was on the shore as he was flying in and saw the crash." Even having discovered her love for Gabe, it was still difficult to talk about losing Jack. As it should be.

"You have." He pressed a kiss to her neck.

Needing to see his face, she turned halfway between his legs, resting her hands on his knee, the other knee at her back.

"While I was back in the States, one of the things I learned was that the rescue mission Jack was coming home from when he crashed was—was yours." She smiled sadly. "You survived that storm thanks to Jack."

Gabe stared at her, the sting of her words lessened by the fact that she didn't move from his arms. Her sapphire eyes, brimming with tears, were still full of love for him. He opened his mouth—to say what, he had no earthly idea—but was stopped by her fingers on his lips.

"In saving you, he gave me a gift so I could survive a world without him—a gift it took me awhile to find, but I found it."

Her kiss was filled with promise, he responded with promises of his own.

*   *   *

In celebration of Rory's good health and Gabe and Charlie's marriage, The Painted Parrot rocked out the biggest Welcome Home/Wedding Party the island had seen in a long time.

Gabe saw to it that Troy and Cassidy were welcomed with open arms and the promise of a cottage anytime they wanted to visit, their earlier mistrust of him finally fading.

The night waned, the crowd dwindled, the little girl slept between her new big brother and sister and, stepping away from their cluster of friends, the husband drew his wife to the dance floor. As the notes of "Dance the Night Away" filled the now dimly lit bar, he held her close, his head bowed against her cheek. He could truly breathe again and it felt so good.

Charlie smiled as his breath tickled against her ear. "Your place or mine?"

What a gift this man was. Welcome home, indeed.

THE END

About the Author

Once upon a time, a sassy Kentucky girl fell in love with a handsome Hoosier boy. What followed is a still-unfolding story filled with laughter, love and pizza—yes, pizza.

When Dana Britt is not writing stories of hope, home and happily ever after, she can usually be found porch sitting with a book in hand. Her idea of a perfect day is a road trip that includes sunshine, taking pictures and spending time with her own personal Hero and two young adult children. Dana often shares bits about it all online at DanaBritt.com—she'd love for you to stop by.

Acknowledgments

raises sweet tea glass

My mother, Charlotte Tanaro, for teaching me to read and encouraging my love of reading. All those library trips and the stealing of her romance books...oh, how I wish she were here.

Jay and Meghan—the best two kiddos I could have ever hoped for. Thanks for putting up with Momma, my babies.

My mother-in-law, Georgianna Britt, for all those times she asked about my writing and always replied, "As long as it makes YOU happy."

I come from a long line of love, as evidenced by my great big, incredible family. From my grandparents to my parents and siblings, nieces and nephews, to my stepmother and all my aunts, uncles and cousins, in laws and outlaws included—what a menagerie we are! I love you all. xo

Madeline, my bonus editor, your help and friendship have been invaluable, my dear. I very much look forward to working with you again.

My friends—you know who you are. I appreciate y'all so.

And last, but never least, my readers (especially if you read this far!) With all my heart, I thank each and every one of you for reading my stories.

www.ingramcontent.com/pod-product-compliance
Lightning Source LLC
Chambersburg PA
CBHW051245250626
47155CB00009B/3169